DARK
LANDS

By

Autumn Dawn

Futuristic Paranormal Romance

New Concepts   Georgia

Be sure to check out our website for the very best in fiction at fantastic prices!

When you visit our webpage, you can:
* Read excerpts of currently available books
* View cover art of upcoming books and current releases
* Find out more about the talented artists who capture the magic of the writer's imagination on the covers
* Order books from our backlist
* Find out the latest NCP and author news--including any upcoming book signings by your favorite NCP author
* Read author bios and reviews of our books
* Get NCP submission guidelines
* And so much more!

We offer a 20% discount on all new Trade Paperback releases ordered from our website!

Be sure to visit our webpage to find the best deals in e-books and paperbacks! To find out about our new releases as soon as they are available, please be sure to sign up for our newsletter (http://www.newconceptspublishing.com/newsletter.htm) or join our reader group (http://groups.yahoo.com/group/new_concepts_pub/join)!

The newsletter is available by double opt in only and our customer information is *never* shared!

Visit our webpage at:
www.newconceptspublishing.com

Dark Lands original publications of NCP. This work has never before appeared in book form. This work is a novel. Any similarity to actual persons or events is purely coincidental.

New Concepts Publishing, Inc.
5202 Humphreys Rd.
Lake Park, GA 31636

ISBN 1-58608-843-2
© 2006 Autumn Dawn
Cover art (c) copyright 2006 Eliza Black

NCP books are available at special quantity discounts for bulk purchases for sales promotions, premiums, fund raising, or educational use. For details, write, email, or phone New Concepts Publishing, Inc., 5202 Humphreys Rd., Lake Park, GA 31636; Ph. 229-257-0367, Fax 229-219-1097; orders@newconceptspublishing.com.

First NCP Trade Paperback Printing: September 2006

TABLE OF CONTENTS

Fallon

Chapter One

It hurt. Rain glanced over her shoulder, crouched on the gritty ally floor. The fall had skinned her palms and knees, and the wounds stung. But they were coming--she could hear them over the sounds of midnight traffic, though she didn't try to peer past the black ally into the glare of streetlights. She ran.

But then it seemed she'd been running all of her life, ever since she'd discovered who she was, what she was. The vigilantes in the cult that chased her were determined to catch her and use her to wipe out the rest of her kind. Their war had been going on for millennia, and the cult was winning. Rain knew she wouldn't be able to resist their torture if they caught her. She'd talk. They'd find out about the others, and they'd kill them. Human and Haunt could not coexist.

Breathless, trembling with adrenaline and exhaustion, she forced herself into a stumbling lope, ignoring her cold, sweat-soaked jeans and t-shirt. She would have loved to ditch her ragged black jacket and pack, but didn't dare; they comprised all of her worldly goods, and she needed them in the chill London fog.

Her father wouldn't have felt the cold. He'd simply have changed into his werewolf form. Faster and more powerful than humans, the weres were called Haunts by the humans who knew of them. If Rain had been a full blood, she might have been able to leap up onto a rooftop and escape the hunters. While she had the speed of the Haunt, on foot in the streets she was loosing the deadly race.

Scaling the chain link fence at the end of the alley was easy--evading the snarling Doberman who went for her throat was not. With no time for regret, she got in a hearty kick, sprinted across the lawn and jumped up, grabbed the top of an ornate stone fence. Barely making it over before the dog sunk teeth into her, she slipped over the top, landing in another empty ally.

Trying to catch her breath, she moved cautiously down the white-lit brick canyon, praying she'd lost them. Already she felt her strength failing, and the next time she fell, she might not make it up.

Listening, straining her preternaturally keen ears to catch any noise, she searched for sounds of pursuit. Finding none, she slowly relaxed and sank against one chilly wall, ignoring the trash at her feet. She'd made it.

Suddenly light exploded into the ally. Deafened by the shouts of men and barking dogs, blinded by the sudden glow, Rain saw death coming and despaired.

* * * *

"Wake up!"

A slap accompanied the brutal voice, jerking Rain from the comfort of darkness. Moaning, she pried open her eyes and blinked at the murky cell. She didn't remember coming there, but she did recall being jabbed with something. Cuffs bound her wrists behind her, and her rear was planted on a hard wooden chair. Did they mean to question her? The word *torture* flitted across her mind, and she shuddered. *Please, God, no!*

Her tormenter--a scarred blighter in working class clothes--took a narrow-eyed look at her, then glanced at a the other man in the cell, an older gentleman in a suit. What hair he had left was iron gray, perfectly matching the winter coldness in his faded blue eyes. He looked her over, then smiled without humor. "Rain, is it? Daughter of Rian Miller?"

She shivered. "Who are you?"

"Taught you some unusual things, didn't he? Lock picking, shooting ... how to run and how to hide."

Nervous now, she felt the cold sweat start again. Her father had been dead for a year, killed by the very people she now suspected held her, but few people had really known him, known *what* he was. These people were not so blissfully ignorant.

By the chill satisfaction in his eyes, he was enjoying her torment. "I have a few questions for you, my dear. Rory!"

A tall, dark man entered at his command, favoring the gent with a cold look. "I'm not deaf, Trent."

"*Mr. Trent,*" the scarred one said aggressively, stepping toward him.

Mr. Trent held up his hand, stopping his goon. To Rory he said, "Question her."

Rory sent a cold look her way. "Question is all I'll do. I'm getting bloody sick of your games, *Mr. Trent.*"

"Strive to remember what happens when you fail me," Mr. Trent said coldly, "and remember who gets hurt."

His lip curled, but Rory turned to Rain. Softening a little, he asked gently, "What's your name, love?"

Rain hadn't lived twenty-two years without seeing some good-looking men. This one, however, put them all to shame. Black hair, deep green eyes and a face to make an angel weep were temptation enough, but there was something more, something she couldn't place. Did he wear cologne? That had to be it, for a scent of tempting power hung about him, though she'd never known a fragrance to addle her so. Just breathing it made her tired blood stir, and the longer he stood by her, the worse the sensation became. *Sex in a bottle,* her muddled brain exclaimed, trying dimly for a warning, but whatever it was trying to tell her became lost in his eyes.

The goon said something to Mr. Trent. The haze she was under dulled their words, but she thought she heard the goon say, "This one's got it bad."

Pheromones, her mind whispered, but the warning was blanketed by a rush of sensation. Dully, she remembered the warnings about rare human women who were born with pheromones so powerful to the male Haunt that they could render him powerless. The male would be so muddled that he'd give his questioners the names and locations of even his dearest family. The cult sought and used those women, but she'd never heard of a human male with the pheromone. This Rory couldn't be one, could he?

Rory smirked at her, but the scent seemed to mess with her perceptions, because her heart insisted it was an expression of sympathy. "I don't think we'll need these, will we?" he said, moving slowly around her to touch her cuffs. She felt a key slide into the cuffs, then they fell away, granting her blessed freedom. Rubbing her aching arms, she felt gratitude swell. He was so beautiful he made her feel weak. "Thank you."

Rory looked her over. "What's a sweet thing like you done to get yourself in this mess? Don't you have mates who will be looking for you?"

In the background, she could hear the goon asking Mr. Trent, *"I'll bet he asks for this one when he's done. She'd be a looker if she cleaned up, and our Rory does like to have his fun before you dispose of them."*

She heard, but the words meant nothing. So long as she could smell Rory, feel the thunder in her blood from breathing him in, nothing else mattered. "Friends ... no, I have no friends."

Rory frowned. "How can that be? A fantasy like you must have lots of friends. What about your father's mates? Won't they help you?"

She thought, very willing to tell him everything she knew. "I ... I haven't seen anyone since my father died."

He smiled comfortingly. "But you know where they are, right? Those mates of his?" He glanced at Trent, then moved closer to whisper in her ear, "I can help you. Tell me where to find your father's friends, and I can help them find you."

The touch of his mouth against her ear sent shockwaves down her spine. Longing seized her. Just let him touch her....

"Like animals for him, I hear. Scream and scratch while he's riding him, and beg for more, they say. Makes me wish I were the Sylph. Lucky bloke."

"Shut up! And make sure that recorder is working. We want to get every name."

Blocking her view of the men with his body, Rory hunched down to her level, tracing the skin of her face with one finger. "Tell me the names, sweetheart. Tell me how to find them."

It was too much. Breathless, desperate to please him, she opened her mouth. "My father's cousin used to live in--"

An enormous blast shook the cell, obliterating her words. Screaming, she threw her hands up and ducked her head, instinctively protecting her face. Dust clogged the air and Rory cursed as soldiers in black burst into the room, killing the goon and capturing Mr. Trent.

She didn't spare a thought for him, but instantly got in front of Rory, protecting him with her body. The pheromones had her convinced that he was her mate. She didn't care what happened to her, but she had to save him.

A tall man strode through the dust, and everything around them stilled. Command shadowed him, powerful as the desert sun, though impossible to see. Not all of his size was in his legs, either--those powerful shoulders of his were enough to give her pause. His long blond hair was tied back, and though it was too murky to tell the color of his eyes, the expression in them chilled her.

But those eyes were not fixed on her. "Hello, Rory." Cold menace vibrated in every word.

"Fallon. Fancy meeting you here," Rory said flippantly. "Come to shoot the breeze, or is this business?"

Fallon looked at Rain, and she quickly inched back. Rory was directly behind her, but she wasn't taking chances. "Leave him alone!" she warned the stranger.

Rory laughed. "Feisty, ain't she? What can I do, mate? Your women all love me."

"Move out of the way, Rain," Fallon ordered her calmly, looking her in the eyes.

Beyond the point of wondering why he knew her name, why he was here, she tensed to fight. "No! You won't touch him! He was trying to help me." She saw one of the soldiers inching to her left, but was too distracted by the menace in front of her to do anything.

Slowly, Fallon's eyes lifted to Rory. "How many women has it been now, Rory? How many of us have you helped to kill?"

"He's a liar," Rory told her soothingly, when she shot a quick look at him. "Don't worry over it, love."

She relaxed and glared at Fallon. "I won't listen to you." There was a game afoot, though she was oblivious to its rules. Somehow she was the center, though why was elusive. *Caring* was elusive. In this close proximity, with Rory's scent teasing her nose, it just didn't matter. The pheromones were her drug, and their source her only god. She would die for him.

But Rory's distraction had proved fatal. With a sudden roar, the soldier who'd shifted to their left charged, taking Rain down in a flying tackle. Shots were fired, but she was so tangled up she couldn't see. Twisting, the soldier managed to land on the bottom, taking the brunt of their fall, and as they landed, she saw Rory jerk. His gun discharged, the bullet striking stone, and he toppled to the floor on his back.

Rain began to scream.

* * * *

Fallon's jaw clenched as he watched two of his men trying to subdue the wild woman. Taking Rory down had taken precious time, and they couldn't allow this. Pity she hadn't seen the gun at her head, threatening her life, but he wasn't surprised at her fury. The Sylph's pheromone was a dangerous thing, and she'd already been in his power when they'd arrived. A nap would do her a lot of good.

Striding to her side, he evaded her kicking foot and applied pressure to her carotid artery. In seconds she collapsed like a doll.

"Bring her," he ordered them. They had to extract to the choppers in a hurry, before the cult figured out their bird had flown and sent reinforcements. They wouldn't like losing an informant; though to his knowledge the cult had already killed most of her friends and family, thanks to her cousin's unwilling help. Fallon was determined that the Cult of the Black Sylphs wouldn't get another shot at her, even if he had to shift her off-world himself.

His fellow Haunts, as humans had labeled them long ago, closed in around him and their precious cargo. Females of their species were well protected, and not a man there approved of what had almost happened to her. Rory was Trent's truant son, and he'd had a bargain with his father. He'd used his sexual pheromones and suggestive abilities-- effective only on female Haunt--to question the women. The names of other Haunt were coaxed from her, his father went on a killing spree, and Rory used the women until he tired of them. The bodies were disposed of when he'd finished.

It was reason enough to take a man's life, and Fallon had enjoyed doing it.

They made it to the choppers, thankful that the blast had taken out the portion of Trent's estate that had housed his troops. The snipers that remained were picked off by Fallon's own men. They needed no night goggles to pierce the inky night, and all of them were expert marksman.

Fallon glanced at Trent and the girl. Trent would be questioned and disposed of like the carrion he was, and Fallon had to find a safe place for the girl. Off world was best, but he didn't know how much she knew, or even if she'd be willing to use the gate. It was going to take time to settle her, and there was only one place he would have leisure to do that.

Chapter Two

Rain woke in the chopper, but was wise enough to stay silent. She couldn't have said much over the chopper's blades, anyway, but she kept her mouth shut until they'd landed and herded her toward a sleek private jet. Dawn was beginning to lighten the horizon and a chill breeze had kicked up when she demanded, "Where are we going?"

The one called Fallon glanced at her. "Home. Wait until we're in the air and I'll answer your questions."

Having no choice, she obeyed him. By his accent, he was an American, so she assumed she was going back the States. She'd been born there, but had run to the UK when her father had been taken. That gambit hadn't worked, but it no longer mattered. Whoever these men were, she wasn't going to get away from them easily.

Thinking of her father still caused a dull ache. She missed him, even as she wavered between blaming his aggressive marketing of her inventions and her own foolishness in making them. She'd been born with an IQ off the charts, and invented gadgets that made investors drool. She'd been too young to understand the dangers some of them held, so entranced by her curiosity, the thrill of doing the impossible. Before her father could market her last invention--which she hadn't wanted; even she could see the danger of it in unscrupulous hands--he'd been killed by someone trying to steal it. She'd escaped, only to spend hellish years running from the Cult.

If she'd been just another dumb teen, her father would still be alive today. If she'd been fully human, a chance encounter with a Cult member in Scotland wouldn't have mucked up the rest of her life. She still didn't know if the thieves and the Cult were the same people.

Fatigue sapped what energy she had. She'd been running for thirty-six hours, and the strain was devastating. Whatever would happen next was beyond her control, and even her first sight of the inside of a private jet gave her little joy. Cold, hungry and parched, she sat where she was asked.

"Water?" Fallon handed her a bottle, which she sucked down greedily. He gave her another.

"Bathroom?" He raised his brows in question, then gestured toward the tail of the plane.

Grateful, she made her way past the half-dozen others settled into deluxe chairs and locked herself in the bathroom. The face in the mirror shocked her. Dirt smeared her skin, and her greasy hair was half-out of her braid, hanging around her face in shaggy brown hanks. There was nothing she could do about the clothes, but she washed up, pulled her hair back into a proper tail and ignored the shadows under her eyes.

Dinner was waiting for her. It was hot and she didn't remember the last time she'd eaten, so she attacked it, uncaring at that point whether it was drugged or who served it. Besides, her pack was gone, and she didn't delude herself that her "rescuers" had come in with explosives and M16's to collect her, only to use her for their amusement. Whatever their agenda, she was safe for the moment. After they got on the ground ... she'd deal with that later.

Exhaustion hit hard. She needed to lie down, but a few facts wouldn't kill her. "Why did you come after me?"

Fallon studied her. "We'd heard a rumor about one of our females being hunted. By the time we found your trail, the Cult was a step ahead of us. You know why we broke into the compound--they would have used your information to locate and wipe out others of our kind. Too many have died already."

He was right. The human bigots wouldn't stop until all the Haunt were dead. Their motive? A simple dread of anyone different than they were, a fear that the Haunt would rise up and take over the world.

Yeah, right. She'd seen the world, and they could have it.

Sluggish as it was, her mind was still awake enough to connect a few dots. "Rory was a Sylph. How? I was taught that only human females had the pheromone, and only one in a million, at that." The Cult of the Black Sylph had been in existence for a long time, and they were frighteningly competent at wiping out her people. They used the Sylphs-- willing or not--to capture and control the shape-shifting Haunt males, using them as informants. To her knowledge, there'd never been a human male with the pheromone. Discovering him hadn't been a pleasant experience.

Grimness tightened Fallon's mouth. "Apparently they come in different flavors now. Our friends in the Cult are dabbling with gene splicing."

Oh, joy. Too tired to dwell on it, she grabbed a couple of the pillows that had been laid out for her and arranged them, reclining her chair as much as it would go. She had very little time before sleep snared her. "Where we going?" she slurred, closing her eyes.

"Alaska. That's where I'm based."

November in Alaska--not exactly a thrilling thought. "Am I free to leave?"

He hesitated. "The Counsel of Elders will want to speak with you first."

The Counsel was the Haunt equivalent of parliament. Most of them were quite old, clan heads and respected leaders. A powerful group, they had final say in all Haunt business.

So, she wasn't free. She knew what happened to anyone who was rescued from the Cult's clutches. Once their face was known, they were bustled through the gate to "protect themselves and others." The Cult had a world-wide network of affiliates; shape shifter hating psychos who'd stop at nothing to see her people dead. Not that she wanted to be captured again, but she wasn't wild about letting the counsel dictate where she could live. Her father had raised her to take care of herself. She wasn't going to be dragged to an alien world, and good intentions be hanged.

It wasn't as if she was really one of them, anyway.

Sleep sucked her down, and she went without a fight. When this thing landed, she wanted to be ready to bolt. Once they got her under formal guard, her chances of escape would sink out of sight.

* * * *

It was forty below and dark, with a sharp wind blowing. Scratching her idea to run the moment her feet hit pavement, she ducked her head instead and pulled the blanket, she'd been given, tighter. How did people survive in this frigid climate?

A black Jeep was waiting for them. Fallon opened the door for her and she slid into the passenger side, grateful for the warmth. Had she been thinking faster, she might have thought to hit the auto-lock and attempt to steal the Jeep, but the cold and her awkward blanket distracted her. Just as well--she'd never learned to drive a stick.

Fallon slid into the driver's seat. One look at his big body convinced her that she'd been wise not to try and run. Guys didn't like women messing with their autos. A guy like him … she had a feeling he'd go through the window.

Curiosity made her ask. "What would you have done if I'd driven off?"

He glanced at her mildly. "My insurance premiums would have gone up, but the body shop guy would have been very happy." He looked back at the road. "You're not that stupid."

Annoyed, she sniped, "I thought your type didn't hurt women."

"We practice discipline, especially of our women. If you were mine, you wouldn't tempt me." This time his glance was speculative.

If he was trying to unnerve her, it worked. She didn't want any part of his 'discipline,' and she sure as fire didn't want to date him. A second glance confirmed that he was cute--no surprise she hadn't noticed, considering--but good looks didn't make the firearm at his side disappear.

Frozen scenery and ice fog flowed past her window, along with occasional traffic. It was only four in the afternoon, and already dark. She had no money and no friends. Running for her life had sucked away every last dime, and it was hardly conducive to maintaining friendships. For that matter, even her last change of underwear had been lost when she'd been seized, and she expected the day to go downhill from there.

She felt tired. A year was a long time to run, and she was beginning to feel like the rope in a tug of war. The bad guys had her, then the ...well, she wasn't ready to call Fallon a good guy yet, but at least he hadn't tied her to a chair. She sighed.

"What's wrong?"

"I lost my toothbrush."

He choked, probably on a laugh. "We'll get you another one."

"Are there any banks open? Trent and his buddies didn't bother to check my pockets, and I've got a little money I'd like to exchange." Two shillings was a little money, after all.

"I'll take care of it for you. Wouldn't you rather shower first? You've had a rough day."

Debating the merits of escaping him in a bank while exhausted, nearly penniless, and hampered by freezing weather, she reluctantly grumbled, "Where are we going?"

"My place. I've got good security, and it will make it easy for the counsel to speak with you."

"About that ... I'm not real eager to chat with them."

He looked at her. "You have nothing to fear. You've done nothing wrong."

Her lips tightened and she stared back out the window. He was wrong there, but she wasn't going to argue with a stone wall. Assuming she could refuel and evade him, she was going to run the moment she got the chance.

Not everybody hunting her was human.

* * * *

Fallon watched her out of the corner of his eye. Something was scaring her, something other than the obvious. In spite of her attempt at careless chitchat, she was still wound tight. One wrong move on his part and she'd be off at a sprint, never looking back.

Did she fear extradition? The Darklands, where many of their people had fled, was a wondrous place, but dangerous as well. It abounded in massive lightning storms and dangerous native flora and fauna, but their people were taming it acre by acre. Reached only by a portal located in Alaska, it demanded strength from its people, and gave richly to those with the heart to rule it. A spirited girl like her would do well there, but perhaps she didn't know that. The few of them left here were increasingly ignorant of Darkland lore.

Like his father before him, Fallon was the guardian of the portal, and he divided his time between the two worlds. It was necessary to know politics on both sides of the border, for his job was often complicated by bickering between the Darkland rulers and the Earth based Elders. Despite the tensions, his job was to protect the gate from criminals intent on escaping human justice and regulated the flow of emigrants fleeing the increasing power of the Cult. Because of this, he found himself playing ambassador and politician more often than he'd like. He was a warrior, not a nursemaid.

Only a few families lingered still on Earth. Almost all that remained of their young men had chosen to receive special combat training, protecting their people and the gate until the stragglers could make up their mind to cross over. Fallon hoped it would happen soon. Those that were left couldn't escape the vigilantes for long.

He checked on his passenger out of the corner of his eye. She was cute, in spite of the shadows under her eyes and eye-watering stench. Not that he begrudged her that--she'd had a rough day. A good shower would take care of the grime, and sleep would restore her color. A faint grin played around his mouth as he considered what rest would do for her feisty attitude. She'd be a handful, and he wouldn't mind the distraction. Life had been dull of late. He had a feeling her visit might be just what he needed.

The sound of gravel crunching under the Jeep's wheels woke her from her light doze. Squinting with lingering sleep, she blinked as the motion lights clicked on, illuminating the miniature castle Fallon called home. She stared at the mullioned windows and round tower as one of the three garage doors slid up. He smiled in amusement when her eyes widened at the bad, black, and very expensive Lamborghini Diablo and custom made Harley parked on either side of the Jeep. Women had a thing for sports cars, even if most of them knew little about the specifics. Looked like she was no exception.

"Bachelor," she muttered to herself, eyeing his toys with misgiving. The odds of him having a wife and kids tucked away in here had just drastically diminished. Fighting the urge to squirm at the thought of them sharing his house unchaperoned, she paid close attention to his quick tour.

"Laundry room. Toss your clothes out the door when you hop in the shower and I'll throw them in. You can use one of my shirts and my robe until they're dry. You'll be comfortable sleeping in the shirt, and there's no way my pants are going to fit you."

She cleared her throat and suggested uneasily, "Boxers might." Heat rose in her cheeks, but she did *not* feel comfortable strutting around without underwear at the best of times, and especially around him.

"Don't wear them," he answered easily. They passed through a spacious kitchen. She glimpsed a roomy living room with leather couches, overstuffed armchairs and a big screen TV as he guided her upstairs. He paused before a door and swung it open, revealing a sparkling bathroom with a huge tub, a shower stall and double sinks. The words 'wife' drifted through her brain, but she shook it off. There were no feminine frills, no soft touches of womanly possession. "You've got a housekeeper, right?"

"Right. Look in that drawer there--should be spare toothbrushes. Soap and shampoo are in the shower, all the towels are clean. Be right back with some clothes."

Grimacing at her reflection in the mirror, she made good use of the toothbrush, thrilled to have clean teeth again. She'd been running hard for the better part of a week, ever since the Cult had picked up her trail again. She'd slept in alleys, hay barns and even broken into a church once to sack out on a pew. Even before, she'd been constantly on alert, taking odd jobs and staying on the move in a chess game that had spanned much of Europe before it had ended abruptly in London. For her, little things like pure water and the prospect of a clean, soft bed held the emotional appeal of a vacation at Club Med.

"Here you are. I'll be in the kitchen working on dinner when you're done." Her host deposited a pile of clothes on the counter and left her to her business.

Stripping naked, she gratefully tossed her dirty clothes out the door and locked it, suffering a brief pang for the mess she was about to make of his tiled shower. She stepped in and cranked up the heat. Hot needles of water rained down on her, heavenly forerunners of a hopefully restful evening. It took three shampoos and lots of soap, but finally she felt squeaky enough to brave the kitchen.

Borrowing his brush, she worked the tangles out of her waist length hair, wishing in vain for a hair dryer. His shirt slid over her bare skin like a caress, making dormant senses prickle uncomfortably. "Stop it," she muttered, belting on his maroon silk robe. There was no lotion in the bathroom, so ignoring her itchy skin, she took a deep breath and opened the door.

True to his word, he was in the kitchen, stirring something in a wok. Ignoring her flash of awareness at the sight of his muscular back, and the way he turned and looked her over slowly, as if surprised, she cleared her throat. "Mind if I borrow this?" At his slight headshake, she took his bottle of olive oil and spread a drop on her palms, rubbing it on her face and hands. Spying a clean dishtowel, she used it to wipe the excess from her face. "Dry skin," she explained at his curious look.

Nodding, he gestured to the kitchen island and a plate of raw fruit and veggies. "Help yourself. This will be done in a minute."

Fallon was … surprised. He's suspected she'd clean up well, but he hadn't expected sable hair that gently waved down to a trim little waist. Baggy clothes and sweat streaked grime had disguised a clear complexion and nice curves. Full lips and smoky blue eyes that occasionally glowed green peeked at him warily from a frame of thick lashes. The girl was hot, and he was interested. Her fear was a hurdle, but time would cure that.

A faint whiff of smoke caught his attention. Saving their dinner before it could burn, he tossed a heating pad on the island and drew up a stool. He'd already set out plates and sundries, and Rain was making good use of them.

"Care to pray?"

His request caught her off-guard. Guiltily swallowing the bite in her mouth, Rain looked at him expectantly. With a self-deprecating smile, he moved around the island and reached for her shoulders.

She grabbed a fork and spun around, breathing hard, jabbing the utensil threateningly into this stomach. "What are you doing?"

He looked at her strangely. "I was about to bless the meal." He looked askance at the fork, then up at her. "Do you always react this strongly to displays of religion?"

"You d-don't have to touch me to pray," she said warningly. Touchy-feely men had not been a pleasant part of her last years.

"I am not going to hurt you," he said slowly, confidently. Never taking his eyes from hers, he carefully reached down and closed his hand over hers, directing it away from his belly. Then, as if she weren't still quivering with adrenaline, he softly intoned a short blessing. Releasing her just as leisurely, he moved away and reclaimed his stool.

When he said nothing, simply served himself, she slowly uncoiled. The pattern of the fork was still imprinted on her hand, but she unclenched it with an act of will and returned to her eating, keeping a wary eye on him.

"Wine?" he poured a glass and offered it to her, then filled his own glass.

Rain knew about wine. It had little effect on her kind and went down like water, so she was surprised at the rich flavor and depth of her first sip. Drawing back, she eyed the golden liquid, then the decanter in front of Fallon. "This can't be wine."

"Darkland wine. Careful, it's stronger than you're accustomed to." His green eyes were amused.

Taking the caution to heart, she sipped curiously at the otherworldly liquid. "What's it made from?"

"Dream flowers. It's a very rare and special vintage."

"What's the occasion?"

"Saving a woman is always an occasion."

She looked away. "I suppose it was worth it--I might have known some names, caused some needless deaths."

It disturbed him, the scant belief in her worth. As transparently as a glass, her expression said death hadn't been such a fearful thing. It was very bad when someone looked at death as a release. Maybe he could shake some sense into her. "If we hadn't come, Rory would have abused you in ways I wouldn't describe to my least favored dog. The pheromone would have ensured you got some pleasure out of it--at first. The sexual pleasure it evokes is phenomenal and impossible to resist, but I've seen what was left of the women he used. Their minds are gone long before their body goes."

She still wouldn't look at him. Her voice was hollow. "I know what he was. I'm glad he's dead."

"The pheromone really shook you up, didn't it? That's normal. Time and a real lover will cure that."

Her eyes widened in shock. "I'm not--" she sputtered, then seemed to flail for words. "What is this, Dr. Fallon's Rx for love?"

"If you like. I've had some experience with female Sylphs. The only real cure was lengthy separation and...." he trailed off, smiling with fond remembrance. The cure had been intensive, the relationship short. She'd sent him away, claiming affectionately that he'd exhausted her, but there'd been a smile on her lips as she wished him well. The smile grew wicked as he remembered what else she'd said. *Find a woman who can keep up with you, love. I'll be content with lesser wine from now on--you've proven how exhausting it is to drink from your vintage."* Rain's presence reminded him that it had been months since he'd last shared pleasure. Interest crooked her siren finger, making his smile grow. "I could help you, if you like."

"I don't like," she snapped, far too quickly. "A cold shower works just as well."

Judging from the look in her eyes, that wasn't the whole truth, but some playful flirting might be just what she needed to overcome the fear he read there. The girl needed to lighten up. "What about a massage? I've been told I have the magic touch."

Had she been a porcupine, her quills would have gone up. "Do you understand rejection, or do I need to get you a dictionary? I don't bedrock with anyone, and definitely not total strangers."

That made him study her. A virgin? Untouched at twenty-two? Or so battered she refused to acknowledge want and need, possibly even emotion? His mood grew more serious. "Has someone forced you?"

Anguish flashed in her face. Her jaw tightened as she hid her wounded eyes. "Not exactly."

Protectiveness made his voice darken. "You were attacked."

"Nobody finished what they started," she said quickly, staring at her plate. "I'm not that helpless." She sent him a quick, fierce glance, then stabbed a bite of dinner, pushing it around on her plate.

'Nobody' implied more than one attacker, perhaps more than one incident. When had it happened? After her father's death, while she was on the run? She was too tightly wound just now to question further, but there would be another time.

It grated that any woman would be attacked, but bit even deeper with this one. She was under his protection now, whether she cared for it or not, and he took that responsibility seriously. She couldn't stay on the edge she was walking--one wrong step, and the knife's edge would cut her in two.

Fortunately, he was a man of many talents. Taking care of women ranked among his best.

They were finishing their meal as the doorbell rang. Excusing himself, he answered it, then returned bearing the delivered packages. He set them on the counter before her. "Your clothes have arrived."

Clearly puzzled, she reached for a bag, then stared at the contents. Slowly, she drew out a pair of folded jeans and looked at the tag. "These are in my size."

"I glanced at the tags on your cloths before I tossed them in the wash. We can exchange anything you don't like, but I wanted you to have selection to choose from." He watched her as he casually started clearing the table. She looked overwhelmed.

There was nothing extravagant in the bags; not knowing her tastes, he'd had the sales lady pick up common designs--t-shirts, a clingy knit top, a sweater. The white athletic shoes would do until she could choose her own, and though more personal, the packages of underwear and socks shouldn't embarrass her beyond recall. Annoyed, he realized he'd forgotten to order a coat, but she could wear one of his when they went shopping tomorrow. He glanced at her to say as much, and stilled. Her eyes were wet.

She was staring at a new hairbrush, but didn't seem to be looking at it. "Thank you." The words were strained, almost whispered. "Nobody's ever--" she broke off and swallowed.

Awkward. He didn't do tears well, but Fallon instinctively understood the basics. Moving to her side, he gingerly wrapped an arm around her, carefully patting her shoulder. He was tempted to say, "There, there" like some inane fool, but resisted the urge.

Rain sucked in a breath and stiffened her spine. "Too much wine," she said a trifle damply, wiping her eyes with the back of her hand. "I need to sleep it off."

Relieved, Fallon stepped back. "Good idea. You've had a rough day. I'll carry this stuff up for you and let you get settled."

She leapt on the idea, padding behind him up the stairs. He entered one of the guest rooms and set the bags on the floor. For a moment they just stared at each other. "There's a lock on the door, but you won't need it. Nothing is going to bother you here." He looked at her gravely, hoping she'd believe him. The girl deserved a little peace.

She wouldn't quite meet his eyes. "Thanks. I mean it. You've been … really nice."

Hm. He'd had more gushing comments made about him, but none quite as warming. The girl was refreshing--he wouldn't mind keeping her around for a while. "You're welcome, and good night." Closing the door softly, he left her to her dreams.

Chapter Three

It wasn't that she wasn't grateful. Rain cast a guilty look up the stairs. At 2:00 AM in the morning, it was deathly quiet save for the muted hum of appliances. Stealthily, she lifted the phone from its cradle and dialed the cab company. With great care, she shut the phonebook and tucked it back in its place in the hall secretary.

Leaving this way rankled. She hated taking anything he'd given her--it just drove the guilt deeper--but she'd desperately needed the socks and underwear, so she'd left him the last of her European money with the rest of her new clothes folded on the bed. She'd doubted he'd want the toothbrush back.

She had a vague plan to head south, out of the cold. It would mean hitchhiking, maybe with a trucker. If she could make it that far, she felt certain she could leave the whole lot of them behind, maybe start a new life. The Haunts and Cult could have each other. All she wanted was peace.

It had been a trick to lock her door from the outside, but she was resourceful, and it made the illusion of her sleeping in more real. She had to get away from there before the counsel found out where she was. If she waited that long, it would be too late. Her father had waited on the counsel and paid for it with his life.

"You've reached the Artic Cab Company. How can I help you?" A sleepy voice answered on the other line.

Straightening, Rain opened her mouth to give directions--

"Put it back."

Swearing, Rain whipped around at the cold words and stared. Just beyond the reach of the desk light's glow, Fallon stood there in jeans and nothing else, staring at her with a hot golden glow in his normally jade eyes. Shivers chilled her. Even with her sharp ears strained for any sound, she hadn't heard him coming.

"Hello? Is anyone there?"

Fumbling with the phone in her lax hand, Rain quickly said, "Wrong number," and hung up. Guiltily, she shifted from foot to foot, waiting for Fallon to explode.

His eyes narrowed. "Am I such a poor host that it's worth risking frost bite? It's cold as sin out there, and you've got nowhere to go."

She drew a deep breath. "I had a plan."

"So do I. Get back to bed." The lethal words warned of impending retribution unless he was obeyed.

There was nothing else for it--she wasn't stupid enough to attack a full-blood Haunt in his prime--so she eyed him, wondering if he'd move or force her to slip past him, passing through his personal space as she did. Intimidating thought, and she was already nervous.

Slowly, he moved aside, never taking his eyes off of her.

Giving thanks to his sketchy sense of chivalry, she slid past, holding her breath until she made the stairs.

He stalked after her.

Eyes widening, she hurried along, juggling her lock picks in her haste to get her door unlocked. Difficult become impossible when he paused behind her and stared at her hands.

Giving her a look, he slipped the tools from her damp fingers and did the honors. Blinking at him in surprise, she slid into the room, unsurprised when he kept her picks.

He drew her door key from his pocket and tossed it on the carpeted floor. "You'll feel better having that, though there's little point, is there?" He looked at the bed and his brows rose. Moving closer, he frowned at the piles of folded clothes and the foreign currency resting on top. He glanced at her.

"I paid you back," she said defensively. It wasn't much money, but it was all she had.

"Did you put a price on your rescue, too? I could present you with an itemized bill, if you like." Arms folded, he looked at her with an unreadable expression. The posture did sinful things to all that naked muscle.

Tamping down on her sudden urge to weep, she looked aside. "I can't pay you back for that. I can only say thank you." A pitiful, inadequate phrase, but all she had.

"That was all I wanted for the clothes, too. If you really want to return the favor, then stay here and get some rest. I'm not in the mood to track you through the ice fog." His tone had softened. Firmly, he reached out and lifted her chin. "If you leave, I will find you ... and you won't like my mood when I do." With that final warning, he released her and strode out of her room.

It was a minute before she could breathe normally again. Just standing next to him sucked all the air out of her lungs. Standing next to him while he was half-naked....

Groaning, she moved the clothes off the bed and onto the dresser, then threw herself down on it. How did he manage to make her feel like an erring child and a hormone plagued teen at the same time? It confused her, added to the stress in an already stressful moment. Now he thought she was ungrateful. That hurt. Maybe she hadn't stopped mentally running long enough to really consider what he'd done for her, but she didn't have time. He was going to make her speak to the counsel, and she had to stop it.

Her father's murderer was on the counsel. She couldn't prove it, had no idea who it was, but the last time she'd spoken to her father he'd told her he was going to share one of her inventions with his friend on the counsel. The next thing she'd known, their home was being raided and her father was dead, his workshop ransacked. She'd barely gotten away with her life that time--she wasn't dumb enough to tempt fate twice.

Just thinking about the night her father had died chilled her. They'd played chess that evening to decide who got to pick the movie. She'd won and picked *A Knight's Tale.* To make up for it, she'd made her dad popcorn. She'd gotten up to use the bathroom halfway through and had no sooner finished that she'd heard the danger alarm go off. With no time to waste, she'd opened the door concealed in the back of the shower wall and jumped down, locking the tunnel from the top. Then she'd raced to the surveillance cameras and watched as their house swarmed with werewolves.

She'd seen her father die.

There'd been no time to linger, to absorb the shock. She'd simply grabbed a emergency pack and bolted like she'd been trained to do.

Her paranoid father had always worried about things like their neighbors finding out what they were and coming to lynch them. She didn't think he'd expected to go at the hands of his own people.

If he couldn't trust them, neither could she.

How was she going to escape Fallon? Clearly sneaking away would be bloody difficult. Killing him wasn't an acceptable option, even if she could manage it--a doubtful prospect at best. Incapacitating him might work, but he was wily enough to make that tough. Getting the drugs to make him sleep, let alone getting him to take them, would tax even her sneaky mind, and coshing him on the head ... She shuddered, imaging his expression if he weren't knocked out, or worse, his retribution if she tried to bash him and failed. Haunt men made Navy Seals look like babes in nappies, and her pitiful street fighting wouldn't save her. If he wanted to, Fallon could power through her moves like a full throttle locomotive, smashing her in the process. You didn't take on a Haunt male unless you were suicidal, and she hadn't reached that point yet.

She could seduce him. As soon as the notion presented itself, she rejected it. Stupid idea. Bedding him wouldn't relax his guard, especially when she'd flinched from him like a caged pidgin at dinner. Not only would he not believe it, she just couldn't do it.

Men scared her. It wasn't because she'd suffered any hideous hurt at their hands. Her father had been her best friend, but she'd always been shy, not the kind of girl that appealing males made up to. As a result she'd had no boyfriends, had experienced only a couple of forgettable kisses. Someone like Fallon wouldn't even want her, and she didn't need to deal with rejection on top of everything else.

Left with no options, she settled on waiting on opportunity. A distraction would come, giving her the chance to bolt. As a plan, it sucked, but she'd worked with less on shorter notice. She'd make it work. She couldn't afford not to.

* * * *

A blood curdling roar jerked Fallon out of a deep sleep. Half scream, half battle-cry, it had him out of bed, gun in hand before his mind registered why. Tearing open his door, he bolted down the hall to Rain's room. Before he could kick the door open, it flew inward, and a wild-eyed fury burst out. Eyes wide, golden-lit with fear and rage, she snarled at him and converted her charge to a flying kick. Habit made him dodge, surprise made him stomp on his instinctive reaction. She was in her nightshirt--his shirt-- and shaking with adrenaline. A nightmare? Flashback?

Kirk, a friend and one of the men who'd helped with her rescue, charged up the stairs, a wicked blade in his hand. He'd arrived on a late flight and his body clock was still set time zones away, so he'd volunteered to guard the TV and fridge while Fallon went to bed. His entrance spooked the girl. With a snarl, she ran down the hall, flinging open the door to his study.

"What's up?" Kirk demanded, looking around for someone to disembowel.

"Check her room. I think it's a flashback," Fallon supplied, dashing after his houseguest. Peeking around the corner of his study with a great deal more caution than he'd approached her door, he barely saved his face as the small statue of a knight whizzed by his head. Swearing, he slipped into the room, dodging missiles as he went. "Rain!"

No response. Looking around wildly, she noticed the moonlight coming through the diamond paned window and raced for it.

A fleeting prayer ran through his head as he dove for her, tackling her just over the chaise lounge. The velvet cushions broke her fall, but his weight sent a fresh rush of panic through her. Damp with cold sweat, blinded by her loose hair, she fought against his hold, trying to bite.

In the end, she exhausted herself, unable to defeat his superior strength. Only then did he relax his rigid hold, fractionally giving her freedom as he shifted more of his weight off her. "Rain?" He brushed the wet hair from her eyes, careful not to release her wrists yet. "Did you have a bad dream?"

She blinked and drew in a shuddering breath. Slowly she looked around, dawning bewilderment in her eyes.

The study light came on. Kirk stood at the door, gingerly avoiding broken pottery and debris with his stocking feet. "Doozy of temper you've got there, love." He started picking up the mess.

Fallon relaxed a little more as she stared at Kirk, comprehension emerging. Certain she was no longer going to attack, he moved off her, sitting beside her on the chaise. "Bad dreams. What were you dreaming of?"

She slowly sat up, shivering. The borrowed shirt barely covered her thighs, and it was cool by the window. "The night my father died."

Fallon snagged the throw blanket and covered her. "What happened?"

"We were swarmed with Haunt. My father had sensed something and made me go down the emergency shoot. He didn't have time to follow without being seen. I didn't dare go back--they were watching the house. I saw what happened through the spy hole." She shivered.

Fallon and Kirk exchanged glances. Carefully, Fallon asked, "Would you recognize anyone?"

She shook her head, still lost in memories. "They were all shifted. They looked alike to me."

The strangeness of her statement made him frown. Shifted or not, every Haunt had recognizable and unique characteristics. "Nothing stood out?"

She shook her head again.

"Would you recognize a scent?" All of them had infallible scent memories and sharper than human noses, even without shifting. She should be able to do at least that.

Avoiding his eyes, she muttered, "I couldn't smell anything. My nose isn't very keen."

What did that mean? Even with a stuffed up nose--and they rarely suffered from illness--she should have scented something. Was she suppressing the memories?

The color had leeched from her skin. "I-I'd like to go lie down now."

Wincing at his impatience in the face of her distress, he picked her up and headed for her room, grimacing as the shards Kirk had missed while he'd been cleaning cut his feet. They'd heal in a day or two, and she didn't need cut feet.

"I can walk," she said shakily.

"Humor me." The last thing they needed was her playing tough and independent. It wasn't going to hurt her to be cosseted a little. Tomorrow was going to be a rough day for her--she needed to rest for what remained of the night.

Stiffening when she saw her bed, she actually turned her face to his chest. Brows rising, he paused, then realized that she might fear falling back into the dream. He thought for a moment. "Would you like me to get a radio for you? The music might help. Either that or you can sleep on the couch. I'll even wrestle the remote away from Kirk for you."

She actually smiled and risked a glance at him. "I'd like that."

Pleased by that small smile, he turned and headed for the stairs. She stiffened when she saw he planned to carry her down.

"Ye of little faith," he chided, not pausing. In moments she was deposited on the couch, the lights on, remote in hand. Raising a brow at the impressive array of snacks Kirk had lain out, Fallon fetched her a glass of juice and a blanket. "Just yell if he tries to change the channel. I'll bring you a stick." Leaving her smiling wanly, he went to find Kirk.

Kirk raised a brow when he stepped into the study. "Get some clothes on, mate. I'm surprised the girl didn't run screaming at the sight of your tallywacker hanging out."

Fallon actually looked down before he caught Kirk's smirk. "Funny. You know I always wear pants when I'm expecting trouble." Not that he liked the black silk pajama bottoms, but they were cooler than flannel. Besides, any man would feel ridiculous facing down attackers with his better parts hanging out.

Kirk grunted. "Our pigeon remembers nothing and has flashbacks that make my sister's PMS look like a Brady Bunch reunion. I'd say toss her back, but she's a menace to society."

Unamused, Fallon sat down in his office chair and started picking splinters out of his feet. "Someone thinks she remembers something. One of our own had to have tipped her hand to the Cult. She's too good at running."

Kirk laughed. "Bold move, calling a taxi on your own phone."

"She's not listed as a genius for nothing. She failed half of her high school classes, then made perfect scores on her GED. Intelligence found texts on computer hacking, advanced electronics, chemistry and physics in her room, along with a host of gadgets that made the hair stand up on the investigator's heads. If her father hadn't got in their way, whoever had raided their house would have had their own captive prodigy."

No longer amused, Kirk dumped the last of the shards in the trash. "Trying to market her inventions was the dumbest thing her father could have done. Probably would have saved his life if they'd continued to pretend she was nothing special."

"He couldn't have known." Fallon watched the blood run from the cuts on his feet and frowned. It was going to stain the carpet.

"What was her father like, anyway?"

Fallon thought about it. "We don't know much about him. Apparently he was a recluse, both from humans and his own kind. He was a widower, and not much of a warrior, according to his family. No real ambitions, no children other than Rain. He raised alfalfa and beans or something. Pretty solitary."

"Did he see Rain as his ticket to early retirement?"

"Who knows? Her inventions brought in a lot of money before she used it up running. The fortune might not have helped him out much, but it helped to save Rain's life."

"Good thing for her."

"Yeah." Tomorrow was going to be busy, and Fallon could use some more rest. Kirk would be up for hours yet. "Keep an eye on her. I'm going back to bed." Answers would come in the morning.

"I fixed your VCR."

Fallon blinked at his sleepy-eyed guest. The VCR had been broken for weeks, and he hadn't gotten around to buying a new one. A glance at Kirk revealed him smirking over his breakfast. "Oh?"

"Kirk got me the tools."

Kirk saluted him with his toast. "She knows her way around a Philips and a soldering iron, I'll give her that."

Debating the possible attractions of the Brit's close-cropped black hair and rakish goatee in the eyes of his female guest this early in the morning was beyond him. Fallon put her ease in Kirk's company down to bonding over too much late night TV and junk food, then ignored it. Kirk wasn't interested, and Fallon was too old for childish displays of jealousy. "Thanks."

She smiled at him, and he blinked. The girl was beautiful when she glowed like that.

Hiding his smirk behind his coffee mug, Kirk caught his eye. His expression seemed to say, *"Too young, too green, too available, my friend. This one will trip you up yet."*

Uncomfortably aware of just how well Kirk knew his usual tastes, his usual liaisons, Fallon frowned and concentrated on eating. He'd seen what a fresh young thing had done to his jaded friends; not that it was a fate to fear, but it certainly wasn't something he had time for. As an ambassador between worlds, he wasn't looking for a young consort, and this one carried a lot of baggage.

Baggage that was going to get publicly rifled through in about fifteen minutes.

He waited until she finished her toast before speaking. "The Council of Elders will be meeting very shortly. It's a video conference via satellite, so we don't have to leave the house."

A sickly shade of gray replaced her normal color. "Why do I have to meet with them? Don't they have something more important to do?"

Fallon studied her. "They have to decide whether to extradite you to the Darklands. You're in danger now that the Cult has identified you."

"I won't go."

He let that go. She wasn't going to have a choice, and it was his job to carry out the transplant. Standing up, he offered her his hand. "It's time."

Ignoring his hand, she pushed her chair out with angry defiance, pointedly keeping her space from him. With a sigh, he led the way, allowing Kirk to bring up the rear, boxing her in. They adjourned to his study. While Fallon raised the wall hiding a big screen TV, Kirk seated Rain in a leather chair that swallowed her, taking up guard behind her. In moments the screen began to fill with faces, some very old, a couple apparently in their middle ages. In moments seven faces stared back at her, studying her with curiosity or dispassion, depending on the Elder.

It was all she could do not to claw her way up the back of her chair and escape.

The most ancient of faces, a man with a white beard and the dignified essence of Sean Connery, looked at Fallon. "Good morning, my lord. Felicitations on your latest mission. I trust all goes smoothly?"

Fallon inclined his head. "As can be expected, Elder Azion." He glanced at Rain. "This is Rain Lilly Zephyr Miller, daughter of the late Rian Miller."

Rain winced. She hadn't known he knew her full name, and thanks to her hippie mother, it was a gruesome mouthful.

Ignoring her reaction, Fallon introduced the seven elders. "Elder Azion, Elder Traforte, Elder Rite."

Most of the names were quickly forgotten, but Rain remembered Azion and Rite. Azion had the advantage of first introduction, and Rite ... the man was creepy. Middle-aged like her father would have been, but with night black hair and startling blue eyes, his face was average, but the intensity in his expression was anything but. Against her will, her gaze kept darting to him, and she felt grateful that he wasn't there in person.

Azion's words drew her attention back to the conversation. His gaze steady, he said calmly, "As I'm sure you've been told, we're here to decide on your future, on whether you'd be better off here or installed in the Darklands."

Her eyes narrowed with defiance. "I'm an American citizen, and I choose to remain here."

"It's not that simple. You're now a target of the Cult and a danger to the rest of us. How do you propose to defend yourself?"

"I'm skilled at making myself disappear," she said grimly. This time she would stay that way.

Kindly, Azion asked, "But what kind of life is that-- running and hiding? Living in fear? Do you feel you'd be happy?"

"I'm happy if I'm free." She tried to ignore the hollowness his words invoked. It had been so long since anyone had cared, so long since she'd had friends. Experience told her that friends would be difficult to make on the run.

"If even large families with many warriors have difficulty resisting the Cult, how do you plan to stay free of them? Our war with the Cult is costing too many lives. Soon there will be none of us left here on Earth, either because we've moved on to the Darklands, or because the Cult has won."

Even she had to admit the man was logical, but she'd had so much taken from her. She didn't want this forced on her, too. "It should be my choice whether I go or stay."

"What of a family? Most of our young men have already left for the Darklands It will be difficult for you to find a mate here on Earth."

He would use that argument. Her heart twisted, and she answered harshly, "I choose not to have one."

Her words caused a murmur to go through her audience. Azion's brows rose. "Why is that? You are young, pretty enough to easily attract a husband. Even if you aren't ready for children now, you may be later."

Feeling sick, she looked aside. She wasn't going to win unless she confessed.

Her father had warned her, once she'd finally learned the truth. It had been horrible enough finding out what he was, but he'd warned her that his kind wouldn't take well to knowledge of her. Some of them might be incensed enough to kill her, and he'd loved her too well to let that happen. He'd installed the escape tunnel in the house and secrecy in her heart. Flinging it away now was ten times worse than giving away her virginity could ever be.

The silence stretched. They were content to wait her out. Clearing her throat, she said hoarsely, "My mother was human."

A flurry of murmurs followed her confession, making her shift in her seat. Almost she expected someone to strike her dead on the spot. Shape-shifters hated mixed blood. Her father had told her so. After all, humans and Haunt had never shared a world gracefully. In their way, Haunt could be as bigoted toward humans as the Cult was toward Haunt. Her father had lived apart from his own kind ever since her birth, encouraging her shyness. He hadn't wanted to risk exposing his daughter to the uncertain mercy of his kind. Little as she knew of the race, she didn't doubt they could hate her. Surely this would result in freedom--one way or the other.

Personally she hoped Fallon would kick her out. Her blood would make an awful mess of his carpet, and he *had* gone through a lot of trouble to save her hide in the first place.

Her father had told her that mixed-blood children rarely survived the first trimester, as the seed did not mix gracefully. She'd been born two months premature and her mother had never really recovered from the pregnancy. She'd died when Rain was five, leaving a grieving husband and a sad little girl in her wake. Her father had concealed the knowledge of what she was from her when she exhibited little of his race's characteristics, thinking that she'd be happier believing she was fully human. He'd been right, for the day she had learned otherwise had sent her world into a tailspin from which she'd never recovered.

The murmur died down. Azion considered her thoughtfully, and she had the sudden suspicion that he already knew about her mixed blood.

"Interesting revelation, but to my mind it makes little difference. You've got our blood. As rare and impossible as that may seem, when combined with your susceptibility to the male Sylph, it makes you our responsibility. I do not believe you will be happy here. Indeed, it's clear that you have been miserable for some time. I move to extradite you to the Darklands." One by one, the Elders voted to send her through the gate to the new Haunt world, sealing her fate.

Her lips parted on a silent protest. They were crazy! She was not about to meekly go along, dumbly complying with their stupid decree. She knew nothing about the Darklands, only that it had a creepy name and was inhabited by a race of beings her father had warned her wouldn't appreciate her existence. Gritting her teeth, she fought the urge to tell them where they could shove their verdict. The less she said, they less they would know of her plans.

She was *not* going to the Darklands.

Azion's eyes shifted inquiringly to her left.

That brought Rain to her feet. Fists clenched, she gritted out, "I'm twenty-two years old, far past the need for a guardian. I--"

"I accept the responsibility," Fallon's calm voice cut off her tirade.

She whirled on him, within a fingernail of attacking him. "I do not want you as my keeper! I don't *need* you as my keeper, so why don't you just--"

Azion cut her off this time. "Lord Fallon will be protecting you until such a time as you find a mate and he can hand the responsibility over. He will help you to get established and will see to your well being until you are settled. This is the will of the Counsel. Good luck, and good day."

Mute fury riveted her to the spot as the screen went blank. Ignoring Kirk and her new "guardian", she stalked to the exit, whipped open the door, strode down the hall and slammed into her room. Locking the door, she threw herself on the bed and screamed into her pillow.

* * * *

"That went well."

Fallon shot Kirk an annoyed look and dropped into his office chair. He could see the hallway and Rain's bedroom through his open study door.

He hadn't known she was a half-breed. It explained a lot, but made little impact on his decision to protect her, other than to make him more certain that she needed it. Elder Azion was right; she wasn't happy here. No matter how she felt about the move, she was sure to have a better chance of survival in the Darklands.

Retirement had been looming for him for some time--he'd be glad to go home. Kirk was ready to replace him, and there few enough of them left on this side of gate to warrant Fallon's continued presence. He had lands and duties in the Darklands, both of which had suffered his absence for over a decade. Dealing with one small woman wasn't going to tax him.

Toying with the latch on his laptop, he let his eyes wander over the shelves of books. The sun shown through the window Rain had almost leapt through, reflecting off the snow and illuminating the red velvet couch. Three moons rode the sky in the Darklands and the climate was tropical. He'd miss this place, but it had never held his heart like his home.

He pictured Rain in the Darklands and smiled. She'd probably attack the first shifted soldier she found, and since all males remained in their more powerful, mute form when on duty, she'd see one almost immediately. Growing up around humans might even have made her fearful. Frowning, he considered how long it would take her to become acclimated.

Chapter Four

It was still dark when Rain woke up, but that wasn't unusual for Alaska. Sunrise wouldn't happen until ten-something that morning. Growling at the dark, she flipped back the covers and hunted for her socks.

She wanted to slap herself for her tantrum last night. Granted, for the last year she'd been hunted, sleep-deprived, half-starved and almost seduced by the bad guy, but that didn't excuse her childish behavior. You'd think the last few years would have pistol-whipped the remains of giddy youth out of her.

She was going to the Darklands. She hated to admit it, yet there it was. With the entire bloody Counsel against her, the Cult's deathwatch waiting for her to show her face and Fallon and Kirk babysitting, there was no way she was going to be able to run. Then there was the little matter of the trinket she carried....

Rain slipped her hand into her frayed leather jacket and pulled out a red rubber ball. A lopsided smirk curved her lips as she peeled it apart at the seams and spilled the contents into her palm. A heavy as gold, the intricately carved metal ball slowly warmed in her palm. Topaz gems winked at her from their settings, inviting her to touch, to wake them from their slumber. Giving in, she held the device next to the bedside lamp, giving it just enough light for its advanced solar battery to operate.

With a hum, the device lifted from her palm and hovered, slowly rotating. The gems lit up, began their opening notes.

Rain shivered as unearthly music, barely heard, intensely felt, vibrated in the air. The sounds physically pleasured the listener, shimmering with the radiance of the aurora, invisibly intense, seductively sweet. Piercing. Addictive.

She hadn't meant to make the Bell. It was supposed to be a gate key, a teleportation device that would open the door to the Darklands and allow her to take a peek without being trapped; her pocket wormhole. She realized too late that one actually had to go to the Darklands before it could be set--problematic, since she'd had no intention of applying for her green card. By then, of course, she'd been addicted, unable to abandon her seductive little toy and its hypnotic sounds.

The idea of it falling into another's hands put her into a cold sweat. Think of how easy it would be for a thief to use it, or a murderer. Able to pop in and out, he'd never be caught.

Her father had been killed just for hinting that the Bell existed.

Someone on the Counsel had committed murder to possess it, and if she weren't careful, she'd be next. Stealing was the least a man could do with the gate at his disposal. Murder would child's play if he could learn to set it. Imagine the devastation if the Bell fell in the hands of an assassin. She wasn't blind to the potential disaster.

Unfortunately, she couldn't destroy it; physically couldn't do it. In its own way it was every bit as bad as Rory's pheromones had been. Her nerves went weak every time she thought about smashing it--the thing had become her lover. The resonance bound even as it gave sweet pleasure, and like a puppet, she danced attendance on it. God forbid a man should ever have such sensual power over her.

Shivering at the final whisper of notes, she closed her hand over the Bell. Breathing deeply, she sealed it in its hiding place and shoved it in her pocket. At least she had an out if things got ugly in the Darklands. No one would think to look for her back here.

It was time to go and face Fallon, and her future.

* * * *

"I'd rather drive." Rain eyed the snow machine as Fallon strapped on his saddlebags and duffle. She knew how to drive one, but she had serious misgivings about letting him. He had that look about him that said he only had one speed--warp velocity. His full face black helmet hid his face and his winter gear only emphasized his height. Kirk was just as bad--both of them made her feel like a round midget.

Glowering at Kirk, who was strapping on his skis, she grumped, "The machine will bog down." Not that she would mind the delay.

"Not this one, baby." Fallon's eyes crinkled, though his grin was hidden. "We've added a few Darklands upgrades. Things are a little more advanced on the other side of the gate. Hop on."

Arms crossed, she eyed him, then grudgingly gave in. No doubt his weight on the back would overbalance them anyway, should they go up any hills. Settling on back, she lightly grasped his waist, holding on by her legs by habit. She'd spent much of her childhood on snow machines and hated to ride double, preferring to be the one in control. It was no fun staring at the back of someone's head--or in Fallon's case, at his back. It blocked out a huge chunk of scenery, and if he hadn't set the shocks stiff enough, guaranteed a jarring ride.

Fallon took off slowly, and she was relieved he wasn't novice enough to dig a hole by gunning it. The thought had no more than crossed her mind when he opened throttle. Rain grunted and held on, rolling her eyes at Kirk's whoop. The blinking idiot was going to find himself wrapped around a tree and he was enjoying it.

Frosted birches and snow cloaked spruce flashed by, giving Rain more enjoyment than she liked to admit. It had been a long time since she'd rode, and Fallon proved a better driver than she'd suspected. He took jumps like a madman, laughing all the while, darting off into the powder now and then for the sheer thrill of it. Kirk shouted encouragement, unintelligible over the roar of wind and engine, but understood. Their pleasure caught under her armor, sinking into her blood until it sang, too. Were all men like this in the Darklands? Maybe it wouldn't be so bad.

All too soon, the wild ride slowed. Disappointed, she looked around at the unassuming stand of birch, seeing nothing more interesting than a fleeing grouse. Fallon dismounted. Twisting around on the seat, she watched Kirk dusting off snow. Fallon took off his helmet, tossing it to his friend, then stripped off his snowsuit, tossing it for sport, too. Kirk laughed and tossed it back. "Feeling the heat already?"

Fallon grinned. "Know it." He turned to Rain. "Take off the helmet and suit and follow me. I promise you'll be more than warm enough in a minute."

Wary of his wicked grin, she slowly obeyed, glowering as the cold bit into her exposed skin.

He unbuckled her duffle and slung it over his shoulder. "Leave the boots and gloves on--Kirk will get it later.

There's just less for him to carry this way." He held out his hand. "Ready, Dorothy?"

"Careful, Toto. I might just make a coat out of you to keep from freezing out here." Giving him her hand so he could help her through the knee-deep snow, she followed, grimacing as powder worked its way down her boots. At least it was growing warmer.

A shadow caught her eye, and she froze, staring at the unusually big tree to her right. Was that a wolf?

Fallon tugged her on, and she noticed the snow thinning under the shadow of the trees. The warmth continued to build, and she looked up as the light dimmed, greened. Well, that explained it. The trees had grown huge, and their leaves blocked the sun....

Rain stiffened and looked around. Redwoods. She was in a redwood forest. Ferns and moss provided a soft cushion on either side of the faint dirt path. Mushrooms the size of ottomans dotted the forest floor, adding color like bright red vases full of poppies in someone's sitting room. A wolf-like creature wove in and out of the trees, a silent watcher to her personal drama. Rain just stood there, looking, ignoring the snow melting into her socks.

Fallon smiled and handed her a pair of shoes, then slowly peeled off her gloves. "Welcome to the Darklands. We'll pitch this stuff back through the gate, then I'll take you up to the Citadel and introduce you around."

Dazed, she looked at him, blinked when she noticed him stripping off his sweater. Underneath was a black leather vest that buckled across his chest. A red embroidered Celtic knot decorated his left breast. She recognized the black pants from this morning, but she'd never seen the weapons belt he buckled on, nor the gun in the low holster against his right thigh. A silver dagger hilt rode his left hip. She stared.

He grinned. "Standard uniform--you'll be seeing a lot of it. Come on, let's go blow your mind."

He'd originally intended to take her straight to her quarters to settle in, then slowly introduce her to his world. Seeing the wonder in her eyes changed his mind. Why not build on it? This magic, the mystique of stepping into an alien world that was now her own, this is what she needed. Let her first moments be full of pleasure and the rest of her days would be colored by it. Tossing aside his mental itinerary, he took her hand, threw her a grin, and headed for the market.

Rain's eyes lit up when she first caught sight of the colorful tents and booths nestled against the curve of the Citadel's stone wall, facing the bay. Rows of merchants selling everything from produce and crafts to weapons and livestock greeted shoppers with cheerful invitations to try their wares. Women with baskets did the household shopping, haggling with shopkeepers as their children scurried around, ogling the goods. By the look on her face, Rain couldn't wait to explore.

Fallon grinned, congratulating himself on a great idea. All women loved to shop.--this one was no exception.

Rain was in awe of the colorful costumes and elaborate hairstyles of the local women. While the men seemed to prefer darker colors and simple pants and tunics, the women swept around in the full spectrum of the rainbow, in styles ranging from harem pants and cropped vests with tulip or full sleeves, to exotic robes and Grecian style gowns. The crowd wove around them, the packed sand under their feet muffling some of the noise as the scent of baked goods and savory delights filled the air. Butchers with their logs of hanging sausages and crocks of cured meats stood next to venders with colorful jars of layered dried fruits and nuts, glass cases full of confections and rows of fat-bellied wine bottles. Several stands with steaming kettles and carved wooden boxes full of bread served customers in a pavilion-covered dinning area, filling their wooden bowls full of something that smelled good. Dishwashers accepted the bowls and cups, keeping the area clean as diners left.

"Yellow arches, eat your heart out," Rain murmured, her mouth watering. Before she could ask what they were serving, her attention was captured by the stall on her left. She gasped. A beautiful jacket of wine-red velvet was displayed on a wooden mannequin, complete with matching choker and earrings. Cropped, close-fitted at the bust for a woman's body, it was decorated with a one inch band of red and white crystals at the edges and fastened with a gold clasp between the breasts. The sleeves were full and made of a sheer, burgundy fabric with ruby and diamond colored crystal cuffs. At least she assumed the stones were crystal--she wouldn't dare display real stones like that in an open market. A black silk sarong and gorgeous sash were tied around the mannequin's hips, teasing the shopper with visions of trying it on.

Rain took a deep breath and put it out of her head. Where would she wear it, even if she could afford it? Ignoring a tempting embroidered gold and silver sheath displayed next to it, she lowered her gaze and tried not to drool over the jewelry in the case below it. A vine necklace with marquee cut white crystals sparkled next to matching earrings displayed on black velvet. The rest of the jewelry was impressively designed, but nothing, in her eyes, matched that pretty set.

She glanced at Fallon, found him near, yet conversing with another man as she window shopped. He caught her eye, smiled, and waved her on. Since he seemed content, she was more than happy to keep looking.

"Good morning. Would you like a manicure or a haircut?" an older woman with a hopeful smile greeted her as she moved to the next stall. Before Rain could decline, Fallon stepped forward and paid the woman.

"Pamper her," he told the shopkeeper. "My ward is being very patient with my preoccupation and deserves the reward." Giving Rain a dazzling grin white enough to keep her blinking, he turned away and resumed his conversation.

The shopkeeper's eyes widened at the coins he'd set in her palm, and she beamed. "Come, dear, have a seat. My daughters and I will make you the loveliest girl in the Citadel."

Before Rain knew what was happening, she was seated in a comfortable chair and bombarded with questions about split ends, what color nail polish she preferred and how long it had been since she'd had a pedicure.

"Er, never," she admitted, trying to catch a glimpse of Fallon before the beautician tackled her ragged ends. It had been a long time since she'd been to a salon, and never had she had three women hovering over her like the personal maids of some pampered duchess. It felt marvelous and novel, and was a far cry from how she'd expected the morning to go. The girls even massaged her hands and feet, which tickled, but felt shockingly good. When they finished painting pretty silver and gold designs on her nails, the elder woman handed her a fruit drink, then beckoned in a man with clothing cradled in his arms.

"For you, milady, compliments of Lord Fallon," he said, displaying his wares with a flourish. A midnight blue top very like the red one she'd admired was draped over his arms. This one had short tulip sleeves and was embroidered in silver and gold with a silver and crystal butterfly clasp.

Her attendants "ooohed."

The man offered an apologetic bow. "We are very sorry the one you admired is not in your size, but we would be happy to have one made for you, or to offer you a look at our other inventory."

"Oh, this one is beautiful, but...." she looked around and tried to catch Fallon's eye. He allowed her to hold it for a moment, smiled slightly, then turned his attention to the man he was speaking to, a different one than last time.

Rolling her eyes at his generosity, she accepted the clothing with shy thanks, going behind the curtain in the back of the tent to change. There were even matching sandals. Wondering what she looked like, for she'd yet to see a mirror, she drew back the curtain.

Fallon glanced at her and froze. Very slowly, he inhaled, his eyes wandering from her head to her feet. By the time they met hers again, they were a glowing, brilliant green.

Beaming, the shopkeeper took her arm and pulled the breathless Rain in front of a full length mirror. Rain gasped.

That had to her, but she couldn't believe it. Her hair was prettily braided and swept up from her face in a princess's coronet. She hadn't paid much attention when the shopkeeper had applied makeup, other than enjoying the attention and praying she wouldn't look like a clown when she was done. Instead, the woman had used a light hand to highlight and conceal, achieving an exotic, ethereal effect. Rain touched her rouged lips, startled by the jewel effect of her silver and gold nails. The girl in that mirror was lovely, and this had to be a dream.

Fallon hadn't planned on giving Rain the vine necklace until later, but she was so breathtaking that he couldn't resist. Her lips parted when he removed it from its velvet pouch and clasped it around her neck, and her breath came faster as he slipped in the matching earrings. Then he drew back a few inches and admired her glowing skin and ruby colored lips. It was her eyes that gave him pause, though. The shining green hinted of tears, an emotion he hadn't meant to invoke.

Slowly, she reached up and closed the distance. A kiss like a soft summer breeze brushed his lips, hesitated, was gone. It shook him more than he expected.

She lowered her eyes. "Thank you," she whispered.

Unable to bear the currents between them, he raised her face. "The least you deserve." Vaguely aware of the avid curiosity of the others, he lifted his head and offered his arm. "Are you hungry? There's a restaurant in the Citadel I think you'd enjoy. I'm starving, myself." Arranging for her clothes and his other purchases to be sent to her quarters, he led her from the shop, keeping the conversation light until she'd recovered.

It was mildly embarrassing and intensely satisfying that he'd been able to move her. While glad she was enjoying herself, he was a little worried. Turning her head with gifts hadn't been his plan--he was surprised he'd managed to spend what little he had on her so easily. Perhaps the shock of her surroundings had thrown her off enough to make it work, but it had been easy enough to pamper her. Would she grow used to it? Demand it? Needy women made him ill, and he prayed that he hadn't just created one. On the other hand, she needed clothes, and creating a pleasant mood on her first day had helped immensely.

He hadn't been wasting time while she shopped. He'd summoned his personal secretary to him the moment they'd entered the market place, then spent his time catching up on events and organizing his household. He had a suite of rooms next to the vast Citadel gardens, and had arranged for Rain to occupy the room next to him. Security would be easier, and she'd have easy access to a familiar face. The idea that he'd like having her close he ignored.

Rain tensed as they neared the massive Citadel gates, currently raised for the day. It was not the sight of the multiple rows of iron gates or the long tunnel cut from the blue mountain that was the Citadel that made her stomach flip, though. Guards stood at the gate--Haunt guards. Fully shifted, with wolfish faces and bodies covered with hair, they might have come straight from the cast of *Howling III.* Each guard wore black pants, boots, and buckled leather vests similar to Fallon's, though none she saw had his red insignia. Armed with pistols and wicked looking knives-- one Haunt even carried a tomahawk at his side and had a rifle holstered on his back--they gave new meaning to *intimidation.*

Nausea from the adrenalin dump threatened to embarrass her. Shaking from battle instincts, she shifted her weight to her toes and cursed her new clothes. Stupid fool! How could she have been so easily sweet-talked out of her sturdy jeans and running shoes?

"Easy," Fallon said, equal parts command and soothing in his voice. He kept moving toward the portal. "They're not holding the gate against you."

"The last time I saw these things, they were tearing my father apart," she snarled bitterly, unable to stop the low growl rumbling at the back of her throat. She could feel her canines lengthening, sharpening, the change that came without her bidding when in danger. The guards were looking at her, and she knew her eyes were glinting gold. Not that they'd care--they made her useless little changes look like costume makeup. Her eyes jumped around, looking for handholds in the smooth rock face, searching for the most likely nightmares to plow over if she had to run.

The Haunt at the gate never took their eyes from her.

"You've been surrounded by us for days now. Your father was one of us. You carry our blood," Fallon said softly. Ever calm, he watched her as if she were no more deadly than a child with monsters in her closet. He kept them moving toward the gate.

Pain made her fingers curl as her fingernails thickened, lengthened. "I'm not one of you," she rasped, the change making speech almost impossible.

Humor coloring his voice, Fallon glanced at her, noted the tell tail changes that had tipped the Cult off in Scotland. "I can see that."

She didn't even think. Turning on him, she aimed for his belly with her deadly nails and tried to shove him over backwards, hooking her foot behind his knee. One shove and she could run, race for the forest portal....

It didn't work. Instead, Fallon crushed her to him, shifting her balance so she was plastered to his chest. Fury and fear had her sinking her nails deep into his back, through the leather of his vest. He grunted, and she felt the warm flow of blood seep from the gouges. Shocked, she released him and backed off. Blood stained her hands. Sickened by the sight, she stared at him in horror.

He grunted again and flexed his back muscles slowly. "We need some ground rules for these arguments of ours, sweetheart."

Miserable, she turned her head and stared blindly at nothing, her mind a careful blank. As shock calmed her, she felt her body change back to normal.

Fallon took her arm in a firm grip and strode for the gate while she was still biddable. Loudly, for the benefit of those watching, he said, "If you're not hungry, all you have to do is say so. I can be dense with women, but even I understand a 'no'."

Heavy with irony, his tone only made her feel lower. Panic attacks with claws could be deadly enough, but she'd never attacked a friend before. Of course, she'd never had a friend to attack, and even now, she wasn't sure that Fallon was one. That didn't stop the sickness tearing up her guts, however.

Fallon didn't need to hear an apology, not with her bowed shoulders and hidden face shouting it out. A surge of pity mixed with lingering irritation. That half-change of hers was unsettling. Their kind was either-or, not an odd mix of both states, and by the look on her face as she'd changed, she had no control over it. Maybe that had contributed to her fright. In human form, Haunt had human senses, except for sharpened hearing. In Haunt form, they had the keen senses of wolves coupled with superior strength, speed and agility, though they sacrificed the power of speech. Rain seemed to be stuck in between, and it had looked painful.

She didn't look up as he guided her up the steps of the citadel and down the stone corridors. Arched windows let in light, showcasing the parquet flooring and colorful castle inhabitants. Five minutes of walking brought them to his private wing and deep into his personal security, security that had been tightened to protect his ward. Briefly wondering what the guards at her door thought of his grim expression and Rain's bowed head, he took her into her room and walked straight through it, exiting out into her private pleasure garden. Once there, he released her. "I find the sunshine calming. I suggest you remain out here until you've settled in." He accompanied the "suggestion" with a fierce look, then he left to attend to the holes in his back.

Rain watched him stalk off, then closed her eyes. Hideously embarrassing, that emotional display of hers. Bad enough it had happened in public, but she was still tense from her view of the Haunt soldiers. Logic told her she'd grow calmer around them, but she'd never love them. Fallon was one of them....

She shivered.

He'd left her in a garden. Walled, roughly the size of a school bus, it had a winding path that led to a bench set under a shady fruit tree. A small pool provided a place to gaze. Pear trees had been trained against the walls, alternating with a pink flowered vine she couldn't identify. Flowering bushes alternated with herbs and mixed flower clusters, providing washes of color. Well clipped grass formed a soft carpet between the flowers and the walls.

With a sigh, she slipped off her shoes and padded over to the bench. She was still tired from long months of running, and though she'd been too long in the London fog and Alaskan chill, the sun was beginning to show its strength. She used the pool to rinse her hands. To her surprise, she found brilliant blue and gold fish swimming in the water.

"Pretty," she murmured. Someone took good care of this place. From what she'd seen, she figured that Fallon could probably afford the best help.

As if summoned by her speculation, a young woman appeared at the door to her apartment. "Mistress?" Her dusky yellow sarong swayed gracefully as she moved closer, giving a glimpse of her straw sandals. Her matching, sleeveless top hung around her neck with a scarlet cord. A sash of the same color decorated her waist as she paused at the pool. Long dark hair flowed free to her waist, and she had an enviable tan. "My name is Malian. Is there anything you would like? A meal, perhaps? The master said you might be hungry."

Rain sighed. "How is his back?"

Malian was slow to answer, but returned a gentle assurance. "He is fine. In two days, the marks will have healed. But come! The change to the Darklands must be difficult. How may I help?"

"I don't know. I guess I'm a little hungry. What is this fruit above me?" Rain didn't feel like putting the girl to any trouble.

The girl smiled. "Hairy sugar fruit, but it is not yet ripe. I took the liberty of bringing you a light meal, if you're interested."

Rain sighed again. Well, if the girl was determined to feed her … she followed Malian into the apartment, surprised at the simple elegance. Decorated in ice blue and yellow, with touches of white and plum, it was cool and inviting at once. Two couches faced each other in the sitting area, and a bed with a silken coverlet promised a good night's sleep. A roomy tub, surrounded by unlit candles, offered a tranquil soak. A mirrored armoire with one glass door showed linens ready for her use.

Malian had set a wide, flat soup bowl on the table. A delicate, wonderful smell arouse from it as Rain took a seat. Malian poured her some juice from a frosty beverage and smiled. "Allow me to put your things away in the wardrobe while you refresh yourself, mistress. Enjoy."

Rain did. The soup was fish in a clear broth, both tangy and sweet. Whatever it was, she would definitely like it again. While unfamiliar, the yellow juice was also very good. "What is this called?"

"The juice is nectar from the yellow leaf stalk, mistress, and the soup is called 'sour pot.' Do you like them?"

"Definitely. This is good stuff."

"I'll be sure to share that with the kitchen. Tell me, what things do you most enjoy doing? It will be my pleasure to see if we can duplicate them here."

Rain thought about it. "I like to take things apart and see how they work. I read science, history and biographies. I do some martial arts, but not really for fun. I like to swim and go fishing … and eating. I always like to eat."

Malian laughed. "Well, the eating is easy. We have an extensive library here at the Citadel, and excellent fishing on the bay. As for the other, I think something can be arranged. What would you like to do first?"

Rain thought about it, thought about the Haunt outside her room. "Uh, the books sound good. Could you bring me a stack? And maybe, if you know about anyone with a broken gadget, I'd like to have it. Tools, too, if you can borrow some." She might never have had a go-fer before, but Rain didn't feel hesitant to use her services. If Fallon wanted to pay for a servant, fine. He was part of the reason she was stuck here, anyway.

"Yes, mistress."

"Thanks."

Rain went back outside to look at the fish as Malian cleared the table. When she was sure she was gone, she took out the Bell and set it. Now that she was here, she could flash back to Earth at anytime, at any of the various points she'd set it for. Unwilling to risk the noise in the garden, she quickly slipped the device back into the casing. She stared at it, considering.

No money. That was that hardest thing on the run, getting money honestly. Whatever passed for money here, she was almost certain it wouldn't fly back home. Basic elements like gold and silver or gems she could cash in, but short of stealing them, she was out of luck. Without them, she would be back where she started, scared, tired and hungry. How could she earn some?

She grimaced. She was going to have to leave her room, see what was in demand, what there was to work with. Her father had believed her inventions would make them rich-- now was a good time to test his theory.

She took a deep breath for courage. She was going to have to face the Haunt.

She made it as far as the door before chickening out. Always bad with directions, she told herself she'd probably get lost. Maybe she could wait for Malian.

Unfortunately, it was Fallon who opened the door scant minutes later to find her still dithering. He raised one blond brow. "Going out?"

"Maybe. I haven't made up my mind," she said defensively. She glanced at his midsection, wondering about his back, but her eyes skittered away from his buckled vest. That thing was a subtle form of torture.

"Allow me to escort you, then. I thought you might enjoy a tour of the grounds before dinner."

"Ah … are there a lot of … of Haunt walking around out there?"

"Yes, but I think I can protect you."

She shot him a look for that comment, but maybe he deserved a little revenge. "I'm not a coward."

"Aren't you? Let's see," he murmured. He stepped closer and kissed her.

Stunned, she froze as his mouth brushed hers. More confusing, he stopped there. Lifting his head, he said softly, "Maybe you aren't."

Confounded, she stepped back. "Don't do that!"

"Do what?" he asked innocently.

"That! You know what. Don't do it again." More rattled than she liked to admit, she braced to resist if he tried it again.

He shrugged and headed for the door. "You don't have to feel inadequate, you know. I'm sure you might get better at it with practice."

Outrage had her following him, railing as she went. "I don't need practice! If I did need practice, I wouldn't get it from you." Confused, she frowned. That sounded like an admission of some kind.

His smile was cocksure, designed to enrage. He threw it over his shoulder and walked slowly on.

Tripping on her skirt, she hurried after him. "If you can't behave yourself, I want you to stay out of my room. I won't let you in if I can't trust you. You're supposed to be my guardian!"

There was no one in the hall, and Fallon took advantage of it, backing her to the wall. Bracing his hands on either side of her, he said huskily, "You can trust me." His eyes dropped her lips. "I promise."

She didn't think he was promising what she wanted, not with that look in his eyes. She shook her head, hating the dizziness in her blood.

His head dipped closer until she could feel his breath against her lips. "No?"

She shook her head, realized it wasn't enough. "No." It came out wrong--breathy and weak.

He moved his mouth to her ear and whispered, "Tell me if I change your mind."

She shivered.

Her stomach felt odd as they walked on--fluttery and unsettled. Keeping her eyes from his, she placed her hand on her abdomen. Obviously he wasn't good for her--he was making her sick. Distracted, she didn't even realize they were passing by Haunt until about the third one. Terror made her draw a deep breath. Her muscles locked up--

Fallon slid his arm around her waist and breathed in her ear. She almost jumped out of her skin.

"What are you doing?" she demanded in a strangled whisper.

His hand slid dangerously low on her hip. "Distracting you?" he said in that oh-so-innocent tone.

She grabbed his hand and threw it off, veering right to an archway with the doors flung open. She didn't have to look to feel him sauntering behind her.

It was a bad sign when she could feel a man like that.

They came to a small field enclosed by a low stone fence. Breathing deeply, she gripped the top and stared out over it. Just beyond it, a series of stone and adobe huts began.

She felt Fallon's arms go around her, gripping the wall beside hers. Again, her muscles locked.

He sighed and let go. "We'll work on it."

She grit her teeth, too angry to answer as he straddled the wall to her left.

"As a man and a warrior, I see something I like and pursue it. I think most men are like that," he said reflectively, looking over the field. "The feelings confuse you, don't they?"

"I have no trouble understanding anger," she growled.

He smiled. "You haven't been pursued by anyone with honorable intentions, have you?"

Eyes narrowed, she dared him to lie to her. "You have no honorable intentions. I doubt you've ever had a lasting relationship in your life. I'm not a plaything, and I'm not a fool!"

"No, you're not. You might know that I'm not a liar, though."

"No, I wouldn't know. When in the last few days that I've known you would I have figured that out?"

"Ah. You need time, and I'm rushing you. My bad."

She breathed deeply for strength. "I've got no interest in a relationship with you, however brief. Don't tell me you're desperate for female companionship. I'm sure there's a few women around here you haven't bedded. Probably a teen or two who came of age while you were away."

"Ouch. You have a barbed tongue. I haven't been as busy as all that. I'll bet there's ten women, at least, who I haven't bedded here."

She walked off.

He hopped off the wall and joined her. "I was joking, you know."

"I don't joke about this kind of stuff. Find some beer buddies to share your gutter humor with."

He let out a gusty sigh. "I--watch out!"

She hadn't been watching were she was going as she turned a corner. Unfortunately, she ran right into a Haunt taking the same curve from the opposite direction. Fallon grabbed her arm to steady her, but it was too late.

"Ah-choo!"

"Rain? Are you okay?" Fallon asked with concern. The Haunt reached for her, perhaps in an effort to help.

"Ah-choo! *Ah-choo!*" She backpedaled, tripping on her skirt. She would have landed on her bum if Fallon hadn't caught her.

"What is it? Are you allergic to Haunt?"

"Dog fur!" she gasped, then sneezed again mightily. Her eyes were watering.

Fallon choked on a laugh. "You're serious?"

She sneezed in answer. "W-thin two feet, I … ah … ah--"

He coughed, clearly dying to laugh. "Okay, we'll take you to the medics and get you something for this. We can't have you running around sneezing all the time. You might blow off your nose at this rate."

"You're not funny!" She really was miserable, and it was hard to breath.

He sobered. "Come on. You need medicine."

Rain balked. "I don't like doctors."

One arm behind her back, he moved her relentlessly on. "You're getting one anyway. Get used to it."

"I hate you," she muttered, and sneezed again for good measure. She was getting light-headed from lack of air.

"Do I need to carry you?"

"You do, you die," she promised.

"Feisty, aren't you?"

She did make it to the medics. To her disgust, she was too winded to argue with him about the bitter medicine he made her take. It did ease her breathing, though.

The medic looked at her, a smile lurking around his mouth. "An unusual allergy, but one we can deal with. Repeated exposure should build up immunity, and we have several herbal mixtures that will help. We'll try the mildest one first, then work up to the more powerful doses as needed. Be sure to note any uncomfortable side effects--we want to make sure the medicine is not worse than the disease."

"That's a first," Rain muttered.

The man smiled. "Is there anything else I can help you with today? No? Then take care, and have a good day."

She sulked all the way back to her room. "I hate medicine. I don't need to take it unless I run into any more walking carpets."

"You'll take it. The doctor said it will help you to build up immunity."

"So he claims."

"And we're going to test those claims. I'll watch you take them with every meal, if I have to. If I can't be there, then I'll make sure Malian sees you do it."

"You're awful bossy," she sniffed. Her eyes were still a little watery.

He opened the door to her room for her. "As you pointed out, I am your guardian. You look tired. Would you like a nap before dinner?"

"I guess."

"All right, then. I'll see you after you rest. Pleasant dreams." He dropped a kiss to her lips, then let himself out.

Rain stared at the door, too tired to chase him down and yell at him--as if it did any good the last time. If Fallon wanted to kiss her, he was going to kiss her. Maybe her best defense was not to react.

Pondering her new strategy, she changed into the linen pajamas laid out on the bed and fell asleep.

Chapter Five

Someone was stroking her hair. Vaguely annoyed--it tickled--she snuggled deeper into the covers.

A man chuckled. Fallon. The man was always laughing, smiling ... you'd think his life was all roses. "Go away."

"It's almost dinner time."

Food. Dinner was a good thing. She sighed sleepily. "Five more minutes."

He laughed again. "You've slept for an hour already. We're having fresh bread, a roast with herbs, tender young vegetables ... I think there's dessert, too."

"Okay. You've convinced me." She didn't move right away, though. She liked to get her brain in gear before she climbed out of bed.

His hand moved deeper into her hair, massaging until she looked at him with sleepy eyes.

"Rain? May I kiss you?"

A 'no' hovered on her lips, but the way he looked at her stilled it. It was the first time he'd asked.

Her gaze dropped to his lips. Could it be that bad? Curiosity stirred. "Ah ... I guess."

His lips curved at her uncertain answer. Gently, he brushed his mouth against hers, not once, but many times, until she found his light touch a tease and sought his lips, seeking deeper contact. Obligingly, he gave her more ... but not enough.

She made an impatient sound. While she'd never liked kissing, if he was going to kiss her, he should *kiss* her. This game was frustrating. Grabbing his head with one hand, she pulled him closer.

This time his mouth opened over hers, gave her full contact. Now his tongue swept inside, surprising her with his controlled passion. This wasn't like the others--it felt ... good. Really good. So good, she started to lose her head.

His hand was cradled behind her head, gently holding her steady. When his body joined hers on the bed, she blinked in surprise, but the kisses soon drug her back down. There were covers between them, after all. One hand curved behind her back, pulling her closer, showing her how good it felt to press against him. She whimpered her encouragement.

Boldly, he swept down the covers and snuggled closer. The kisses alternated on her lips and ears, trailed down her jaw and caressed her neck. The hand on her back slid down to cup the curve of her behind, massaging, pulling her closer.

She should have objected. Should have said no. Instead she gasped, unable to remember why this was a problem. It had just been so long since she'd felt pleasure, and he was giving her his full attention. Pitiful, but she was starving for his touch … *any* touch. More importantly, he was more than willing to give it.

If she couldn't have love, then at least she could have this.

Heaven help her, the man was gorgeous, nice, and he wanted her. It was all she could ever hope for, then she would take it.

Her sleeveless linen shirt twisted around her, the soft fabric suddenly chaffing. Fallon sat up and pulled it off her, sinking back down into a kiss before she could object to the exposure. His weight was so good, the sensation of his leather vest on her breasts exciting, scary in its newness, but to hard to stop.

He lifted from her slightly and stared at her breasts, then slowly licked his lips.

She shivered and covered them.

Smiling wickedly, he covered her hands with his own and rotated them.

Shocked, she yanked hers away, then gasped as his hands took over, massaging, pinching her nipples, causing wicked fire to race through her blood until she arched under his hands.

He kissed her, took his time to deeply explore her mouth, then lifted again to watch her. "Want it, sweetheart? Need it?" he whispered rakishly. "Have some." His mouth closed around her nipple, gently bit.

Rain's body arched off the bed. She growled and yelled his name, closing her eyes as his hands came under her to grip her butt.

Bursts of pleasure raced through her, causing white hot flashes of light behind her lids. What was this? It went on and on, then ebbed, only to rise again and consume her.

She was so hot. Couldn't get enough, but when she tugged at his vest, wanting closer contact, he slipped down her body instead.

"No, love. Tonight's all about you. You want to invite my pleasure another night, I'll be happy to oblige. For now ... just enjoy." His tongue caressed her belly, lapped at her navel, dipped inside. Kissed the skin just above her pants. Taking his time, he untied the bow of her drawstring trousers.

Rain knew what came next, trembled in anticipation. She'd heard about it, wanted it. Wasn't about to tell him no if he wanted to do it. This was better than the Bell, better than--wait! What was she thinking? If he was going this far, he wasn't going to stop there. The Bell was safe, in its way. *He* was not. "Wai--! Uh. Oh. *Ahhh.* ... His fingers had slipped below the pants, which he'd inched down. He had her clitoris in between his thumb and fingers and was gently massaging.

"More?" he said suggestively, and lowered them a fraction. "Do you want my kiss there, too, baby? Say it."

"Say what?" She couldn't think.

"Tell that you're wet, dreaming of my kisses. Tell me that you want my kisses there."

"I can't!"

"Yes, you can. Say, 'Fallon.' "

"Fallon."

"I want your kisses."

"I ... I want your kisses." She moaned in pleasure as he rewarded her, then squirmed when he stopped.

"Fallon, I'm wet, dreaming of your kisses."

"That's embarrass--" she broke off with a squeal as he dipped a fingertip a fraction into her. Sadly, he stopped again.

"Say it. Say it all, or I'll stop now."

"No!"

"Say it."

"F-fallon. I ... I'm so wet, dreaming of your kisses there." Just saying it made a gush of liquid heat wet her thighs.

"That's my sweet kitten," he murmured. Deftly, he flipped her onto her stomach and tucked a pillow under her hips, raising her up. He stripped off her pants, leaving her totally exposed, totally naked to his vision.

She tried to sit up. "What--"

He spread her thighs and licked her, right where she'd told him she needed it.

It was too good, but she couldn't get away, couldn't stop him with her hands. The more she squirmed against the sheets, the worse the friction teased her. Her butt was high, her thighs clamped in his big hands, spread wide for his pleasure … and hers.

Such sweet pleasure. Such a relief to surrender. She couldn't fight him, didn't want to fight him. Could only buck and squirm as he sank deep into her, crying out when his deliberate moan vibrated inside her.

Fallon knew that he could have anything he wanted at that moment, but he wasn't about to take it from her. She was passionate and needy, needing a lover who would put her needs first. This first loving was about healing, about teaching her the power of trust and pleasure. It was also a binding, though she wouldn't recognize his power over her at first. They would have plenty of time for more, and he was a man with self control. So instead of bringing her higher, driving her mindless, he brought her down easy, left her floating on a plain of pleasure. When she had drifted down enough not to hurt when he stopped, he got off the bed and pulled her up. "Come on. It's time for dinner."

She wobbled in his arms. "W-what?"

"Dinner. Oddly enough, having dessert first always whets my appetite."

She blushed and looked around for her clothes. Happy to keep her off balance, because he didn't want her to think--it was always a headache when women thought in these situations--he helped her into her dress. Mm, he liked that blue outfit on her. He was tempted to buy her that style in every color of the rainbow.

She still looked dazed when he brought her to his suite and seated her at the long table. Larger than her own apartments, his was furnished in soft greens, bronze and tan leather. It had three bedrooms, suitable for the family he'd one day have. The houseplants were few, but well cared for thanks to his housekeeper. He looked at Rain, but whatever she thought of the place, she seemed too unsettled to comment.

The meal had just been laid out on the table. Content to leave the unfocused expression on her face, he filled her plate for her and poured her wine before serving himself.

She ate, but kept her eyes on her plate. He let her have silence for a little while, then said casually, "I thought we could fish on the bay in the morning. I've arranged to borrow a small sailboat, and the weather promises to be fine. We should enjoy it before the storms come in the fall and we're forced indoors much of the time."

She risked a glance at him. "Storms?"

"Fierce electrical storms. How do you like your dinner?"
She looked down at the half-eaten roast. It's good."
"And did you enjoy making love with me, too?"
Rain looked at him with a stricken expression. "You're so casual about it."
"Not casual. Frank. I enjoyed it. I don't want it to be swept under the rug. Preferably, I'll like to share it again with you … at your invitation, of course."
She remained silent, her eyes on her plate.
Fallon waited.
"I think you'd better find someone else," she whispered.
"I've no interest in somebody else."
"Today." Her voice gained strength.
"You've decided I'm some sort of playboy."
"Aren't you?"
He considered that. "In the past, I've been as wild as any youth. Trust me, the lifestyle pales as a man gets older. I'm thinking differently these days, planning differently. You have nothing to fear from me."
She met his eyes with apparent difficulty. "What's that supposed to mean?"
"It means I'm looking for a wife. My friends have settled down and I like what they've done with their lives. They've got a good thing going."
"Well, if you're looking for a wife, we know you won't choose me," she said bitterly. "Besides, you barely know me. Like I said, find someone else."
He continued doggedly, "There's an appeal to coming home to a place with someone in it. I like the idea of a wife lighting up a house."
"You want kids," she accused him.
He shifted uncomfortably. "Not really. Not right now, at least. Don't misunderstand--I like playing with my cousin's children, but it's a relief to know that they're his at the end of the day."
She raised a skeptical brow. "You're going to have a hard time marrying a girl who doesn't want kids."
"Do you?"
That caught her off guard. "Well, no. Not really. I mean, I don't think I'd be a bad mom, I just don't have the urge, you know? I don't like the idea of being pregnant, or childbirth, or diapers. Myself, I think it would be better to adopt a kid. Someone else has already done the worst stuff, that way."
"What about the teenage years?"

She shrugged. "I'm not afraid of teens. They're easy to talk to."

He smiled. "You see? We'd be perfect--not that anything's decided now. Here, try these fruit jellies. They're delicious." Best to change the subject, let it percolate in her subconscious. "Did I tell you I've officially retired from my post as ambassador to Earth? Kirk took it over. Not that there's much traffic these days. There's only a few families left on Earth, most of which are making noise about crossing over. Some of the Elders are retiring and crossing over, acknowledging that their roles are being phased out. Elders Azion and Traforte should arrive in a couple of days."

She stiffened and cut her eyes his way. "Really?" She wasn't stupid enough to think both of them had suddenly decided to retire following her trip to the Darklands. She was a sitting duck, nicely boxed in by Fallon's protective care.

She suddenly realized that Fallon hadn't asked her any more questions about her father's death and the Haunt involved. He'd seen how much the experience still affected her--for all she knew her allergy to Haunt fur was also psychosomatic.

Granted, he sometimes came off as a flake and a playboy--witness his talk about marrying her--but how much of that was real? Someone had put him in charge of the portal, and that was no position for a fool. He might be easygoing around her, but she remembered her first glimpse of him, wreathed in dust from the bomb. This was a dangerous man. Relaxing around him was hazardous.

Becoming his lover was the act of a madwoman.

"There's going to be a party for them in a couple of days. We're invited, of course."

"Not interested." She picked up her wine and took a slow sip, just to have something casual to do. She had a poker face when she wanted, and these weren't thoughts she wished to share.

Her father had talked to both Elders Azion and Traforte within days of each other. Soon after that they had been swarmed with murderous Haunt. For a girl who hadn't know about them until her teens, nor even seen a transformed one, it was a horrific experience. If she hadn't wanted to be one of them before, she really wasn't happy about it then.

One of them wanted the Bell, and they wanted to keep quiet about its existence. She wasn't eager to reveal it, either. It was her ticket out of there … she thought. After all, it hadn't been tested yet.

"You're still angry at them for sending you here?"

Fallon's casual question made her refocus. "I have no use for the council," she said coolly. "Like I said, I'm a US citizen. I'm here under protest."

He watched her. "You've been very quiet about your protests."

"Who's listening to me? I said it to the council and my stance hasn't changed."

"You enjoyed the market and seemed to like your new garden."

Rain shrugged. "I learned a long time ago to make the most of the moment. Yeah, they were cool. I enjoyed parts of Ireland, too, but I wouldn't want to live there permanently."

"What would change your mind?"

She looked away, toward the glass patio doors, and blinked. There were three moons in the sky. "Whoa!" Unable to resist, she crossed the room and stepped outside, his question forgotten.

Moonlight bathed Fallon's private garden, lighting it much brighter than she'd ever seen the night be. Why did they call this place the Darklands?

Fallon followed her out, lounging against a tree trunk. "Pretty?"

"Beautiful," she agreed, soaking it in.

"You didn't answer my question."

She sighed. "What would make me stay here? I don't know. Whatever it is, I haven't seen it yet."

His eyes glinted in the moonlight. "Haven't you?"

She considered him a moment, then answered him honestly. "You haven't shown me yourself yet. I don't really know you. Maybe you really do want a wife, but you're blowing smoke. Whatever you are, it's not what you pretend to be. You're different since we came here, but I remember what you looked like when you shot Rory."

He looked down with a slight smile. "They said you were a genius." When he looked back up, his eyes were smoky, with flashes of hot embers. "So you want to see the real me, do   you?"

"No." She had a feeling that it wasn't all pretty. No one who did the things he had to do would be all sweetness and light. "You want to know what I want? A boring, suburban existence. I want to fight with the cable repair man, go grocery shopping early to avoid traffic, pay a mortgage. I've lived a life of adventure, and you know what? It's not all it's cracked up to be. I want to sleep in the same bed every night with sheets that I've washed myself and not have to worry about bedding down in an ally where a drunk might stumble in to harass me. I don't want to have to kill anyone else." She looked away. "I'm tired of them trying to kill me."

"I can guarantee the man who wants to hurt you is going to find it hard," Fallon said firmly. "I'm trying to give you what privacy I can, but the security around you is very real, Rain. I am watching out for you."

Her eyes narrowed. "Why would you feel the need? After all, without the cult here, I'm just another penniless immigrant." She watched him picking his words, wondering what he suspected, what he knew.

"Perhaps I should be questioning you. You never did give me any details about your father's murder, other than that Haunt were involved. There aren't that many of us who could have participated. The Earth population is down to hundreds. I know the police investigated the murder and your disappearance. I've seen the reports, but by the time we found out and sent our own people to check into it, the scent traces and such were faint. I can't guarantee that some of those Haunt haven't since crossed over. The council knows this and wouldn't have turned you loose here without a protector."

"So you're just being cautious?"

He scanned the moons for a moment. "You know, what happened to your father was overkill. He wasn't a warrior. One, maybe two Haunt could have taken him out, but estimates are that there were at least four or five." He considered her. "It seems like they were looking for something. What could that be, Rain?"

She rubbed her right bicep. "Maybe it died with him. What little I saw as I was getting away. ...." The memories were stark.

Fallon looked more thoughtful that pitying. "Do you know what I think, Rain? I think you do know what they wanted, and that you carried it away with you. I also think you were pursued by more than members of the cult." He let that statement hang, then added, "I think whatever this thing was, you either hid it ... or you still have it."

Her eyes widened.

He shook his head slowly. "You've got to work on those tells, sweetheart. You're a book. It's a weapon, isn't it?"

"It's not a--" She could have swallowed her tongue, she was so chagrined by her mistake.

White teeth flashed in a predator's smile. "Not a weapon. Are you sure? Men do kill for them."

A growl of vexation vibrated in her throat. "Not your business, Fallon."

"Things that can be used against my people are my business. So?"

"You've been trying to gain my trust. That's what all this has been about. That's why you seduced me." If she couldn't dodge him, she'd go on the attack.

He shook his head, but remained relaxed against the statue. "While I'm not above those kind of tactics, no. I wanted to see what it would be like. Happily, it was all I expected." His teeth flashed again.

She snarled. "If I wanted to make a weapon, I'd test it on you first. I haven't made any … yet."

He shrugged. "Why don't you just show it to me and end the battle? Why all the secrecy?"

"Because it's mine. Because it's none of your business! Not the council's, not yours, got it? It's mine."

"Is the secrecy worth risking your father's murderers going free?"

"If I knew anything about that, I'd come clean. I don't. You werewolves all look alike to me. I didn't smell anything I'd remember, so do me a favor and bugger off, mate!" She stalked off. Oddly, he didn't follow her to her room. Maybe he knew she would be easy enough to find when he was ready to interrogate her again. This reprieve couldn't last.

Anxiety made her restless, and pacing her small room didn't help. She needed out, so she threw on some jeans, a navy sports bra and a long sleeved, black shirt. Dressed for success, she scaled her garden wall.

She wasn't trying to escape the Darklands. It was freezing cold on the other side of the gate, assuming she could find it. Her sense of direction sucked. Even if she could follow the snow machine tracks back, she'd freeze long before she reached civilization.

No, she just needed a break from company, especially Fallon's. Crossing the grassy spot behind the wall, she took a straight line toward the looming shape of an obstacle course she'd seen in the distance that morning. At the time it had been swarming with Haunt, but now it stood abandoned at the edge of the park.

Rolling her neck, she jumped up and grabbed one of the dangling ropes. Wrapping the rope around one leg and holding it with her feet, she climbed up hand over hand to the top beam. Walking across was easy--she'd always had excellent balance and no fear of heights. She climbed down the cargo net and then sprinted over to the pole at the end, climbing it like a palm tree. The next bit was harder, a series of poles spaced at two foot intervals, and not in a strait line. Pretending they were stepping stones, she paced across them, her carriage straight and confident. To dismount, she grabbed the hand bar and slid down the line, over an open pit filled with water.

Enjoying the challenge, she slithered, shinnied and hopped at full speed, then sprinted back to the beginning of the course and did it all again.

About the forth run through, she started to tire. It was late and she'd been running a marathon of sorts for the better part of a year. She turned back toward the garden, and froze. She scented Haunt on the air. There, to her right.

Her nose and ears were keener in human form than when she changed, oddly enough. She looked in the direction of the smell, but couldn't see anything. Whoever it was, they hadn't bothered her yet, and she was looking right at them.

Breathing deeply to ward off panic--or maybe it was controlled hyperventilation--she paced toward her garden. Now that her senses were attuned, she could tell there was more than one following her, to her right, left and behind. Brilliant. She'd have to sprint for it if they moved in, and she'd already used up precious adrenaline.

Reaching into her pocket, she casually removed a little toy of hers, then closed her eyes as she held it up. A brilliant flash lit up the darkness as she broke the modified glow stick, wiping out the night vision of those following her. Opening her own eyes, she sprinted the distance to the garden, leaping obstacles as she ran. Vaulting up, she grabbed the top of the wall and swung over, hitting the ground running. She threw open her patio door and dashed in--then muffled a shriek as the lights turned on.

"You do realize that you just blinded your security detail."

"Fallon," she gasped, blinking at him warily.

"I can tolerate your sneaking out at night if you really must, but not your incapacitating your protection. What did you use on them?"

She looked at her hand dumbly, then recovered and shoved it behind her back. "Just a little glow stick."

"Give it here." He held out his hand.

"No. It's used up, anyway."

One minute she had the stick behind her back, the next he had it, leaving her blinking with the speed he moved. "Hey!"

He examined the glow stick with a slight frown, then stuck it in his pocket. "You said you didn't make weapons."

"That's an overgrown flashlight."

"You just blinded three of my men with it. Had they been human, it would have been permanent. As it is, they'll be days healing."

"Lucky them," she said flippantly. "How was I to know I wasn't running for my life?"

He regarded her steadily. "Let's get some ground rules straight. When you want to go out at night, you tell me or my head of security--I'll introduce you. That way we can avoid your panicking and doing something rash. How many of these things do you have?" He raised the hand holding the spent glow stick.

She shrugged. "I can make as many as I want."

Fallon sighed. "If we didn't already have similar technology, I'd tell you to patent it. In another situation, I would applaud your quick thinking. As it is--take care not to hurt the people who care for you. You're not an island anymore." He left.

Disconcerted by his quiet words, she sat down in a chair. Great. Now she felt bad. Well, how was she supposed to know it hadn't been the bad guys chasing her? Those poor sods probably had families.

Disgruntled, knowing she'd sleep poorly anyway, she sat around and tried to think of something to make amends.

* * * *

Fallon paused in drinking his coffee, one brow raised. Malian had just delivered a piece of paper with a complex schematic. He had to smile as he read the messy handwriting across the top. Rain had designed a night vision goggle to protect his Haunt's eyes from sudden flashes.

So that was how geniuses apologized. A simple 'I'm sorry' would have worked. Apparently her mind worked differently. A point to remember.

"Something funny, my lord?"

Fallon smirked at his head of security and handed over the paper.

Rykarr laughed. "Interesting apology. I'd hire her, if I were you."

Fallon slanted him a glance and went back to his coffee. "You would, wouldn't you? She's a handful."

"Beauty, though."

That earned him another look. "You're looking for me to fall in love and settle down, aren't you? I plan to take her on, but I'm not in love yet."

"Matter of time with that one." To look at him, you wouldn't think Rykarr was a romantic. A mercenary, maybe, with his gunmetal gray hair and black eye patch. Not all injuries could be healed, even by a Haunt.

"A bottomless well of interesting turns, I'll admit. That's largely her appeal."

"Not her fetching hazel eyes. I understand. Her mind is exactly what I'd pursue, too." An old veteran who'd served his father and taught Fallon much of what he knew, he got away with a lot of cheek.

Fallon just smiled. Rykarr could fish all he liked, he wasn't going to get a bite. "How are her replacement soldiers doing?"

"Much warier than the last batch. Any idea what tricks she has left?"

"Expect anything." Her room had already been searched, but they hadn't found anything suspicious. After the glow stick experience, he wasn't sure they would recognize trouble if they saw it. She liked to disguise her tricks.

Must have a thing for secret agents.

He did like the way her mind worked. Combined with the British flavored accent, she more than held his interest. While he wouldn't mistake that interest for love, it was growing. It was inevitable, and he planned to take her down with him. Getting her there, though ... it would help if she trusted him.

Chapter Six

She didn't trust him. Rain unscrewed the housing from a broken communication device and set it down in the clockwise pattern she'd started with the screws. Malian had rustled up an entire basket load of defunct and broken devices, plus a rather nice tool kit. If Rain had been the one paying her, she'd have given her a raise. Instead, she'd praised her ingenuity and sent her out for a list of components, chemicals and lunch. She wondered how long it would take before Fallon showed up to comment on her budding lab.

Not that she was cooking up anything dangerous right now. If she had been, she'd have hidden it among the junk pile, fully expecting him to poke around. The best way to hide something was in plain sight, which is why she'd attached the Bell to a flat gold collar she'd had Malian find. Actually, she'd requested that Malian find something inexpensive--beads, leather--to hang the pendant from. From the weight of the necklace, she didn't think it was made of gold-plated nickel. It looked good, though she'd had to wear one of the dressier outfits Fallon had purchased for her to make it blend in. At least the amber silk tunic and harem pants were comfortable.

As she was pondering the probability of ruining the hardwood floor if she started messing with chemicals, there came a knock on the door. "It's open."

Fallon walked in and frowned at her table full of junk. "Malian requested a soldering gun for you."

"Ah, yes? I'll pay you back. I'm planning to construct a levitating solar light with some of these spare parts. It should sell well."

He waved that off. "This room is not meant to be a hobby shop. I'll get you a proper room set up if you'll be patient for a day or two. If nothing else, you'll need more tables." He surveyed the spare parts spilling off the table, scattered on the floor and overflowing a basket with a frown. "Make a list of what you'd like to have and I'll see it set up. Books, tools, materials ...whatever. I'd rather you had a safe and comfortable working environment than be forced to make do with the kitchen table and a fingernail file."

Stunned at his generosity, she stared at him. Suspicious moisture burned her eyes, and she had the alarming urge to run over and hug him. He probably had no idea what he'd just done for her. "Really?" she whispered.

Slow, confident, his smile lit up her heart. "I don't need to stifle your mind, sweetheart. It's one of the sexiest things about you."

That did it. She got up and crushed him in a hug. After all, he'd broken the touch barrier when he'd made love to her. Like a little girl suddenly shown affection, she seemed to look for an excuse to touch him. "Thank you," she said, strangling on the emotion. If he didn't stop it, she was going to fall in love with him.

He laughed as if surprised, then returned the hug, stroking her back. "Here I thought it would be difficult to convince you to go sailing with me. Will that count as part of your thank you?"

She reached up and pulled his head down for a kiss. There was nothing chaste about it. He took over and seemed to get serious enjoyment from it, then reluctantly raised his head. "Mmm. Hold that thought, honey. I promise we'll get back to it on the boat. Ready?"

The boat turned out to be a thirty-five foot sailboat with blue and gold sails. Rain gaped when she saw it. "Are you sure you know how to drive this thing?"

He laughed and handed her aboard the gleaming white vessel. "It's called sailing when you're in a boat. Do you like it?"

"It's pretty. What are we fishing for today? Tell me it resembles fish."

He dropped a fast kiss on her lips. "It resembles fish. Ready?"

The waters were calm and they dropped anchor in the bay, within distant sight of the Citadel. Fallon baited his hook and tossed it over the side, fixing his pole in the special holder attached to the rail. "Now then, here comes my favorite part of fishing." He leaned over and kissed her.

Her hand loosened on the rod. He'd done something to her with his offer of a lab of her own. It wasn't just the generosity, it was the thoughtfulness of the gesture. He was so easy with his affection, so open handed. If she did ever marry him--

She pulled away, startled by her thoughts. Breathing raggedly, she looked back at her pole.

He brushed a kiss on her temple, then worked over to her ear. "So pretty," he murmured. "You make me burn from the inside out."

"I think--"

He placed one long finger against her lips. "If you're about to make a comment about me and another woman, I promise you'll unleash that hidden side you keep wondering about."

She shut her mouth.

"Better. Let's try this again." This kiss was longer, more satisfying. Hot and restless.

"I got a bite!" She grabbed for the pole. It had almost been jerked out of her hands.

"Throw it back," he suggested.

"Are you nuts? Quick, get the net!"

He sighed, but helped her haul forty-five pounds of thrashing, slippery fish on board.

"Call it a day?" he asked hopefully after the fish had been stored in the live well.

"No way! I'm on a role now."

Unfortunately for him, she was. He let her haul in three more monster fish before declaring she'd caught her legal limit.

She was beginning to think he didn't have much use for fishing.

She smiled at the wind in her face as he steered them back. "We'll have to do this again soon."

Fallon grunted.

"You know what we should do? We should build a fire on the beach and cook the fish over the coals. What leaves do you have that are edible?"

"We could let my cook do it, too. He does a great grilled fish."

She frowned. "I'll compromise. We'll set up a grill in my garden and eat it out there. I'm good at barbeque. I know you have sweet potatoes here--we'll cook a couple of those, too. You can have your cook do a side dish and dessert."

He smirked. "I had no idea you were so domestic."

"Well, I am letting you contribute something, even if you have to pay someone else to cook it. After all, I did catch all the fish."

"I provided the boat."

"Doesn't count."

"How do you figure?"

"I'll think of a reason," she promised.

He laughed.

* * * *

They set up the picnic in her garden. The wok-like grill on the tripod slowly baked their dinner as they lounged on the blanket by the light of the triple moons. Rain considered them as she sipped her dream flower wine. "Can you ever see the stars? There's all this light."

"Sometimes. They have different cycles, but we actually have a few days each month with only one moon."

"Wow. Who named this place the Darklands, then?"

"Someone with a taste for drama. Did you know the elders arrived early? Their party is tomorrow afternoon."

She was silent. While she didn't want to go, it was the best way to get answers.

"Even if you don't want to celebrate for their sake, you should go for your own. There will be other women there, and it would be good for you to get out of your room once in a while and make friends."

"I don't socialize well."

"Practice helps."

"You haven't seen me discuss the wonders of computer hacking or the thrill of magnetics with a room full of bored women before. They don't care about science and I don't care about waxing. You see the problem."

His teeth flashed in a grin. "Discuss men. That's always common ground."

"Not when I agree with the man half the time, and say so. Don't look so surprised. I loved my dad. There are good men out there. You said he wasn't a 'warrior', but I thought he was something much better. He was a good father."

Fallon grew serious. "I did not mean to disrespect him. I regret I never had a chance to meet him. He must have been remarkable--after all, he raised you."

A moody sigh was her answer to that. When he looked as if he'd pursue the subject, she got up to check on dinner. "It's done. Get it while it's hot." Perfectly cooked, moist and flaky, the fish went well with the lemon rice pudding and crisp vegetable salad Fallon--or rather his cook--had contributed. Finished, she lay back on the blanket with a sigh of contentment.

A tactical error.

Fallon's head appeared in less then a minute, blocking out the moons. "Hello."

She turned her head aside to avoid his kiss. It landed on her cheek instead. "Fallon, I'm full."

"Okay. No pressure on your stomach, I promise." He moved her hand up to nibble her fingers.

"I don't think … hey ..." He'd popped her pinky into his mouth and was sucking on it. Maybe she'd had too much wine, or was too relaxed, but she didn't feel motivated to put up a serious protest.

He slowly released her finger, then started on the next. By the time he was done, she was in a very receptive frame of mind.

"I want to pamper you tonight," he said, reaching for a little box she hadn't noticed before. He opened the top, then set it so she couldn't see inside. When she sat up to look, he kissed her, distracting her with slow, persuasive heat. While she was still dazed, he lifted her tunic off, baring her to the waist. Except for her necklace, of course, but *that* wasn't hiding anything.

Automatically, her hands rose to hide her breasts.

"No, no. That's not how this game is played. Lie back." He eased her down to the blanket and put her hands by her side, holding them there for a moment. "Keep them there." His gaze was appraising, frankly appreciative, and she had to close her eyes in embarrassment. Why was she letting him do this?

"Now, then." Her eyes popped open as he moved closer, a small brush in his hand.

"Close your eyes again. This is eye shadow."

"You're doing my makeup?" she asked in puzzlement. "Why do I have to be naked for that?"

"Just close them," he said patiently.

He might be calm, but she was ready to jump with sizzling awareness. "Y-you know, I haven't done this before. How 'bout you give me back my shirt?"

"The sexual tension is part of the pleasure," he murmured, stroking her cheek with a soft brush.

"How can you even see what you're doing in the moonlight?"

"I can see. Make a kiss with your lips. Mm. I do love deep red lipstick on you. Such full, sweet lips." He put away the lipstick and got out a nail file. "Give me your hand."

She was beginning to understand this was going to be a slow torture session. Instinct made her keep her newly polished fingers flat on the ground, even though she desperately wanted to curl them, or use them to shield her breasts. Her nipples were stiff with tension, desperately hoping for his attention. It was all she could do to keep her hips still.

He glanced at them and smiled. "Ready for a little nipple rouge? It will stain them a deep red to match your lips for several days. Hold still--we don't want to stain your pretty white skin." Over her uncertain murmurings, he painted her nipples, taking his time.

By the time he got to the second one, she liked the way he thought.

"Glitter cream," he said, rubbing a new form of torment between his palms. "We need to spread this *all over*." He started at her neck, thoroughly massaged her breasts and rubbed her belly. By the time he removed her pants, she was ready for them to go. When he filled his hands with her butt and lifted and kneaded it, she felt sure she knew what was coming, and she was ready for that, too.

Instead, he massaged his way down her legs, taking his time with her feet and toes. Then he got out the polish again.

"You've got to be kidding," she muttered, leaning back and closing her eyes. The man would kill her.

A perfectionist, he took his time, then deliberately closed the bottle and put it away.

Here it comes, she thought.

Instead, he took what she thought was a necklace out of the box. "This is a virgin's belt," he said, showing it to her. It had smooth gold links and a string of dangling pearls hanging from it. The first few pearls were medium sized, but there was a large one hanging at the end. "Plant your feet and lift your hips for me."

She obeyed, shuddering with the feel of the night air on her hot, wet center. He fastened the links around her waist. She was so damp she was dripping, and had been for some time. That had never happened to her before. *None* of this had ever happened.

While her legs were spread and open, he dangled the pearls between her legs, then popped the big one inside her.

She collapsed on her back in shock and reached for it.

"Leave it!" he ordered her, and she'd never heard that tone from him before. Stunned, she stared at him. "But--"

"Leave it," he said more calmly. "It's getting you ready for me. Close your legs and squeeze. Feel what it does to you? Go ahead and squirm. Feel how the strands tighten against your peak? Feel how they rub? It's pressing against the special spot inside you; it's going to make you climax at any minute."

The chain anchored the end of the beads, keeping the line barely taunt as they slid wetly between her legs. Knowing he was watching, knowing he could see ... as if to prove his words, she came right then, lifting off the blanket.

He smiled savagely and stripped off his clothes. "Leave it!" He ordered her again when she tried to stop the special torture. He took her hands in his and flattened her body to the ground, closing her legs together with his own. "Do you want me yet?" he snarled in her ear.

This was the side of him she hadn't seen before, the one she'd feared ... and wanted. He wasn't playing games now, wasn't blowing smoke.

She knew what it would mean for him to take her virginity. Her father had explained that once Haunt couples joined flesh, it was forever. Fallon really was going to take her to wife ... and he had the means to make her desire him. No court would annul a marriage consummated in mutual passion.

The pearl between her legs pressed again on that special spot, making her lift off the blanket with a hot scream.

Fallon muttered something jealous sounding and pulled it out.

She whimpered at its loss.

"I have something better," he growled, and spread her legs. Suddenly there was a fullness, a sweet hardness.

She decided she liked it. "Ohhh. More." Her bright red nails flexed on his back.

She felt him smile against her neck. "Anything for the lady."

It burned, it hurt ... but there was just enough pleasure to make her want his invasion. He was big, and hard, and at the moment, everything she wanted in the world.

So she let him ride her, let him fill the tight hollow between her legs as he tortured her mouth with kisses. He was sweetly savage, controlled yet dominate until the end, when the control slipped completely away and he rode her fiercely, throwing his head back as he roared his own climax.

Well earned, if anyone wanted to know.

* * * *

She lay in bed later that night, tucked in the hollow of Fallon's arm. He'd carried her limp body inside and bathed her, then taken her again in the tub after crushing the pearl.

It was symbolic, he said. Nobody was ever going to enter her body again but him.

She very nearly let him have her a third time, just for that.

Promising to get to it after her body had a chance to heal, he'd kissed her and carried her to the bed. Now she lay there, wondering how she'd ever gotten to this place.

Dangerous. She'd always known the man was dangerous. Exhausted, she slid into sleep. Tomorrow would take care of itself.

* * * *

Rain awoke to wine and a bed strewn with flower petals. Brushing a petal from her cheek, she surveyed the bed strewn with pink and white botanical confetti with sleepy surprise. "Are we having a party?"

Fallon sat on the edge of the bed, clad only in his black pants. "I felt a celebration was in order." When she blushed, he added mischievously, "Are you very sore?"

Avoiding his eyes as her face got hotter, she brushed the petals from her lap. "If you're looking for an encore, then yes, I'm pretty sore."

He smiled. "Good thing I filled the tub, then. I also put some healing herbs in it."

Risking a glance, she asked dryly, "In a hurry, are you?"

"With you, always." He held a white silk robe out to her and helped her into it. "Unfortunately, we do have a party to attend later, and I have to introduce you to my mother." He said it offhand, like an afterthought.

Her eyes snapped to his. "Your *mother?* I didn't even know you had one!"

They'd stopped at the tub, and he whisked off her robe with quick efficiency. "Didn't want to jinx the deal."

Loathe to stand around naked in front of him, she slid into the water. "Yeah, but you could have dropped a clue! How am I supposed to face the woman, knowing that I just found out about her hours before I met her?" Knowing what she'd just spent the night doing with the woman's son. Yikes!

"I wouldn't worry about it. She's been nagging me for years to marry--she'll be delighted about you. Oh, she'll scold me, but she'll take to you like a duck to water." He sat on the edge of the tub and trailed his fingers in the water. "She'll probably start in about grandchildren right away."

Rain opened her mouth, then closed it, thinking before she spoke. "We talked about that."

"We did, and I still feel the same. I'm an expert at circumventing her schemes, so just follow my lead. Direct opposition just strengthens her, I warn you."

"Great. A controlling mother-in-law," Rain muttered, sinking further into the water. Whatever he'd put in the bath was invigorating, just the thing for what was sounding like a tough day.

"It's not that bad. Like I said, she'll love you. I'll the one who will suffer if you two ever join forces against me. I don't get any sleep as it is." He sent a smug look her way, and his eyes slid to the clear water.

She sank up to her chin and crossed her arms over her chest. "Go away. Make yourself useful and order some breakfast or something."

He laughed and dropped a kiss on her hair. "See? It's started already."

* * * *

She wasn't laughing an hour later as Fallon swept into his mother's apartment, one arm firmly anchored around Rain as if to prevent her from running. She might have, too, but he shut the door too quickly.

Apparently his mother, Lady Portae, had been forewarned. She hurried up to Rain with a cry of delight, enfolding Rain so deeply in her plump arms that Rain felt she was drowning in her mother-in-law's perfumed bosom. "My dear girl!" Mercifully, Portae released her and held her back at arm's length, examining her with hungry eyes. "So you're the clever girl that *finally* snared my Fallon." Her eyes teared up, and she quickly applied a handkerchief. "Come in and tell me all about it." Her brilliant purple robe swished against Rain's side as she linked arms and led Rain to a place of honor on a flowered sofa.

As Fallon joined her on the couch, Lady Portae sank down on the one opposite. A tea set and refreshments were waiting on the table between them. Apparently Fallon's mother was prepared for a lengthy visit. "Pour us some tea, Fallon. We have so much to talk about."

Most of the talking consisted of Portae--she'd insisted on Rain calling her that, since she couldn't bring herself to call Portae 'mother'--grilling them for the story of how they met, fell in love, and how soon they intended to produce grandchildren.

With frequent glances at Fallon, Rain edited and hedged, leaving out the parts that weren't fit for company. Eyes sparkling, Fallon supplied the bits where she'd tried to run away, the rat. It was hard to resent him, though. He'd dressed to impress today, and his loose trousers and gold trimmed tunic, cut in the Chinese style, made the gold of his queued hair all the more striking. While she wasn't one to drool in public, she caught herself dwelling on his beautiful green eyes.

Portae smiled as she sipped her tea. "I'm so grateful you changed her mind, Fallon. I can see you're looking impatient, though, so I'll stop interrupting your honeymoon. I can't wait to speak to my friends! Lady Vectrex will be so jealous! She's been trying to get her son married off *forever*."

Fallon just smiled and kissed his mother's cheek. "Don't forget the party this afternoon."

"As if I could," Portae said fondly. "It isn't everyday my son is honored for serving his country. I'm looking forward to it."

Rain waited until the door had closed behind them before saying, "You didn't mention that you were being honored."

He shrugged. "It's nothing. How about a light lunch before we get ready? There'll be food there, but I'm starved."

"How can you be hungry? You just got done eating an entire plate of cookies at your mother's!"

"You call that food? I need something with some meat."

They passed too close to a pair of Haunt guards, making Rain sneeze.

"You haven't been taking your medicine, have you?"

She frowned in annoyance, ignoring the guilt his frown triggered. "I'll take some when we get to my room."

"Which is now my suite," Fallon informed her. "I had Malian transfer your clothes over there this morning. We'll move your tools and such once your workroom is finished."

She wasn't sure how she felt about that. Moving in with Fallon was weird, even though she knew that they were married according to his customs. Not only had she not expected to ever marry, she'd certainly never expected to end up with someone like Fallon. While he did listen to her, his tendency to take charge was disconcerting. She had a feeling she'd spend a lot of time in her workshop, distracting herself from the complications of living with someone like him.

The truth was, she hadn't thought at all. She'd just cruised along, too shell shocked to think anything through. It had just been easier to let someone else do the thinking. At the time that someone had been Fallon. Time would tell if she'd live to regret her complacency, but honestly, she wasn't together enough to do anything different yet.

They didn't make love before the party. She told herself she hadn't been looking forward to it, anyway. Instead, they talked, and Fallon massaged her feet until she fell asleep on the couch. He woke her with a kiss that almost made them late, then hurried her into a striped sarong of olive and burgundy with black print. While not what she would have chosen herself, together with the sleeveless black top, it looked far better than she expected.

"You know, these clothes keep appearing in my closet," she said tentatively as Fallon helped her dress her hair.

"Do you like them?" He closed a hairclip over the back of her hair and brushed the loose ends off her shoulders.

Feeling her way, she said carefully, "Yes, but I don't need so many of them."

He wrapped his arms around her from behind and breathed in her hair. "It pleases me to give them. Permit me to provide for my wife."

She frowned and turned around.

He stopped her with a finger to her lips. "We haven't talked about money, Rain, but I have a lot. If you want to spend the rest of your life lazing on the grass, watching the birds, you may. However, I know you're both smart and driven, so if you want to turn your talents toward helping others, you may. Spend every dime you make on charity or public works, if you like. It's what I did with the ambassador position, in a way. You're in the position to do a lot of good, if you so choose.

However, don't begrudge me the chance to spoil you if I like. You're invited to do the same for me."

She couldn't help but smile. "You want a closet full of dresses?"

He kissed her nose. "I was thinking along the lines of you being a light in my home, but if buying me dresses makes you happy ..." They laughed.

What he'd said about her doing good stuck with her. She'd never thought much about what she'd do if she had the wealth to do anything she chose. She definitely didn't want to spend her days lying around--she'd get fat--but she'd never seen herself as working in the public eye. Maybe she could be an anonymous donor or something. Surely there were worthy causes out there that could use an influx of cash. There always were.

Her thoughts served as a good distraction as they entered the chamber where the party was being held. Once they'd passed between the Haunt guarding the door, though, she stiffened. The glittering crowd within daunted her, unused as she was to company. Even when Fallon linked arms with her and sent her an encouraging smile, it still took courage to step into the crowd.

Right away they were swarmed by a mother and her three young daughters. Thanks to the slow aging processes, it took a little observation to tell who was which, for the mother didn't look a lot older than her children. It helped when Fallon introduced them. "Rain, this is Lady Septis and her daughters, Justice, Fleur and, ah … forgive me, I've been gone a long time."

"Jael," Lady Septis said with a smile. "I don't believe you've met before, as she has so recently come of age." She turned the smile, a trifle too bright, on Rain. "And you are Lord Fallon's new wife! Word has traveled fast. Congratulations on your new alliance. But you must find it lonely here in the Darklands. You're from away, aren't you? You must come and visit us at your leisure. It's never too late to make new friends."

Rain couldn't help a twinge of suspicion. She wasn't the type to make friends easily, and that overdone smile of Lady S's made her uncomfortable, but she didn't know what to call it. Peeking at Fallon's easy expression didn't help, either. Sometimes she hated that façade of his.

The next lady who accosted them helped Rain to solidify the sensation she was having of something wrong. Young and bouncing, with a husband in tow, the girl nearly smothered Rain with overtures of friendliness. "Do you like shopping? Oh, but of course you do!" The girl laughed giddily. "We should go together sometime and stop in for lunch. I know this wonderful little shop …"

Rain frowned, her suspicions now knee-deep. The girl was social climbing, and while the Rain didn't consider herself of any importance, she did resent the friendship offered under false premises. When the girl started to trail off, her face showing uncertainty in the wake of Rain's cool expression, Rain said slowly, "You have something green in your teeth."

Horror widened the girl's eyes. She slammed a hand over her mouth, then looked in chagrin at her husband, who'd been startled into peering at her.

The unfortunate lady's hand dropped, then flashed back up to her mouth. "Oh, I'm sorry! I didn't realize ... Come on, Gari! We have to fix it."

Rain did feel a tiny stab of guilt as the girl rushed off.

Fallon looked at her with reproach, but there was laughter lurking in his eyes.

She shrugged irritably, then said in her defense, "She was ... well, I'd swear she was brown-nosing for some reason."

"Get used to it. That one isn't all that bad once you get past the gushing, though." He lowered his voice and murmured in her ear, "The thing about a sword, love, is you have to know when to use it. You posses an especially powerful one. Try not to annihilate too many defenseless young things."

She sighed, feeling too old for this kind of torture. "I'm getting the picture that you're somewhat admired here." These people surely weren't sucking up to them to get closer to *her*.

Fallon laughed.

The laughter attracted his mother. Rain wasn't sure if that was bad or good, because while she at least knew that Portae liked her for her good sense in marrying her son, she also preceded to introduce her to everyone in sight, dragging her around the room with dizzying speed. Her traitor husband quickly found a group of friends to hide behind, chatting with them while his mother showed her off, occasionally gesturing to Fallon for emphasis.

To Rain's relief, she got to sit down at a table reserved for Portae, herself and Fallon while those being honored, including Fallon, took turns making speeches at the head of the room. Grateful to be in the shadows, Rain sat back and studied the two elders who were also retiring.

Elder Azion took his turn at the pulpit, looking more like Sean Connery than ever. Uncertain of his guilt, she sat there torn between hating him and giving him the benefit of the doubt.

Elder Rite was easier to hate, though again, she could prove nothing yet. Middle aged like her father would have been--a fact that made her bitterly resent him--his hair was still black, his eyes still a piercing blue. He wasn't handsome, but he was big, even bigger than Fallon, and built like a concrete pylon. That black hair gave her pause, though. There'd been no black Haunt the night her father was killed--or she didn't think there'd been; it had been a confusing night.

She was going to have to speak to them. Her guts clenched at the thought, emotion riding high.

Her chance came later, as people were starting to clear out. She'd told Fallon that she wanted to speak to the men, then whiled away the time as best she could with a group of Portae's friends.

"--so then I made his house glow in the dark," she related to the amused group of matrons. The story was a about a bully who'd teased her about being a geek when she was a kid. The boy had made her life miserable on the bus, and she'd repaid him by making the neighborhood think his house was haunted. "I also made howling noises start up when anyone walked up the drive. He never bothered me again." She smiled with satisfaction as the ladies laughed.

"I'll have to mind my manners around you then, young lady," a gruff voice boomed from behind her. "Obviously you make a dangerous enemy."

Rain turned and smiled coolly at Elder Rite. Heart pounding, she offered him the barest of nods in respect to his status. "You wouldn't do that, would you, Elder?"

His heavy brows rose. "Still taunting a bear with a stick, young Rain? I see marriage has not taken care of your recklessness yet."

"I learned when to take chances after my father died." Her heart was in her throat, waiting to see a glimmer of guilt, something that would convict him once and for all.

Instead his face softened. "I am sorry for your loss. Your father was a good man. There should have been something we could have done to find justice for you."

To her horror, she felt tears prick her eyes. He was making her feel young again, and she hated it. She never wanted to be a child again. "I survived."

He sighed. "You did well to marry Fallon, child. He'll make you happy." With a nod of farewell, he was gone.

Well, that sucked. Disgusted with her emotions and the pitying looks she was getting, she turned her face away while she regained control. Happily, the ladies took pity on her and took up their conversation again.

She'd been aware of Fallon nearby, and no doubt he'd caught their conversation. By the carefully neutral expression on his face as he came up to them with elder Azion, she'd swear he had.

Azion didn't seem affected by the somber mood. "Lady Rain! I'm happy you seem to have settled so well into your new home. What a pleasure to see that the Darklands held something for you after all."

Pompous, she thought. Certain he was right. "So it seems." Remembering her purpose, she bared her teeth at him in imitation of a smile. "Fallon is even helping me to set up a new lab. I plan to jump into my work right where I left off. The first thing I plan to do is build a new Bell."

Azion's eyes gleamed. She would have missed it if she hadn't been looking.

"Really? I hadn't known you were into musical instruments."

She smiled like a wolf. "It also plays music." Almost daring him, she reached up and stroked the Bell pendant at her neck. His eyes followed it, glued themselves to the golden sphere.

Almost strangled, he said, "What a lovely piece of jewelry, my dear. Did you make it?"

She just smiled, that cold, hard smile that said, *I've got you, you murdering bastard.* She could feel that subtle change in her eyes, the one that meant they were glinting gold. For once, she didn't care. She wanted Azion to know she hated him.

Fallon stepped into the silence, taking her arm. "My wife has many talents. If you'll excuse us, Elder, ladies." He steered Rain out of the room at a slow, deliberate pace.

"That was stupid, Rain. Azion is a powerful man," he said once they were alone in the hall. Though his voice was quiet, the anger carried clearly.

"He murdered my father," she hissed. "It's no accident he's 'retired' now. That bastard followed me here to the Darklands, and he wants to finish what he started. Keeping my mouth shut won't make me safe."

"You don't know for certain it's not Rite. Just because someone is nice to you, doesn't make him innocent."

"Don't I know it. But you tell me, how many Elders are there who could have been involved, just coincidently arriving in the Darklands within days of me?"

He was silent for a moment. "We're going to raise the security around you. It's going to be close and visible."

"Telling him you know there's danger? I say we let him try to come after me and pick him off. I've outwitted him before."

"No."

"I think--"

He looked at her, and this time his eyes were gleaming gold. "I said no." Slow, deliberate, his words held the weight of finality.

A muscle ticked in her jaw. She was going to have to get creative.

Chapter Seven

Fallon wasn't going to give her the chance to do something stupid. The minute they entered his rooms, he summoned Rykarr. While Rain listened with interest, Fallon brought his captain up to speed.

Rykarr heard Fallon out, then started issuing orders over his com unit.

Rain slouched in her chair and walked a coin through her fingers.

Fallon felt a burst of anger as he watched her. She was willing to put herself at risk for the sake of her revenge. Justice, she called it. Maybe it was, and overdue at that, but she didn't need to get herself killed to obtain it. They had plenty of time, and he was patient. They could see this thing resolved easily enough.

"Who's the head honcho around here, Fallon? The guy in charge of justice?"

Surprised out of his plans, Fallon focused on her. "Jayems, Lord of the Haunt."

She considered. "You have an in with him? Seeing as how you were an ambassador for him?"

"He's my cousin," he said cautiously, wondering where she was going with this.

"I'd like to talk to him." She sat up, closed her fingers around the coin. She looked at him expectantly.

The men looked back at her.

"Okay, but why?"

"I want to tell him what's going on ... and a few more details you don't know about all this."

Fallon frowned, feeling an unwelcome twinge of jealousy. "You can't tell me first?"

She shrugged. "Two birds, one stone, you know? Introduce me to him and I'll let you in."

Let him in. Interesting phrasing. "Rykarr should be there, too."

"Okay."

Fallon looked at her a moment more. "All right. I'll see if he's available."

* * * *

Rain was a lot more nervous than she let on. Fallon didn't say much as they walked toward Lord Jayems' suite, an escort of Haunt before and behind. Unfortunately, the combination was making her eyes water with the urge to sneeze. The medicine must be wearing off. The only good thing about it was that it was hard to be fearful in the middle of a sneezing attack.

Fallon looked at her as they approached a set of double doors guarded by yet still more Haunt. "You didn't take your last dose of medicine, did you?"

She held her finger on her upper lip, trying to fight off another sneeze. Just as the doors opened, she sneezed powerfully, then three more times in succession.

Rykarr chuckled and moved slightly left, out of the line of fire.

Muttering something, Fallon led her to a chair and sat her down. Sniffing, determined not to lose it again, Rain looked up--and sneezed again.

"Excuse me," she said to the dark haired man standing in front of her. "I'm allergic to dog fur."

His stern mouth twitched. "I see. How uncomfortable for you."

"You've no idea," she muttered.

Fallon sighed and introduced them. "Rain, this is my cousin, Lord Jayems, though you'll call him Jayems. All in the family, you know. You probably saw him at the ceremony, though I didn't get a chance to introduce you."

"My apologies," Jayems said gravely. "I was only there a brief time. Our daughter is ill, and I wanted to check on her and my wife."

"Nothing serious, I hope," Rain said politely.

"Just the usual childhood malaise, but she is very uncomfortable," Jayems said. He waved Fallon and Rykarr to seats, then took the one behind the massive carved desk. "I was told you had something of interest to tell me?"

Rain took a deep breath. Whatever the man said, his little girl was sick enough to make him cut short his appearance at an important ceremony. He wouldn't like to spend much time dallying with her. "I think Elder Azion killed my father." She gave him the cliff notes version of her life before the murder and after. "During the murder I saw a gray Haunt. Fallon tells me that's rare."

Fallon cut a look her way. "You hadn't told me you'd actually *seen* the gray Haunt!"

She met his eyes. "We've got a lot of unresolved issues. Listen and you'll hear what else I didn't say." Beyond him, she saw Rykarr wince.

Fallon straightened and his nostrils widened, but he kept his peace.

She looked at Jayems, who regarded her with a curious gleam in his eye, and quoted her conversations with Rite and Azion in as closely as possible. "Azion murdered my father," she finished simply.

Jayems regarded her without expression. "You've mentioned that a couple of times. What I don't know is, why? What was his motive?"

She drew a deep breath and removed her necklace, slipping the Bell from its clasp. "Meet the Bell." Out of the corner of her eye, she saw Fallon staring at the thing as she passed it over to Jayems. He had to be burning up about now, either with frustration or curiosity.

Jayems examined it. "What does it do?"

She smiled. "I'd heard rumors that you wanted to close the gate when all the immigrants crossed over. I'll tell you now, I doubt all of them will. I wouldn't have, if I hadn't been … pushed." Out of the corner of her eyes, she saw a muscle jump in Fallon's face. There's also the problem of how to close the gate. Your site is remote, unmarked, but accidents happen."

"The volti take care of 'accidents,' " Jayems said coolly, referring to the wolf-things that prowled the woods around the gate.

She shook her head. "You need a better way. The Bell can lock the gate for you. As a matter of fact, it's a gate in itself." She let the silence build.

Finally Fallon ground out, "Are you saying you could have left at any time?"

"Two problems to that. No money, for one, which slowed me up the first time. I need time and peace to build that up, and I've yet to get either."

"I gave you money this morning!" Fallon sounded as if he were chewing gravel.

"Prismatic silver is not an easy currency to convert, let alone explain," she said tersely.

"Just as well, as you were going to use it to leave me!" Fallon's eyes were glowing gold.

"Ah … you said there was a second reason?" Jayems said, interrupting a doozy of a brewing quarrel.

A little abashed, she looked at him. "I haven't tested it yet."

"Ah." He set the Bell carefully on his desk.

Fallon picked it up and looked at it. "So this is what I spent weeks of frustration trying to figure out."

Rain shrugged. "If it makes you feel better, it frustrated Azion for years."

The look he sent her throbbed with so much fury that she finally shut up. Taunting him was beginning to look hazardous to her health.

"So," Jayems said, drawing out the word to get their attention. "This Bell could be used for escape, theft ... even murder."

"An assassin's dream," Rykarr said, speaking up for the first time.

"That's not why I made it," Rain said with a frown.

"It's how it'll be used," Rykarr answered. "I'd say it's best left locked up in Lord Jayems' safe."

She smiled without humor. "Nice thought, but it doesn't eliminate the central problem. Azion knows I can make another one any time I want. Hundreds, if I liked."

Her words met with deafening silence.

It was almost funny, sharing the irony of her existence with three men who looked as stumped by the problem as she did.

For a moment, anyway.

"Azion will have to die," Fallon said coldly. "I won't tolerate his continued threat to my family."

Surprised by that, she shot a look at him.

Jayems held up a hand. "Peace. We haven't proved beyond doubt it was him."

"I can't afford to wait," Fallon answered.

Rain let them debate, following her own lines of thought. When she'd traced them somewhere interesting, she spoke them aloud. "What makes an object valuable? It's rarity. In the case of technology, it's good only until it becomes obsolete or common. One day a spy is killing for it, the next every guy in America is using it in from the comfort of his couch."

"You can't put a Bell in every house," Fallon argued, looking alarmed at the possibilities.

"No, not as it stands. I can modify the technology, though. Think about it," she said, getting excited. "What have you got for transportation here? Shoe leather and pack animals, some boats. Okay, what if I made Bells for emergency or official transport, limiting their use to on world, secure sites? The Bells could be programmed as single use units, or better, single destination"

Fallon said slowly, "Azion would still know they could function as off-world destination devices."

She shook her head. "Not if I published the disappointing results of my off-world attempt, made it very public, stressed the local applications as if I'm trying save face. Half the appeal of the technology is its secrecy. Once it goes public...." She let them work it out for themselves.

"All of this still leaves you lacking justice," Jayems pointed out. "While your sighting of a gray Haunt is incriminating for Azion, I'm told you have no scent memory. Without it, your testimony is still his word against yours."

She drooped a little, thinking of that. The world sucked sometimes. "Well, Fallon was against plan A. I compromised by solving his problems instead."

There was silence as the men regarded her. When he spoke again, Jayems' voice had gentled. "You still aren't certain it works."

"It'll work," she said gloomily. "I always make these things work."

Jayems looked at Fallon, who still held the Bell. "Well? Do you want to keep charge of it?"

Fallon looked at Rain. "Do you need it?"

She swallowed. She hadn't used the Bell in days, was afraid of what the withdrawal would be like. On the other hand, maybe Fallon's ... attentions ... would mitigate any lingering problems. Making love to him did seem to give the same sort of pleasure, only deeper and fuller.

She blushed just thinking about it. "No. Better keep it here, just in case."

Fallon studied her color, then handed the Bell back to his cousin. "Very well. Are you ready to go, Rain?"

Rykarr stayed behind at Jayems' request as Fallon escorted Rain back to their suite.

She hesitated at her own door. "Would you mind? I'd like some time to myself for a while." She was feeling depressed. She hadn't meant to sacrifice her interests like that, and the backlash of emotion wasn't pleasant.

Fallon looked at her for a long moment. The dynamics had shifted between them in the last twenty minutes. "You're certain?"

"Yeah," she said on a sigh. "I want to hang out in my cave for a bit."

A grave smile curved his mouth, but didn't last. He kissed her. "For a little while."

She shut the door to her room, alone at last. She'd meant to work on a plan B while she had the time, but found she really was too disheartened to bother. Her emotions had been stressed for so long, it had been hard to really mourn her father. So much adrenaline and fear was bound up within those years that it was painful to look back, to examine the feelings.

All this time she thought she'd gotten past the worst, and now she discovered she'd yet to really grieve. She was afraid.

Maybe it helped to feel sorry for herself. Maybe it was a kind of letting go, giving up her dream of justice, but something about tonight's mix of emotions let the tears begin to roll. No one was chasing her. She didn't have to muffle her sobs, choke them off. For once the grief didn't hit her on a crowded bus or subway.

Once the tears began, they came in a flood. Years of pent up pain came out, years of hiding in the dark, fearing what she was, fearing what hunted her in the night. In a way, she had Fallon to thank for that.

She'd hurt him tonight; wanted to hurt him. Part of her was angry at him for making her come here, for railroading her into a relationship she wasn't ready for. They were both going to cross some rough roads to get to a place where this marriage he'd started could work. He'd taken advantage of her, but she was to blame, too.

She hated admitting that, but she was nothing if not fair. Now, they were stuck. She was stuck, because she'd willingly given up her ticket off this planet. For what? To sooth Fallon's fear. Why had she done that?

Maybe it was because she understood fear. He had been kind to her in his way. Maybe the only thing he felt for her was desire, but he'd been generous about sharing that, too. He didn't make her feel used, just confused. Weak.

Maybe that's what scared her most of all.

Fallon returned an hour after he'd left. Though the lights were out, he had no trouble finding her in the moonlit shadows of the couch. He sat beside her on the cushions and traced the tracks of her tears. "Okay, now we try this my way." He kissed her gently, then scooped her up and headed for the door.

"Where are you going? I can walk," she grumped, trying to sit up. She gave up rather easily when he tightened his arms.

"Humor me. I feel like carrying you." The Haunt at his door opened it for them, and this time she remembered to hold her breath so she didn't sneeze.

Fallon set her gently on the bed, then knelt before her, kissed her hand. "Rain? Thank you for laying aside your own desires this once. I promise to remember it, and I hope to return the favor sometime."

She gave him a lopsided smile. "You think you'll find an opportunity? It's a rather large something."

He kissed her other hand. "Maybe I'll go for a series of small somethings." He joined her on the bed and slid his hand behind her head, holding her steady for his kiss. "For now, let me say 'thank you' the best way I can."

"Thank you, huh?" she said dizzily, when he came up for air.

He skimmed his mouth over hers. "Hm. One of the best advantages of being married. I get to comfort you with my body."

The man knew aid and comfort, she'd give him that. Their first night together had told her to expect wildness in his bed--this night showed her what comfort was. Every caress spoke empathy, every tender kiss, love. Even if he didn't feel it, that's what came across in his touch. Could a man who made love like that feel nothing?

Later, she lay drowsing by his side, thinking nothing in particular. Compelled by a sudden urge, she turned her head and placed a kiss on his bare chest. "I love you."

His body jerked. "Come again?"

Fallon's reaction made her want to laugh. "I must, you know. Mad as you make me, I haven't kicked you out of bed yet."

He peered down at her, his brow furling as her shoulders shook. Reassured that she was laughing, he said gruffly, "Well, I am pretty lovable."

She laughed some more, then made the mistake of meeting his gaze. His was serious and tender, a little troubled.

"I've never been in love before."

"You're not now," she stated. "That's all right." It wasn't, but it had to be said. She wasn't going to force him into any admissions he didn't mean.

"You're wrong about that. I'm something, but I'm not sure what yet."

She snorted and settled back down. "Well, wake me up if you figure it out. I've had a hard day."

His chest rumbled as he chuckled, but he let her sleep through the night.

* * * *

The next morning dawned gloomy, and Rain was out of sorts. Fallon was off doing whatever ex-ambassadors did all day.

What she ought to have been doing was getting to work dumbing down her technology--er, making it more commonly useful. Saving her hide, as a bonus. Instead she moped around, staring out the window, dallying over breakfast, taking a long bath.

Fallon hadn't been in bed when she awoke. Had she scared him with her talk of love? Well, too bad. He'd seduced her into his bed, he could deal with what it had done to her feelings. It wasn't like she planned to get all sentimental or try to psychoanalyze him or anything. She had enough problems trying to figure out what motivated her.

Goaded by anger, she strolled to her rooms, holding her breath as she walked past the Haunt guarding the hall and the door to her suite. Once inside, she actually got some work done, but she never really settled. Still edgy, she gulped some of the vile allergy medicine and braved the hall. "I'm gonna go for a walk," she said defiantly to the Haunt outside. "I need air." When none of them growled at her, she made good on her idea and walked on, trying to ignore the pair of them trailing behind. Once she'd found a way outside, though, she paused in confusion. She knew that the obstacle course was straight across from her garden wall, but where was she now? Hoping it was the right direction, she chose a path to her left.

There were a few people on the stone paths, but her surly expression and the Haunt soldiers trailing her must have discouraged conversation, for nobody tried to talk to her. Just as well--she wasn't in the mood for chitchat.

Once she'd thought it, she suddenly felt lonely. Great. Fallon was mucking with her head now. One more thing to blame on him.

Maybe it was dumb luck, but her ramblings brought her to the obstacle course. To her dismay, it was swarming with soldiers doing exercises. Even if they'd have welcomed her, she didn't want company. Muttering something foul, she stomped off toward the woods across the way. There looked to be a park off to their right and an orchard beyond that. Maybe by the time she'd done the loop she'd have worn out enough to enjoy a solitary lunch.

The park was too crowded, though by no means full. She felt exposed as curious eyes tracked her progress. It was as she entered the orchard and achieved the seclusion she'd hoped for that she began to worry, though. Something wasn't right. Shouldn't her bodyguards have said something by now, questioned her choice of wandering in the woods? She half expected someone to appear, ready to chew her out.

A familiar pain gripped her as the *change* came over her, lengthening her nails, sharpening her teeth and her senses. This time she rode it out, using her nose to test the wind, blessing the ears that picked up sound unavailable to mere human ears. She stood still, looking, scenting as shiny red fruit swayed gently in the breeze. Something....

Her guards picked up on her unease and looked around warily. One reached for his dagger ... and she saw it. A hilt just like that, one with a pale blue stone, had been raised to smash into her father's face that night long ago. The memories slammed back like a freight train rushing through her mind, triggering the panic. With an animal snarl, she turned on her heels and ran.

She was back in the night, alone, afraid, with blood on the wind. The monsters were chasing her, would kill her like they'd killed her father. They were going to get her.

But nobody ran like Rain. Nobody had ever been able to catch her when she'd started to move, could leap as high, dodge as fast. She might not have all the fur of a full blood, but she had all the speed, plus some. Even so, she didn't dare look back.

"Trouble! Backup! She just took off like she'd been shot from a gun. Kial's trying to catch her...."

She heard the words and put on a burst of speed. There were more of them coming now.

Ahead, she could hear the thunder of a waterfall. Water had saved her last time. She'd used a canoe to steal away, letting the water mask her scent, then docked at a waterfront restaurant and taken a cab to the bus depot, just like she'd planned with her dad. There'd be no bus today, but the water could still take her away. She ran to the head of the waterfall--

"No!" her guard yelled franticly behind her.

--and jumped without looking at the landing.

* * * *

Fallon paced slowly along the river's edge, staring out over the foaming water. It was only two miles from the waterfall to the mouth of the ocean, but those two miles were half a mile wide and filled with fast, dark water full of boulders. The falls Rain had jumped from were over four stories tall and the pool at the bottom had rocks the size of Volkswagens. Things that went over that fall did not survive the drop. If by some miracle they did, the river rode over them, dragging away any slim chance for life.

Rain was dead.

They were combing the banks and boats were braving the swift currents at the ocean's mouth, but it was a formality. Nobody expected to find the body.

Her guards didn't know what had gone wrong. Kial had almost grabbed her before she'd jumped and had to be saved from overbalancing himself. He and his partner, Brack, were searching obsessively, unwilling to give up. They'd never lost a charge before, and to have a woman die on them like this....

Fallon looked away from them.

His companion, Keilor, both Master of Hunt and his cousin, clamped him on the shoulder. "Don't give up yet."

Fallon just looked at him. Keilor knew the odds. As the commander of Jayems' armies, he'd seen long odds before, and he'd seen death. Today had brought another one.

Fallon hadn't expected it to hurt so much.

"Sir, they've found her!" One of Keilor's soldiers came up, holding a com unit. "One of the fishermen pulled her on board. She's hurt, but alive." News passed rapidly among the men, resulting in a few scattered cheers.

Fallon took the com unit like a sleepwalker and held it to his ear. "Hello?"

"Hello! We've got the lady and we're heading for the docks. We've already got a medic coming to meet us." There was a spate of cursing in the background, breathless and feminine. There was a pause, then the man said somewhat uncertainly, "She wants me to tell you she's fine."

"Put her on," Fallon ordered, relief making him terse. She was alive!

"Uh, I would, but she's out again."

Fallon cursed, tossed the unit to the soldier and bolted for his stag beast. The ugly reptile looked like a horse on steroids crossed with a stegosaurus, but it had speed to match its grouchy temperament, and that's what he needed.

He reached the docks in record time, then had to shove his way through the crowd that had formed as news of the rescue spread.

The fishermen carefully transferred Rain to the medic's anti-gravity stretcher, wincing as she groaned.

"Watch that knee," he advised the medics. "It's the worst."

"Yes, that one, idiot!" Rain gasped as the medic lightly touched the offender. She dug her nails into his hand, then let go with a groan. She shivered. Her hair was still plastered with salt water and her face held a ghastly pallor. She bit her lip, causing bright beads of blood to well as they jostled the pallet.

"Hey, enough of that," Fallon ordered her, taking her hand as they moved toward the Citadel.

Her eyes flew open to look at him. "It's not that bad."

"I see that."

She tried to smother another groan. "Stupid rocks." She muttered something incoherent and tossed her head. "That water's cold."

"Why did you jump?" Fallon's throat was tight. He was afraid of the answer. If she'd tried to deliberately take her life....

"There was something ... wrong."

"What?"

"Wrong...." she trailed off, breathing shallowly.

"My lord, later," one of the medics snapped at him. "Let's make sure she lives, first."

"Gona live," Rain muttered, but it was clear she wasn't fully sensible.

They wouldn't let him inside the operating room, so Fallon paced the lounge. Keilor joined him, keeping silent vigil as they waited for news.

"Maybe a flashback?" Fallon offered, when upwards of half an hour had crawled by. "She has panic attacks around Haunt."

While Keilor had not yet met Rain, he'd listened just that morning as Fallon had spilled his guts about his wife. "Maybe."

"I know Kial and Breck are reliable. I wouldn't have assigned them if they hadn't been."

"I know."

"She's not going to die. She's too stubborn to just die." Fallon looked at Keilor, almost begging.

He received a glimmer of a smile. "From your description, that's true. I'd focus on what you need to do in the future to prevent these panic attacks, if that's what it was. It's a dangerous habit in someone who can outrun her guard."

Fallon blew out a breath, still amazed at that. He'd never heard of a woman being able to outrun a fully *changed*, adult male. If asked, he'd have sworn it couldn't be done.

He hated learning things about Rain behindhand. All he wanted was a nice, tame married life, yet what he got was fireworks going off under his feet. He certainly couldn't let her keep jumping off cliffs! Yet he didn't want to smother her. There had to be a way to achieve some equilibrium.

An hour after they'd taken Rain into the ER, a medic came out to get Fallon. "You can see her now," the medic advised, "but don't make her talk too much, and don't get her upset. She's lost some blood; not enough for a transfusion, but she'll be a little weak. There's a few cuts and bruises, a bump on the back of her head and of course, her knee. Other than that, she's doing remarkably well, considering." A touch of awe came into his voice. Apparently, Rain's stunt was destined to become legend.

"What's wrong with her knee?" Fallon asked, a little sharply. As far as he was concerned, her behavior was cause for alarm, not admiration.

"Oh, just a bad sprain. It could have been far worse."

"Yeah? Well, stand by. I'm not done with her." His cold words aside, Fallon was relieved to find Rain resting quietly. Apparently the painkillers were working fine.

She sent him a glance. "I'm fine. Don't look so grim."

He raised a brow as he took the chair next to her. "This is fine?"

She shrugged, then winced as she thought better of it. "Well, I'm not dead."

"A near thing, but I'm glad." He tried to hold his tongue, found he couldn't. "There was nothing chasing you, you know."

"Maybe," she said warily.

He sighed. "What sent you off?"

She thought about it, looking uneasy. "I don't know. We were isolated, and the woods … I just got this feeling. Then there was this blue stone in one of the wer--er, Haunt's swords, and I...." she looked frustrated.

Fallon tried to contain his temper, knowing it was born of worry. "Blue gems are very, very common in our sword hilts. I could find you a dozen of them in as many minutes. Now if you'd said a red stone, I could have done something with that."

She grunted and chose not to comment.

Chewing on the inside of his cheek to contain the scalding rebuke he longed to deliver, he took her hand instead and awkwardly stroked it. "I chose the men who guard you very carefully."

"They're not men," she muttered, refusing to look at him.

It took a quick breath to keep from snapping at her. "Would you still feel that way if they took a bullet for you? Would you still despise Kial if he were bleeding out right now? Those *men* put their lives on the line for you! For that matter, I don't understand your prejudice. You're one of us."

The medic came in just as Rain drew breath to scorch him.

"My lord? You were asked not to excite our patient. For her sake, would you please leave until you can control your temper?"

"A fine idea," he snapped, flinging a last look at Rain. "We'll continue this when we're on equal footing."

"You won't win," Rain said sullenly. A hot red flush rose in her cheeks, making the rest of her face dead white in comparison.

While sympathetic, Fallon also felt intense frustration. He'd mistaken her acceptance of them, of their relationship, as an acceptance of who she was and the Haunt in general. Now he knew better, and he couldn't address the problem the way he wished. When it came to his wife, he had no patience.

Keilor had remained in the waiting room, the familiarity of years, perhaps, making him think Fallon would need to talk some more. He took one look at Fallon's face and smiled sympathetically. After all, he had a wife. "Want to discuss it over a drink?"

An hour and two stouts later, Fallon was beginning to relax. "She's stubborn, coz. I never would have thought having a wife would be this taxing."

"I hear you," Keilor said, still nursing his first beer.

Fallon sighed. "It doesn't have to be this hard. She's just trained herself to run at every opportunity."

"She had reason, sounds like," Keilor said reasonably. "I've had vets like that. Look at some of the older soldiers, the one who've really seen action. At least we give them a chance to decompress."

"She can't go on like this," Fallon insisted. "I can't let her keep running."

Keilor stretched out a leg, getting comfortable. "So retrain her. Works on the stags. Don't see why you can't recondition her to be more at ease around the things she fears."

Fallon thought about it. Rain wouldn't appreciate that approach, but it might work. If it kept her from leaping off cliffs....

Chapter Eight

Rain opened her eyes and found that she was alone. Lovely. She'd had unpleasant dreams and would have welcomed a distraction, even if it was Fallon's scowling face. Not that she could blame him; she felt a creeping embarrassment that she'd thrown herself over a four story waterfall without a good reason. She shifted and winced. She must have hit every rock in that blasted river.

The current had been fast, and she was amazed that she'd survived. There had been a couple of times she'd been sucked under and nearly drowned. Maybe somebody upstairs was watching out for her, because there was no way she should have made it out of that river.

If a higher power had saved her though, she couldn't fathom why. Fallon was mad at her, for one. You'd think he'd at least have a little sympathy for his half drowned wife.

As she lay there feeling sorry for herself, the devil himself popped in. Bearing flowers, he handed the bouquet to her and kissed her on the cheek. "Hello. How did you sleep?"

"Terrible. Why are you so happy?" He looked like a man who'd had good news. Feeling hopeful, she asked, "Did Azion die in his sleep?"

He laughed. "No. But you're alive, the sun is shining and the medics say you're allowed to go home. How about it? Would you rather lie on your own couch or here in the hospital?"

"It is a little boring here."

"Great! Let me get you a chair." He turned to go.

"Hold it! There's nothing wrong with my one leg. Crutches will work fine."

He raised his brows. "They said you strained your shoulder, too."

He had her there. The stupid shoulder throbbed if she worked it and she could barely raise the thing. It was going to cost her if she insisted on walking with crutches. However, her left shoulder was fine, and that was her lame side. "One crutch will do it."

Fallon considered her a moment. "All right. If you want to hobble up three flights of steps, a quarter mile of flagstone paths and another quarter mile of hallways on top of that...."

She sagged into the mattress, exhausted just thinking about it. "Okay, you can use a chair. Just this once, though."

"Of course. Let me help you get dressed."

Thanks to the jarring of the wheelchair, she was feeling grouchy with pain by the time they reached their rooms. The sneezing wasn't helping, either. She couldn't help glaring at their Haunt escort, knowing they were the source of her discomfort.

"Let me get you some medicine," Fallon said as he helped her settle onto their couch.

She sneezed in answer, then glared at him just because she could.

He grinned and got the bottle.

Once she'd eaten and napped--amazing how tiring pain could be--he settled down for a discussion. She could tell what was coming when his face got serious. She tried to head him off. "Now's not a good time."

He seemed to consider that, then shook his head. "I'm not going to lose my temper. I've dealt with your near death experience--I'll be okay now. The important thing is that I help you to cope with your fear."

"I don't need help."

"You're going to be here for a long time. We need to make you more comfortable with your surroundings and your heritage."

"My heritage died back on Earth. I'm an American citizen unlawfully transported. End of story."

"Beginning of story. Your life got more interesting, is all. It's my job as your husband to help you with the transition."

"Is it now?" she asked sarcastically. She didn't care for his cheerful attitude or the feeling that he was looking forward to this.

"Absolutely. I figured we could work on proximity first."

She quirked a brow, trying to distract him. "I think we've covered that."

He smiled and kissed her. "We'll get back to that later. You need to relax around the Haunt, at least enough so you don't jump out of your skin every other day." He leaned back and looked at her. "Granted, Haunt soldiers are intimidating. We train hard to be ... but your fear is way beyond what's considered reasonable. I've thought of a way to fix that." He waited.

Not that she was interested in his cure, of course, but curiosity finally drove her to ask, "What?"

He smiled. "I'm going to let Kial into the room. He's going to hang around for a while until you get used to seeing him."

"He'll get fur on the furniture!" she snapped, reaching for an excuse. "I'll be sneezing all day."

"It's leather. It'll clean," he said confidently, and went to the door.

She drew in a sharp breath as the Haunt came in. Was it her imagination, or did he look equally wary?

"So, Kial. Anything interesting happen to you today?" Fallon asked.

Kial responded with sign language, surprising her. Well, maybe it shouldn't. Normal Haunt lost the ability to speak when they had *changed.* Sign language was one way to solve that.

Fallon gave her an ironic look. "He says 'no, not since yesterday.' "

She glowered.

Fallon looked back at Kial. "So, what did the wife have to say about that?"

She blinked. Kial had a wife? It was hard to picture. The idea made her uneasy.

"Really? How old is your son now? Two?"

The unease grew. The werewolf had a son. So? Makes sense that he could reproduce. It didn't mean he had any fatherly feelings. She looked aside, her thoughts making her vaguely ashamed.

With barely a glance at her, Fallon lead the Haunt closer. She could feel her nails digging into the couch. A silent growl trembled on her lips.

They reached the armchairs opposite her. Just as she was poised to climb over the back of the couch, they stopped.

"You know how she is about sneezing, so if you don't mind *changing* before we sit down...."

Kial did as Fallon directed. The *change* itself wasn't dramatic, just a simple melting of form, accomplished in seconds. Underneath all that fur, Kial was an unassuming brunette of average height and looks. His expression was a little hesitant as he addressed her. "Good morning, my lady."

She stared at him without blinking, wary as a kitten suddenly dropped into a box of pit bull puppies. Her abused muscles were screaming at her to relax, but her mind wasn't listening. She'd run hurt before, and she could do it this instant if he got any closer. Amazing what terror and adrenaline rush could do to wipe out pain. She felt herself creeping toward that edge.

Fallon gestured for Kial to sit. "So tell me, are you still thinking about getting your red sash? You're more than eligible."

"I don't know if I want it. I'm happy and content where I am, and so is my wife."

"You know I can't promote you without it."

"I'm not worried about it yet."

Rain found that it was difficult to maintain rigid muscles for extended periods, especially when she was hurt. Despite herself, she was also following the conversation. Fallon's nagging was beginning to wear on her.

"There's more money for captains. Think what you could do with that," Fallon urged.

Rain rolled her eyes.

"We have simple needs. The promotion would mean less time with my family. We're not ready to sacrifice that," Kial said firmly.

"Yes, but--"

Rain couldn't take it any longer. "For heaven's sake, Fallon! Give the man a break. He doesn't want the promotion."

The men looked at her, surprised. Fallon even smiled, very slightly. "He'd really make a good addition, hon."

She scowled and peeled herself from the couch. Reaching for her crutch, she snapped, "He already said no. Why are you so stubborn? Can't you just take a 'no' once in a while?" She hobbled to the bedroom door and slammed it behind her for good measure.

Fallon looked at Kial and smiled. "So, when are you taking the test?"

Kial smiled back. "Next week."

"Good man! You're going to make a good right hand for Rykarr." Fallon grinned. Rain had taken the bait. Now all they had to do was think up a stage two.

* * * *

Rain was drowsing in her garden, minding her own business, when she heard a low growl. It sounded like a puppy in play, somewhere on the other side of her garden wall. She was about to drift back off when she heard the sound of a grunt, then a pitiful whine. The hairs rose on the back of her neck as she reached for her crutch and scrambled up on the bench, the better able to see over the wall. A circle of three young boys were ganging up on a young ... well, he was young. The boys were roughly eight years old, and she guessed that the ... kid ... on the ground was about the same age. One of the boys was sitting on the furry kid, pummeling him with his fists while his buddies cheered him on. It wasn't until she spoke that Rain realized that the kid on top was a girl.

A sense of outrage made Rain's blood boil as she took in the sight. "Hey! Get off him, you little snot! It's not fair to kick a guy when he's down."

The girl looked up in surprise while the hairy fellow lay there, panting. She was missing her two front teeth. "He was teasing me!"

Rain swung up on top of the wall, grimacing as her knee throbbed. "Yeah? Well he's down now, so get off him before I boot you in butt. My word! In my day we beat up on the boy, but we didn't need all our girlfriends helping, too." She raked a scathing look at the boys, making them blush.

One boy, a dark haired kid also missing a front tooth and sporting silver bracelets, scowled at her. "We weren't helping. That wouldn't be fair."

"Whatever." Rain swung down from the wall and carefully got her balance. She poked the girl with her crutch when the kid just stared at her. "Get off and run along. Go find another girl to beat up on." She shook her at her own words, then bent down and gingerly hauled the hairy kid to his feet. "You okay, mate?" Funny how her time in foreign countries came out in her voice when she was under stress.

On his feet, the little guy came up to her chin. If he was eight, he was tall for his age. He looked at the girl--she hadn't bothered to leave--and glared.

Rain felt her mouth twitch. Her reserves of nervousness at the miniature werewolf were fading fast. "Not allowed to hit girls, eh?"

The kid hunched his shoulders.

Rain rotated her aching shoulder and made a stab at acting the adult. "Well, were you teasing her?"

"DJ jumped out and scared her," the boy with the bracelets reported helpfully. "Carri hates it when he does that."

Rain took a closer look at the freckled little girl with the orange bush of hair. Maybe it was a case of puppy love, maybe not. "Whatever, we don't hit people. I should tell your parents."

The girl hung her head.

Yeah, she should, but that would be too much trouble. Rain decided to cut them a deal. "Fine. If you can behave yourself for the rest of the day--especially when I'm trying to nap behind my wall--then I suppose I could let you off the hook. Now, apologize to each other." She poked the hairy kid. "You! *Change* back so you can speak up."

DJ looked aside and shuffled his feet. He made a few indistinct signs.

Rain frowned and shook her head. "I don't do sign language."

"He said he can't *change* back," Bracelet kid said. "He has a hard time *changing* sometimes."

A little slow, was he? Rain felt herself warming to the kid and didn't like it. "Fine. Do your sign language thing, then. It'd better look sincere, though."

DJ made a few quick signs to Carri.

Carri huffed, then mumbled, "Okay, I'm sorry."

Relieved to have the whole business over with, Rain nodded her head and started hobbling back toward home, going the long way around. She didn't feel like trying to scramble over the wall again.

The kids followed her.

"Whatcha doing?" Bracelet kid asked.

"Going home. You should, too. What's your name, anyway?"

"I'm Malix." He grinned at her, showing off his missing tooth. He nudged the unknown boy, another red head. "This is Twix. He's Carrie's older brother."

Rain grinned. Twix, was it? Did his mama know she'd named him after a candy bar?

"What's your name?" Malix asked. He really was a cute little thing, with black hair tumbling into his eyes.

"Rain." She would really rather the kids took off. "Don't you have somewhere to be?"

"No," Malix said innocently. "Do you have any toys?"

She shook her head. "I'm too old for toys."

"You don't look old," Carrie said suspiciously. "I bet you know how to make all kinds of toys."

"Just the exploding kind," Rain muttered.

"Really! That's cool! I want to see," Malix cried.

"Me, too! Me, too!" the others chimed in. All except for DJ, who was looking at her with great interest.

Rain sighed. Unable to take the torture, she grouched, "All right! I'll show you one little thing, but then you've got to find something else to do."

Ahead of them, she could see a couple of Haunt in uniform. By the purposeful way they strode toward her, Rain guessed they were her security detail. They didn't look happy, but then, they rarely did.

The kids quieted down as they saw where she was looking. Rain couldn't take her eyes off the Haunt, and she could feel her breathing accelerate.

Malix tugged on her sleeve. "DJ wants to know why you smell afraid."

Startled, she cut a look at the half pint werewolf. "I don't." It came out more harshly than she meant.

"Are you afraid of Haunt soldiers?" Malix wanted to know.

"No," Rain said curtly, but she could feel the tension closing in on her as the soldiers flanked her.

"But DJ says--"

She cut Malix off. "Have you ever seen a Gauss rifle? You use steel balls and magnets to fire them off. I built one the other day while I was feeling bored."

The inevitable questions helped her to relax somewhat. She wasn't sure if it helped or not to see DJ edging protectively toward her. Or maybe she had it wrong. Maybe he was afraid of the bigger Haunt, too.

Suddenly, she began to sneeze.

"Bless you," Malix said.

She sneezed again.

"Are you all right?" Carri wanted to know.

"Allergies," Rain said grimly, resigned to the inevitable. "I hate taking my medicine." Funny, though. She hadn't sneezed around DJ, and she'd been around him long enough for his fur to affect her.

"What's an allergy? Is it catching?"

Rain rolled her eyes at the questions and hobbled faster. She couldn't wait to unload this bunch.

Once in the suite she shared with Fallon, the kids were fascinated by the pile of odds and ends on a corner table.

They especially liked the simple version of a Gauss Rifle, a grooved wooden board with four nickel plated, neodymium-iron-boron magnets taped to it.

"Cool! What is it?" Carri asked.

"It's a linear acceleration device for studying high-energy physics."

They were silent for a moment. Then Malix piped up, "Can I play with it?"

She snorted with amusement. "Sure. Bring it out to the garden. Carri and Twix, you bring the little table there." She didn't think Fallon would care if they used the marble topped end table. She was fairly certain it was an antique, but it wasn't like they were going to damage it.

She handed a pouch of nickel plated steel balls to DJ and followed the kids out to the garden. She'd set up a board for a target earlier, but hadn't used it yet. Once the rifle was set up, she explained its use. "Okay, we point the rifle at our target, then put two steel balls against each magnet, right in the groove. Good. Now we put a ball in the groove and give it a little nudge and...." The kids cheered as the marble struck the magnet, causing a chain reaction that sent the end marble shooting off the end, striking the board with a satisfying, "whack!"

"Okay, now you try. Youngest to oldest." Carrie started out, then Malix, DJ and Twix. They played for a whole fifteen minutes before the game began to wane.

Rain found herself amused to be playing with four little kids. She'd never enjoyed something like that before. Maybe she was changing.--scary thought!

When she finally told the kids it was time for them to go home, they protested a little, but not too badly.

"Can we come back tomorrow?" Malix pleaded.

She considered, then shrugged. "I guess. As long as your parents know where you are. Now run along, and don't beat up on each other," she said with a stern look for Carri.

"As long as he doesn't tease me," she said pertly, then escaped before she could be reprimanded.

DJ was slow to leave. He didn't seem to want to abandon the Gauss rifle.

Rain eyed him. "You know, it's easy to build your own. Ask your mom and dad if it's okay. I'll give you a parts list if you like."

It was the first time she'd seen a werewolf smile. Unfortunately, it wasn't a pretty sight, even on a kid. She made quick work of the list, then sent him on his way.

* * * *

Fallon slipped the kids each a bag of candy as they passed him in the hall. He'd been eavesdropping, and couldn't have been more pleased with how their little skit had played out. Rain was softening.

For a woman who claimed to have little interest in children, she had a tender heart. He was devious enough to keep that card in play.

Feeling happy, he hummed a tune as he left her alone to dwell on the experience.

Fallon found her in the garden later, finishing up her nap. "I heard we had visitors."

She grunted and sat up. Smothering a yawn, she informed him, "I found this little redhead beating up on a boy. I took pity on him."

"Hmm. I heard about it second hand from Malix." He sat down and began massaging her foot, the one attached to the good leg. "He says you're pretty cool."

"Huh." What he was doing felt pretty good.

He kissed the top of her foot. "His brother gave their parents the part's list. He can't wait to make his own … guess rifle was it?"

"Gauss. Wait. You mean DJ and Malix are brothers?"

"Yes. DJ is the older. His dad's proud of him for not hitting a girl back, but he promised to give him pointers about making her stop without hurting her. He also told him to stop teasing girls."

"Who's his father?"

"My cousin Keilor." He snuggled up behind her on the wide wooden lawn chair. It was a tight fit, but not claustrophobic. When he snuggled his hand low on her belly, she lost the desire complain.

Clearing her throat, she said, "Oh. So they're related to you … sort of."

"Second cousins. They're related to you, too, through marriage. Nice of you to be kind to them." His hand slid a fraction lower.

"Wasn't hard," she said off-hand, distracted.

"Still." His finger began tracing little circles just inside her waistband.

Losing track of the conversation was inevitable, but she gave it a valiant effort. "Kids are okay, as long as they belong to someone else."

His lips feathered over the back of her neck and shoulder, making her melt. "Yes." His hand slid lower, tangling in the curls between her thighs. "If we had kids here now, I couldn't do this." His finger started a slow circle that eased a wordless sigh from her lips. A moment later, he began to lower her pants. Still on her side, she protested, "We can't! My knee."

He chuckled. "I see I need to work harder on your education. Can you think of a position that won't put pressure on it?" To illustrate, he circled an arm around her waist and pulled her bare butt against his front.

"Ah...." she croaked. He was fast taking care of any reluctance she might have felt.

"Mmm-hmm. I'm afraid you're still over dressed for such a warm day, though." He reached up and popped the clasp on her harem style top. He played his hand around her breasts, inhaling like a man deeply satisfied with life. "Ah, yes. As sweet and tender as I remembered." He squeezed a nipple, surprising a squeal out of her. She shifted under his hands and he admonished her. "Uh-huh. We have to be careful of that knee."

The last thing on her mind was her knee as he took his time playing with her silky breasts, gliding his hand over her stomach. She was whimpering by the time he sat up and pulled off his vest, then opened the laces on the front of his pants. He guided himself to her slick opening from behind. "Open up, sweetheart. The doctor wants in."

She still hadn't gotten used to how big he was. Completely vulnerable, she panted as he eased inside, filling her with delicious hardness. No wonder she hadn't missed the Bell's seductive song--Fallon could make a sultana forget her harem.

He was slow but thorough--the man must have been born with self-control. He took his time to tease her, driving her past what she could bear, then easing her down. Nearly insane with desire, she pleaded and begged until he gave in and finished her off. By that time she wouldn't have known she *had* a knee, much less cared if it ached.

It was sometime later--after dinner, dessert and more of Fallon, in fact--that she realized that Haunt weren't so different, after all. It couldn't have been more obvious that her lover was proud of his heritage, and look how wonderful he was. She wasn't ready to see it, but she didn't *think* she'd freak if she saw Fallon *change* now. She'd try not to, at least, because she wasn't a coward. The day would surely come when it would happen, and she figured she could work up to it. Maybe she'd even practice with Kial, watching him *change* and stuff until the thought of being close to a Haunt didn't put her in a cold sweat. Even hanging with DJ had to be a help.

What she had with Fallon was worth preserving.

One matter was left undone, however. The man who'd started her terrors was still alive. As long as he was out there, she'd never feel safe. The man was like a sword dangling by a silk thread, poised over her head whether she ate, dreamed or loved.

Azion had to die.

She'd tried to let go, to live and let live for Fallon's sake, had even managed a measure of resignation. Only now did she see clearly that there would be no peace until Azion had been dealt with. It wasn't like he was going to repent and behave. He'd started the war. She needed to finish it before he finished her.

* * * *

Rain sat in her suite late the next afternoon. Brooding, she lifted her newly constructed short-range Bell and considered it. This model looked like a large ball bearing, etched with a few engravings. It chimed, but she'd modified it to avoid the seductive song. They didn't need to pass on that little trait.

Losing her original wasn't as bad as she'd dreaded. She didn't miss her own Bell's song, having realized that Fallon could give her so much more than it ever could. It had been a beautiful creation, though, and special, and she missed it a little for that. This Bell, though, was going to serve a higher--or lower, if she preferred--purpose. Rykarr had called it the ultimate assassin's toy. It hadn't taken much thought to realize he'd been right.

Rain keyed the Bell and opened a portal to Azion's private rooms. Happily, he was alone at his desk, his back to her.

Allowing him a fighting chance, she said coolly, "You look a lot different when you're not covered in fuzz, Graybeard."

He spun around so fast, he nearly fell out of his seat. "Rain! What the###" he apparently realized he was better off with his mouth shut.

She half smiled. "Hello, Azion. I thought I'd show you what you wanted so badly. What do you think?" She rolled the Bell between her palms, walked it through her fingers like a Chinese exercise ball. "Nifty little toy, isn't it?"

Azion stood up and moved closer to the portal. "How are you doing this?" he looked around her room before his gaze settled on her hands. "Is that the device that makes this projection?"

She couldn't help a smirk. "No projection, old man. See for yourself."

He hesitated. "Why are you doing this?"

She raised a brow, playing it cool. Inside, she burned. "Let's not waste our breath."

He considered her for a long moment. "It was necessary, you know."

Her answering smile was cold, sharp edged. She played the Bell through her fingers, making it sparkle in the light.

The lure of the Bell must have been too much. Azion gave her room one more penetrating look, then reached out to touch the portal.

Rain closed her eyes against the flash. When she opened them, all that remained of him was a pile of rust colored dust. Her hand clenched on the Bell, closing the connection.

Her room was neat, empty. There was no way to trace Azion's death to her.

She felt a little sick. She'd let the man reach out to his own destiny, but knowing he was dead wasn't the sweet relief she'd hoped for. Knowing she'd had a part in it ... abruptly she got up and left the room.

* * * *

Fallon was in Jayems' study, examining a printout of Azion's rooms. He'd been there most of the morning with Jayems and Keilor, trying to find a workable assassination plan. "The man has more safeguards in place than the whole palace put together," he finally muttered, straightening. "You'd think he was king."

"Or planned to be," Keilor said, with a glance at Jayems.

Jayems wasn't saying much. Though physically in the room, his mind was on his little girl and only heir, who was slowly recovering from a nasty bout of poisoning. It had been a close call. If her mother hadn't figured it out, if they hadn't given her charcoal and pumped her stomach as fast as they had ... if the medics hadn't been the best.

Fallon's fist curled. He wanted Azion dead. Knowing the man would like to return the favor, especially to Fallon's wife, made his blood burn.

"Your eyes are glowing again, Fallon. Calm down. Cool heads will solve this better," Keilor cautioned. A battle veteran who was far older than he looked, the man knew what he was talking about.

"It's easier when it's not family," Fallon said grimly.

"I hear you. You should be grateful your woman turned her problems over to you and Jayems. I have nightmares thinking of the trouble Jasmine might get into in the same situation. You're a lucky man."

"Believe me, I get down on my knees and give my share of thanks," Fallon said fervently, relieved again that Rain wasn't involving herself. That had to be hard, and he was so thankful. He couldn't stand the idea of her in danger.

Keilor's com unit vibrated, and he answered it. For long moments he said nothing, just listened. "Okay, I'll be there in a moment. Standby." He looked at his closed com for a long moment, then looked at Fallon with wide-eyed sympathy. "You and Jayems had better come, too."

Dread pooled in Fallon's stomach as he followed Keilor, but he somehow kept his mouth shut. Whatever was going on, he knew Keilor would show him soon enough.

To his surprise, Keilor led the way to Azion's rooms. The door was shut and the guards before it looked agitated. Azion's large, heavyset aid, Dorron, fidgeted before the door. When he saw them, his face lit with an odd mix of chagrin, relief and caution. "My lords! I didn't know what to think. The guards didn't see or hear anything, and there is no scent of anyone strange in the room. The elder had been in there alone all morning. No one but us has been in since we discovered … it." He trailed off, strained.

Fallon exchanged looks with Jayems.

Keilor asked calmly, "Who else have you notified?"

"No one! I didn't want to say anything until someone else had confirmed what we thought. Come in and see for yourself." Dorron opened the door and ushered them in, led them through a room of severely plain furnishings made of the most expensive materials. Behind the massive desk, he stopped and stared at a small heap of orange dust. It looked like someone had dumped a bucket of dirt out on the carpet.

Keilor knelt and studied the dust.

Dorron swallowed. "I'm afraid … I think this might be Azion's remains."

Fallon's brows shot up as he knelt beside his cousin. "How?"

"I'm not sure, but you can see Azion is not here, and this is."

The men exchanged looks. It couldn't be this easy. "I know of nothing that can do this to a body. We don't have any weapons capable of this." Even as he said it, Fallon's brows drew together. He remembered Rain's genius, her inventions. If anyone had motive....

Keilor stood up and looked around, studied the room. After a moment, he *changed* and wandered around. Baffled, he *changed* back. "Could he have wanted to disappear for a while? Could this be an effort to do that?"

"Impossible," Dorron said coldly. "He had plans. He wouldn't just leave, especially not right now."

"Really?" Keilor drawled, looking the man over.

Jayems spoke for the first time. "I want tests run on those remains, and I want this room ripped apart. I want to know the truth, Keilor." His voice was strained, but a thread of relief crept through. "Do whatever you have to, but get answers."

Keilor nodded and ordered a forensic team over his com unit.

It was half an hour later, with the team hard at work in Azion's room, until they were able to return to Jayems' room to talk. Fallon was ready to explode with frustration, desperate to find Rain and shake the story from her. After that he'd just shake her. What was she doing? She could've been killed!

Keilor practically drug him into the study. "Wait! Your Haunt are with her and apprised of the situation. Azion's supporters are still too baffled to act, and they don't know what we know."

"If she did this, I'll give her a crown for it," Jayems said fervently. He was pacing in a fever of anticipation. His personal nightmare was closing.

Fallon's was just beginning. "What if she'd gotten hurt! He wouldn't have hesitated to kill her." Pacing on the opposite side of the rug from Jayems, he was yelling and didn't care.

Jayems shot him a look. "Mind the child," he snapped. "She needs her rest."

"Sorry. Still, when I think--" Fallon clamped his mouth shut. He felt like a bat in a cage, desperate to beat his way out with his wings. He wanted his wife! Wanted to punish her, shout at her, make sure she was okay.

Keilor got in his way and clamped his hands on his shoulders. "Stop! Breathe. Stop thinking like a husband for a moment. This is larger than that. If she'd been a trained soldier, you'd be offering her the moons."

"She's not!"

"Fine, but she did us a service just the same. Don't punish her for that. Have you considered that she might be hurting? Killing is never easy. For all you know, she's afraid of what we'll do if we find out."

"We won't do anything! Well, I might spank her blue, but--"

Keilor actually shook him, then smoothly dodged Fallon's thank-you punch. "Fine, now that you've got your aggression out, you'd better plan what you're really going to say to her," he snapped, then his face softened. "I'm trying to help you, brother."

Fallon dragged in a shuddering breath. Somebody had better help him, because it was going to kill him to do what he had to do.

* * * *

DJ and Malix found her brooding by a fishpond. Among other things, her knee ached.

She couldn't stand to be alone, but wanted to avoid conversation, so she'd chosen to sit by the deserted pond on the edge of the park. For once she'd been glad of the silent company of her guards. As a plus, they even scared off the casual passersby--or maybe it was her expression that did that.

She shouldn't have been surprised to see the kids--they seemed to get around. What did surprise her was DJ. "Hey, kid. Where's your fuzz?"

DJ blinked his dark eyes at her. Black haired, with long, thick lashes, he was destined to break hearts one day. "I didn't want to scare you."

She snorted in amusement and tossed another mangled piece of grass on the ground. "Wouldn't worry about it, buddy. I'm at least as scary as anything running around these woods today."

The boys sat on either side of her. "You're sad?" Malix asked, looking at her face.

She sighed. "Just having one of those moments all mad scientists have."

"You're not mad," a deep voice said, surprising her into looking around. A dark haired man about twenty years DJ's senior stood right behind her shoulder. Handsome in a rugged way, he was looking at her with penetrating sable eyes.

"You must be the father," she said dryly. "DJ couldn't look more like you if he tried."

He shrugged. "Malix takes after his mother. She likes to gloat about it, but DJ and I don't mind. I'm Keilor, your cousin-by-marriage."

"Ah. Nice to meet you." She couldn't summon much enthusiasm.

Keilor looked at the boys. "Now that you've said hello, run over there and play with Kial and Brack. I think I see a tree you haven't climbed yet ."

Rain raised her brows as he sent her bodyguards off to play nanny. Obviously he had the authority. By the look of him he was more than capable of defending her ... or cutting off her head.

Keilor studied her for a moment. "Has Fallon mentioned what I do? My title is Master of the Hunt. I'm in charge of the Citadel's military and head of security. Jayems sent me to speak with you."

She let the shields slam down over her eyes, knowing that he'd pick up on it. "Oh?"

His eyes never left hers. "An interesting thing happened to Elder Azion today."

She let her interest show, knowing it was expected.

"What we assume are his remains were found in his rooms. We're still running tests."

Somewhat strained, she asked, "Why do you assume it's his remains? Can't you sniff it out?"

His smile was sardonic. "It's difficult to do much with a pile of dust. I'm wondering if DNA testing will find anything."

"Wow. Well, if you expect me to cry at his funeral, you'll be disappointed." She looked away, unable to add any color to her voice.

Keilor seemed to chew on that. "We presume he was murdered. Under the circumstances, there'll be a lot of pressure to find out who did it. Officially, I have no body, no witnesses. I doubt we'll ever solve the case." His smile was slow, admiring. "Someone did a very good job of removing an evolving threat, not only to yourself, but to Jayems and his family." At her surprise, he added casually, "Jayems' daughter wasn't ill--she was poisoned. While we had no proof who ordered it, we had our suspicions. There are a great many people who want what he's got." While she digested that, he stood up. He offered her a slight bow. "Welcome to the family, Rain."

The world was a little rosier after that. Apparently the Haunt here held a different view of justice than the government back home. For once, she was actually glad to be in the Darklands. Head held high, she headed back to her home, almost in charity with the two Haunt at her side.

Fallon met her at the door. By the expression in his eyes, he knew. "You've had an interesting day."

She just stood there once he'd closed the door, waiting to see what he'd do.

He studied her a moment, then smiled and handed her a glass of liqueur. "Have a drink. There's more than one toast being made to you today."

By reflex, she took a sip, then had to ask, "You're not mad?"

He looked surprised, then reached behind her head and held her steady for a confirming kiss. "Do I look mad? You wouldn't believe how hard it is to assassinate a man like Azion." He looked into her eyes. "He's a murderer and a child killer, Rain. Not all justice is done in the public eye, nor is it taken lightly. Someone else would have taken him down if we hadn't been beaten to it."

She took a deep breath, then swallowed more liqueur. "Death is an ugly business, Fallon."

He nodded. "Which is why you're a scientist and I'm a politician. With luck, we'll be able to keep bloodshed out of it." *From now on,* remained unspoken. For just a moment, he let her see the depths of worry, and yes, anger, simmering below the surface. He was giving her slack this time, but she could see where his concern would take them the next time. Somehow, that made her feel better. He was not a man who let those he loved trip lightly into danger.

She nodded, hoping he was right, trying not to think about the rest of it. When he put his arm around her, she was more than happy to let him lead her to the garden to unwind.

There were times--right then, for instance--when she really, really loved that man.

Epilogue

Six months later

Rain took off at the sound of the shot, racing for her life. The Haunt fell behind her; one beat, two. The dirt path was smooth and even under her shoes, giving speed to her flying feet. Redemption was just ahead, the scarlet ribbon a promise of relief to her burning lungs. With a lunge, she broke through the line, slowing gradually into an easy lope, a walk, then a stop.

Fallon, now *changed* back to normal, finally caught up and swung her into his arms for a panting kiss. "You did it!"

She laughed breathlessly. "You're not supposed to celebrate losing, you know." He'd talked her into running the race. There'd been lots of interest among the locals, with tales of her waterfall stunt circulating. Her bodyguards had taken a lot of heat for letting her outrun them, and she'd finally given into Fallon's cajoling and agreed to a public demonstration of her speed. She hadn't known how much she'd enjoy hearing a crowd cheer for her. It was almost as nice as knowing that Azion's supports had finally given up on solving his disappearance. No fingers had ever been pointed her way, but it was only in the last month that she'd really begun to relax about it.

The nightmare was finally over.

Fallon smirked and kissed her again, bringing her back to the moment. "Hey, at least I'm still on my feet. Look at them."

Rain looked back and saw the other eight Haunt in the race, some *changed* back, some not. Most were bent over, panting. One was lying in the middle of the track, spread eagled.

She laughed. "Well, you have been training with me."

Fallon gave her another bear hug, then grunted as two little missiles slammed into them. Malix and DJ almost knocked them over.

"Wow! I've never seen anyone run so fast," Malix exclaimed.

"I'm going to run that fast when I grow up," DJ promised.

"Looks like they have a new hero," their mother Jasmine said. She put an arm around her husband Keilor's waist, giving him a smile.

Keilor kissed the top of her head. "I'm not worried."

Rain looked at her sweaty husband and had to laugh. Finally, for the first time in years, neither was she.

The End

DARKLANDS:

HOMECOMING

Authors Note:

This story is a side note to *Teasing Danger*, meant for those of you who wanted to know Wiley's story. It's not meant to stand alone, so if you don't already know how her story ends, you'll have to read TD. ~Autumn Dawn

Chapter One

She hated parties.

Parties were full of happy, smiling people, and Wiley James had never fit into that crowd. So she ditched her boss's birthday bash and ran off to the hills.

Literally. Sometimes a girl just had to go AWOL.

It started out like any other adventure, with her dashing off a note and leaving coordinates for her roommate and best friend, Jasmine. Nearly as crazy as Wiley herself, Jas would roll her eyes, grumble, then load up her Jeep and track Wiley down. Helping her would be Lemming, Wiley's search and rescue dog. It was good training for the dog, and a much needed vacation for Wiley.

It wouldn't be the first time she'd left a note for her good-natured friend to find after work. When Wiley had the itch to move, she waited for no one. Sometimes she thought she might explode if she didn't run into the woods. They were her solace, her grounding place.

Some people relaxed by flying to the Bahamas. Wiley preferred to tackle the Alaskan hills, the USA's last frontier.

She grinned to herself as the cab dropped her off on a deserted highway. She shouldered her pack and wondered how anyone could have dubbed her state, "Seward's Icebox," but she smiled every time she talked to someone who hated it here.

More wide open spaces for her to play in. Less people to notice how odd she was. There weren't many women who liked to explore wolf-infested woods alone, in late September, with winter closing in. Even fewer who would call it ripping great fun to see no one but squirrels and wildlife for days on end.

Jasmine liked to blame her friend's oddities on growing up an orphan, but Wiley knew better. There was something wild inside her, something that needed to be free.

Something more than human.

Oh, she hid it well, she thought, inhaling a breath of crisp, cold air. No one could tell by looking at her that she could smell scent traces of the game that had crossed her path. No one could tell how well she saw in the dark. And nobody, not even Jasmine, whom she loved like a sister, knew what she could turn into in the darkness of the night.

But no one needed to know. That's why she was out there, stomping through the woods. As long as she burned off her emotions with constant work and rigorous exercise, no one would ever know what she was. The darkness inside, the monster that lurked just behind her eyes, that was a secret that only the night could tell.

Rusty red brush crunched under her feet, mixed with golden birch leaves. Though she could move silently when she wished to, she relished the snap of twigs underfoot. Today was a day for noise, for release. She playfully kicked a loose rock ahead of her, and felt herself relax for the first time in days. Coming out there had been a really great idea.

She walked for a long time, until even the long daylight of the Alaskan day failed and she was using night vision alone. Satisfied that she was isolated enough to remain undisturbed, she set up a two man tent and started a fire.

Ringed with birches, the hillside clearing had a lovely view of the night. A half moon rose in the clear sky. Stars, long hidden by the midnight sun, twinkled in the cool black expanse. Somewhere in the valley, a wolf howled.

She shivered and threw another stick on the fire. Closing her ears to the sad wail, she heated some water. Dinner tonight was hot cocoa and Meal Ready to Eat, or MRE. At 1250 calories each, the freeze dried packet of chicken a la king held enough food substance to keep a hungry soldier on the march...or to seriously constipate a couch potato. All she had to do was rip open the packet, add boiling water, close it, and wait six minutes. She'd heard of other kinds that came with their own heating element and were ready to heat without adding water, but they didn't sell that kind at her local five and dime. They did sell trail mix and protein bars, which she'd stocked up on for breakfast. One experience of eating reconstituted egg powder had been enough. Even the dog had put her nose under her paws and whined when Wiley had offered it to her.

While she waited for the water to boil, she pulled out her one-man tent and assembled it. Toss in a sleeping bag and *voila*! All the comforts of home.

She'd just turned back to the fire to check the water when she saw them. Eyes. Dozens of them, glowing just outside the firelight.

Drawing a slow breath, she reached for her sidearm, a .357 Redhawk revolver, grateful she always carried it in the woods. Maybe the fire would be enough to scare the wolves off, but if not, a few bullets should do the trick.

"Get!" she yelled, feeling like a fool. Contrary to the tree hugger's expectations, these were no fat, mellow zoo buddies. Alaskan wolves could and would take down a lone human if they were hungry enough.

"You'll have to do better than that," a man's voice said from the shadows. Suddenly, not one, but three men melted out of the night into the fire's glow.

Sweat made her hands slippery on the gun. The odds weren't looking good in her favor.

"What do you want?" she demanded, trying to look tough. They were downwind, so it was no surprise she couldn't smell them, but why hadn't she heard them coming?

"You're trespassing on private property," the man spoke again. He and his blond companion were both tall, and the third man only slightly less so. All three had long hair and muscles, though his dark hair was tied back. A quick glance showed them all to be armed with sheathed pistols and wicked-looking knives. Hunters? She didn't think so, not running around in their shirtsleeves. They ought to be freezing.

"I didn't see any signs posted," she said warily.

"Maybe you missed them in the dark," the dark haired one on his left said. "Are you alone here?"

"I'm camping. I expect company at any time," she said coldly. "My roommate is coming with my dog." No need to mention that Jasmine was a petite asthmatic, or that Lemming would rather crawl up her leg than take on a wolf.

"What's your name?" The middle man asked again. His steady gaze was unnerving. She couldn't see the color of his eyes, but they were set in a strong, austerely handsome face. His voice was deep, and rang with authority. This was a man who was used to getting answers.

She couldn't think why lying would help. "Wiley James."

He jerked as if she'd slapped him. It was hard to tell through the smoke, but she thought he paled.

"It couldn't be her, Jayems," the blond said quickly. "It's just a coincidence." He glanced her way. "That girl couldn't be more than …" He frowned. "How old are you?"

"Twenty-four," she answered cautiously. It was only a few days until her birthday, but she wasn't going to age herself unnecessarily.

The men stared at her. Unnerved, she stared back. "What's going on?"

"You …" The one called Jayems swallowed with difficulty. "You're the same age as our cousin, who we lost many years ago. Her nickname was Wiley."

A sickening slide of premonition made her shiver, and she started to lower the gun. Her arm ached. "I don't know you," she said with ruthless common sense, trying to shake some sense back into her numb brain. "I'm sorry for your loss and sorry I trespassed. If you don't mind, I'll pack up and leave right now."

The Cherokee look-alike stepped toward her. "Wait." He looked at her stocking hat, noted the brown hair peeking out in wisps around her ears. "You have dark hair, but many people do."

"Yes, they do," she said edgily, keeping her arm loose and ready. One more step and he was in her sights again.

"What was your mother's name?" the blond demanded.

Sweat trickled down her back. The subject stank, and the situation did not feel good. "Don't know; I was an orphan. Stay back!" She pointed her gun at the Cherokee, who'd gotten too close.

"Keilor," Jayems said in warning, halting him.

Keilor stopped, canting his head in acknowledgment.

"Do you know where you were born?" Jayems asked carefully, as if he held himself in check. He almost sounded polite.

"No," she automatically.

"What age were you orphaned at?" Keilor asked, staring hard at her.

"Young. I'm not the one you're looking for," she repeated, willing him to back off.

There was silence for several seconds. Then Jayems said, "We can't take that chance."

In a split second Keilor had leapt the fire, snatched her gun and tossed it to Fallon. Screaming, she struggled, trying to throw him off. Wiley was far stronger than she looked, but he had a surprising strength. He grunted when she stomped his foot, but he wasn't going anywhere.

So she did the only thing she could, an act of ultimate desperation. She *changed*.

Wiley slowly backed up in a cold sweat. She saw her hand, covered in long, silky black hair. Her thick, strong nails had blackened; her hearing, intensified. Her breath came in scared huffs as her sharpened night vision pierced the shadows, counting wolves.

Only they weren't wolves. The faces were all wrong, and they had ridges on their backs like wild dogs.

"Oof!" he grunted as she broke loose and threw him. Barely avoiding the fire, he tucked into a roll and jumped back to his feet in a crouch.

"It is you," Jayems breathed, and his eyes were glowing. He stepped forward, his hand out. "Don't be afraid. See, we're just like you." In a blink, he *changed*, growing dark hair all over, lengthening his nails. His face became the flattened face of a wolf, and his eyes gleamed golden in the firelight.

She screamed, or tried to. She had no voice to shout when she *changed*. She spun and ran, ignoring the animals around her, desperate to escape the nightmare behind her. She was so scared, she shifted back to human as she ran, somehow thinking the dream would end if she changed, if she woke up.

Strong arms grabbed her from behind, lifted her off her feet. Those arms were human.

"Easy," Jayems said, subduing her effortlessly. "Easy, Rihlia."

"L-let me go!" she shouted, freaking out. That name triggered something in her, and she knew that she was dead. The monsters that had haunted her dreams for so long had finally caught her.

Then there was a burst of light, and she knew nothing at all.

Chapter Two

"You shot her!" Jayems stared at the limp bundle in his arms, too stunned to do more than state the obvious.

"She's happier that way," Keilor said, putting away his laser gun. It had been set on stun. "She'll be easier to take home if she's not fighting us all the way." He still looked dazed, as if he couldn't quite take in what was happening. Then he blinked and focused. "You *are* taking her home after all this? Or were you planning to leave her to wake up and think it was all a dream?"

"Are you insane? Of course I'm not leaving her here!" Jayems looked around. "But about her friend? She said someone else was coming. Could he be one of us, too?" The shock of finding his long-dead cousin was still muddling his brain.

His day had started out so ordinary. He'd gone over the books for the Citadel, and then made plans to walk Fallon and Keilor to the gate. Fallon had business on Earth, tending to those of their kind who'd chosen to stay behind. Keilor had been planning to visit, having never seen the planet. He'd been born in the Dark Lands, the world where most of their kind had migrated. His duties as Master of the Hunt, the captain of the Citadel's guards, he'd assigned to another. Jayems assumed that his subordinate would be disappointed to hear of Keilor's sudden return. He couldn't imagine Keilor staying behind now.

He looked at Fallon.

The blond looked torn. He'd been as fond of Rihlia as any of them. "My business can't wait, Jayems."

"I know. Don't worry, you'll be back, and she'll be there. This time, she's not leaving my sight." He looked around. "Keilor? You can hide this camp? We'll need to watch it in case she wasn't bluffing."

"Done." He looked at the girl in Jayems' arms for a moment, and then shook his head. "I'll send the *volti* out scouting. They'll let us know if anyone is coming. I'll join you when I'm done here." Similar to wolves in temperament and appearance, the *volti* shared a unique bond with Jayems' people. Fierce and loyal, they occasionally served as guards or scouts.

Fallon said his farewells and strode off to take care of his business. Keilor dismantled the camp as Jayems hefted the girl and strode for the gate.

It was a subtle transition, the gate between worlds, and you had to walk into it just so, for the path was narrow and only accessible from one direction. Moments after he'd started on the path, the landscape changed. One moon became three in the balmy sky, and *volti* wove in and out of the tall ferns between giant trees. A spicy forest smell wafted on the gentle wind, mixed with the distant scent of the sea.

It took only a few minutes to reach the gates of the Citadel. The Haunt guards, always in wolf form, saluted him with respect even as their eyes lingered on his burden. Remembering how she'd reacted to his own transformation, he was glad she couldn't see them.

Parquet tiles clicked under his boots as he made his way down the hallways to his rooms. The Haunt at the doors opened them for him, and in moments he'd crossed the sitting room and laid the girl gently down on the couch. He studied her, frowned, and then straitened her head on the pillow.

She was dressed far too warmly for the climate. Keeping a sharp eye out for movement, he pulled off her hat, releasing a riot of dark hair plastered with sweat. The heavy coat had to go, too, but he dreaded taking it off. She would not be pleased to wake up and discover him removing her clothing. Taking a quick breath, he pulled it off as fast as he could and laid it next to her hat. While he was at it he dispensed with her boots and the second layer of heavy socks. The rest he'd leave to her.

Searching for a handle on the moment, he glanced out the window that took up an entire wall and looked at the three moons. She was going to wake up soon, and would want explanations. One couldn't just take a woman from her place, dump her on one's couch and expect her to take it calmly.

Practical matters first. She'd been cooking her dinner. She would be hungry and perhaps thirsty. Fetching a tray with a glass of water, bread, cheese and fruit took too little time-- he was left staring at her, willing her to wake up.

When she did wake, her eyes opened with a snap. She took one look at him and tried to back up over the couch. "Don't touch me!" she shrieked when he reached out a reassuring hand.

He spread his hands and backed off a step.

Breathing hard, she stared at him, her eyes wild. Whatever their natural color, at that moment they were swirling gold with stress. Sweat trickled down her temple and dripped down her neck.

"I'm not going to hurt you," he said calmly, willing her to believe him.

"You stole me!"

"Yes, I did. I wanted to bring you here to explain."

"There's nothing to explain. You take me back right now or I'll ..." She looked around, maybe searching for a weapon. When she found nothing more dangerous than couch pillows, her eyes shot to his weapons. She glanced at his face and shivered. Maybe she dreaded the *change* more than she did his gun.

"I don't hurt women," he tried again. "I'm especially not going to hurt my betrothed."

Her expression of horror said it all. "Your wha …wha...?" She couldn't get the words out.

Afraid she would hyperventilate, he snapped, "Breathe! You're going to make yourself sick, woman."

Anger seemed to serve her better than coddling. "You're not marrying me!" she got out. She even stopped shrinking back into the couch.

He looked to the side, searching for patience. "We were betrothed when we were both younger, Rihlia--"

"That's not my name! You've got the wrong girl."

"I hear what you're saying, but a simple fingerprint match will prove it. If that's not enough for you, we can take stronger measures. As for me, I'm convinced. It was no accident that you were there tonight. Things were taken out of both our hands."

She was shaking her head. "You're crazy. Stark-raving nuts."

A muscle ticked in his jaw. "You were traveling with your parents when you were four years old. Their party was attacked. You were lost in the battle and presumed dead. We never found your body, though we searched for days. Now I know what happened--you found the gateway to Earth and wandered through. Someone must have found you and … " He trailed off, unsure how the rest of the story went. "Tonight I found you again."

"You found me, and now we're not on Earth," she said with derision.

He gestured behind her.

She narrowed her eyes, and then risked a peek over her shoulder. She did a double take and stared. "It's a trick," she said after a moment of strangled silence.

Raising his brows, he went to the balcony and threw open the door, letting in the warm night air. "Go outside and look at the trees. Feel the warm wind. Look at the sea below us. Were you anywhere near a sea when you camped?"

She glanced at the three moons through the huge window, then at the open balcony door. She didn't move.

He left the door open and moved away. "It's no less true if you refuse to look."

Slowly she rose and edged to the door, keeping a wary eye on him. She stepped out on the balcony and looked out for long minutes. When she came back in, her eyes were haunted.

"Water?" he offered her when she dropped back onto the couch.

She stared at the refreshment tray, then gingerly picked it up and took a sip.

"It's been a long day for you. You can stay in the spare room for tonight. It has a private bath and a lock on the door. No one will disturb you. If you would like to rest now, we can talk more in the morning." She didn't look as if she could take much more, and he needed to think.

She looked at the water in her hands with a lost expression.

Guessing it was an improvement over her trying to climb the walls, he summoned a maid and sent her to prepare the spare bedroom. After giving more orders to his staff, he sought out his guest. She was watching him with wary tension.

"Your room is ready and the maid drew a bath for you. She's left fresh clothes for you on the bed and will show you the room. If you need anything during the night, you have only to ask. Would you like to take the tray with you?" She hadn't eaten a bite.

When she stood up, but said nothing, he retrieved the tray and took it to her room, leaving it inside. She didn't enter the room until he left, then she slammed the door and locked it.

"So much for a truce," he muttered ruefully.

Feeling tired, he paced over to the balcony and looked out, though he didn't exit the room. Somehow he felt he'd better keep an eye on her door, lest she disappear again.

Had it really been twenty years since her disappearance?
So much in his life had changed. She'd been so young
when they'd been betrothed, but if she hadn't been lost,
they would have already been wed for six years now. If
he'd only known she was alive ...

It didn't matter now. There were things that had to be
done, arrangements to be made. For a moment the thought
crossed his mind that she would have been better off left
alone, but he shook it off. After all those years of searching,
of seeking answers, he couldn't just leave her in the woods.
As hard as it might be for them both, he was going to make
this work.

Chapter Three

The next morning didn't start much better. Rihlia emerged from her room very early, looking as if she hadn't slept. Maybe she'd hoped to escape while he slept, for she didn't look happy to see him.

"Good morning," he said pleasantly, noting that she'd put her freshened clothes back on, though he'd guess she had less layers on underneath. She'd put on the lighter boots he'd ordered for her. It was a tiny start, but encouraging nonetheless.

In the morning light, he could see that her natural eye color was brown, the same as the hair she'd pulled back into a tail. It had been longer as a child, but many things had changed since then.

He'd seen the maid go into her room and come out with the untouched tray. "Would you like some breakfast?"

She said nothing, but slunk like a prisoner into the dining chair he pulled out for her, leaning away when he slid it back in.

"I didn't know what you were used to, so I ordered a variety of things." He said the blessing, then dished a little of everything onto her plate. Normally he would ask what she wanted, but nothing about today was normal.

She looked at the spiced rice on her plate, then poked the curled vegetables next to them. "What is this?"

"Fern heads."

"Ferns." She didn't sound impressed.

"I believe you're familiar with apples," he said, pointing to poached fruit. "They're cooked in wine and honey. The juice next to you is a native berry--you used to love it." It was hard to be patient. She'd once treated him like a beloved brother, and now she thought he was trying to poison her over breakfast. It was almost more than he could stand.

She shot him a look and went back to staring at her plate. "What's this sausage made of?" She looked hideously suspicious and a little green. "You don't eat people, do you?"

His eyes widened. "What! You can't be serious." When she just looked at him warily, he snapped, "It's an animal. A grazing beast called a deerhare." When she still wouldn't eat, he demanded, "What's wrong?"

She considered him. "How do I know this isn't drugged?"

Frustration made him sigh. "Would you like me to taste everything for you? Better yet …" He switched their plates and cups, then handed her his roll. Then he topped off her plate and dug in, ignoring her.

Keeping an eye on him, she finally picked up her spoon. She must have been hungry because once she started she quickly finished everything in front of her in mere seconds.

Relieved to see her fed and feeling less like an ogre, he gestured her over to the sitting room as the servants cleared the table. When they were alone again, he retrieved a folder from his desk and placed it on the low table in front of her, taking one of the chairs opposite. "This is your dossier. We've completed a fingerprint analysis, voice scan and DNA test. You are Rihlia, daughter of Rhapsody and Crewel Sotra. When you were a child, we often called you 'Wiley One,' or 'Wiley,' for all the mischief you got into. Obviously that name was the one you used when you crossed worlds." When she said nothing, he asked, "How did you come up with the last name, Jayems?" The question had been burning him.

She looked away, focused on nothing. "The orphanage gave it to me."

"Orphanage?" Somehow he'd never pictured her in such a place. There'd never been a question that she was loved, and he'd thought she was dead. They all had. The thought of her in such a place chilled him. What other indignities had she suffered while they'd given her up?

"The place where they raise children who have no family. Unwanted children," she said sarcastically, as if he needed a definition.

The bitter edge hurt him. "You were wanted," he said intensely, leaning forward. "You were taken from us. I searched for days myself, trying to find you. There was nothing to be found, no scent or sign of you, and now we know why."

Her face was closed. "So? Now you know where I was. Put me back."

Disturbed by her lack of emotion, he said, "You belong here."

She said nothing.

Lost, seeking a way to reach her, he asked, "What do you do in your world?"

"I'm a clerk in a hardware store."

He puzzled that out. It didn't sound too enthralling. "Do you enjoy it?"

She shrugged.

"Do you have a lover?"

"No!" she said vehemently. "I have a life. I was enjoying it."

Relieved, he said with less intensity, "Do you have many friends?"

"Some. Enough."

"And this roommate you mentioned …?" When she remained silent, he decided she needed more facts. "We moved to this world to avoid humans. Our kinds never mixed well. We killed each other. Humans fear us. I assume they're the ones that taught you to fear yourself."

No response. Normally that wouldn't bother him, but this wasn't the ordinary sort of inquest. Her feelings mattered to him. "This friend of yours would turn on you if she knew who you were."

"You don't know Jasmine!" she exploded, killing him with her eyes. "She's not just a friend, she's the sister of my heart! She was raised with me, went to school with me … she even stayed in Alaska just to be with me, and she hates snow! She's the closest thing to family I've got, and you're not going to talk trash about her." Then she added grudgingly, "Besides, she's got my dog."

He smiled. "A dog is not a problem; if that's all you want. Your friend is." He thought for a moment. "We can fake your death."

She blanched. "Don't you do that to her! She has no one else. If she thought--" she broke off, apparently to unwilling to finish the thought. "You don't know what it's like to be alone."

"You're not alone." He leaned forward, putting intensity into the words. She would never be alone again if he had his way.

It only made her angry. "I am! Was … listen, I'm talking about Jasmine right now. I won't let you hurt her like that."

He settled back in his chair. They were on familiar ground now. He had a bargaining chip, and he waited to see what she would suggest.

It didn't take her long to offer a deal. "Let me see her and explain, and I'll … I'll promise to listen to what you're saying."

"You're already listening. You can't help that."

She blew out a breath. "I won't try to escape if you let us talk."

"You won't run off regardless. There are dangers in the woods around here, and I'm not about to permit you to charge off heedlessly into them." There were political dangers aplenty inside the Citadel, too, but she didn't need to know about those yet.

He didn't need to add that he had the manpower to make her stay where he put her.

Her eyes narrowed. "I'm not going to marry you over this."

"That's not an issue we'll bargain over." That was an issue he'd tackle after he'd gotten to know her better. They had enough to deal with at that moment. "As I said, I don't hurt women. That includes forcing them to share my bed. If you find yourself there, it will be because you choose to go."

She flushed and avoided his eyes. She muttered a curse.

He raised a brow. "If that was meant to remain private, it didn't. My ears are as sharp as yours." Ignoring her evil look, he said, "This is what I'm offering: a new home, a new world and a family who loves you. All I want in return is your willing cooperation. Be pleasant. Try not to view us as the enemy."

"And you'll let me talk to Jasmine?"

"I will."

"And you won't hurt her?"

"I won't, though it's not a promising beginning that you would have to ask."

She looked at him hard. "I don't know you."

"But you will try to keep your promise?"

"I will keep my promise."

"Thank you. When did you expect her?"

Chapter Four

She had to give him credit--Jayems did not push. Other than insisting on calling her Rihlia, he was all that was pleasant. He didn't crowd her or try to touch her as he took her on a tour of the Citadel. He didn't comment when she looked at the guards with wild eyes, nor did he try to comfort her. He treated the guards with indifference unless he dealt with one directly. Those interactions were matter of fact, with various degrees of familiarity depending on who it was, not that she could tell what was said. All those who were changed used sign language, a fact she took keen note of.

"Why can't they speak when they're a werewolf? Is it part of the curse?" she finally asked.

"It's not a curse, girl," he said with frown, as if she were talking about the ability to walk. "It's part of who we are. Being unable to talk is just another part of the *change*, like being fast and strong. We also can't mate, for that matter, and we're a little color blind."

"I never noticed," she muttered.

He looked at her speculatively. "How often do you *change*?"

Darkness filled her eyes. "Twice, I think. Maybe three times, when I was really little. Whenever I couldn't help it."

"Couldn't help it? When you lost your temper? What do you mean--twice a month?"

"In my life." Her mouth was a flat, grim line.

He stopped walking. "You only changed three times in your life." He was staring at her as if she'd just announced that she was gay.

She looked at him out of the corner of her eye. "Yeah," she admitted, shamed to remember the times she'd lost control. She'd worn sunglasses everywhere when she was a teen, trying to shield her eyes. They'd been banned in class, of course, so she'd perfected the art of blanking out in school. Her peers had all thought she was a perfect freak. Thinking back, she couldn't believe even Jasmine had befriended her, unless it was because Jas was even more lonely than she'd been.

"How did you ..." He seemed to be searching for a neutral phrase. "Er, how do you bleed off the hormones, then?"

"Hormones?"

He looked at the sky, then around at the trees. They'd stopped just shy of the exit to a courtyard. "The emotions and needs that build up in your body when you cannot or do not change for some reason. We're not like humans--we have a physiological and psychological need to *change* at times, or we grow sick. It's the way we're designed. How did you manage?"

Seeing they were close to a bench, she exited, crossed the grass and sat under a shady tree. She fixed her sight back on the gray Citadel walls and tried not to think. "I signed up for every sport known to man. I drank, smoked, got stoned and made out. Eventually I gave up on the drugs and laid off the booze--they made me more likely to lose control. After that I just exercised until I dropped and had a string of boyfriends. Eventually I gave up on that, too. Too much frustration. I could never complete ..." She trailed off with a glance at him. "Mostly I had nightmares."

A shiver ran through her, thinking of those. Some nights she awoke with black hairs all over the bed and clawed sheets. In the orphanage she'd learned to sleep with the sheets over her head no matter how hot it got. As an adult she'd had a lock on her door.

The nuns at the orphanage had thought she was possessed. She still remembered them crossing themselves against her.

He took a deep, slow breath. "Now that you're here, it's safe to *change*. You no longer have to suffer."

She just looked at him.

A muscle flexed in his cheek. "You will change, in your room if you must. I don't want you getting sick."

She looked back at the walls, tuning him out.

Jayems squatted down in front of her and looked her in the eyes. His were hard and glowing gold with emotion. "You are not a monster. You have needs. Now that I know what you went through, I'd be shot before I ever let you go back." His tone was quiet and final.

Fear froze her to the bench. She couldn't help it--he looked like her nightmares.

He drew another slow breath, and gradually his eyes darkened to normal. He blinked and seemed to regain control. "Come. I wanted to show you our kitchens."

Careful not to upset him again, she walked at his side, keeping a measured distance between them. Not friendly, but not too rude. She didn't want to see those eyes again.

Too her surprise, there was a man holding a beast outside the kitchens. About the size of a pig, it had a body like a cross between a large kangaroo and a deer, with hoofed feet. The head had a distinctly jackrabbitish look about it, and the ears were long. The body was dull brown with white markings on its legs, belly and tiny, tufted tail.

"This is a deerhare," Jayems explained. "You know him better as sausage."

She grimaced at him as the handler led the animal away. "Ugh. Do you always introduce your guests to their breakfast?"

"Only when they think we're serving infant instead," he said dryly, opening the kitchen door for her.

The kitchens were huge and immaculate. Entire rooms were devoted to baking, butchering and processing vegetables. There were sinks and stoves in each room, as well as various kinds of pantries and cold storage. The staff was polite, though they only stopped what they were doing when directly addressed. It was hard to believe the amount of food they processed in a day.

"The Citadel is vast. The kitchens supply all the food for our garrison, my personal household as well as their own families," Jayems explained. "There are many young apprentices here, learning how to provide for their own families. It's not just a kitchen, it's also a classroom."

"Wow." Wiley thanked a young man who handed her a tiny tart, then took a bite. Warm citrus curd and buttery shell melted on her tongue. "Mmm! Where do I sign up?"

Jayems grinned. "You're welcome to take lessons here in the kitchens, or I'd be happy to arrange a private tutor."

Unwilling to acknowledge that she'd be there long enough to attend the lessons, she made a noncommittal sound in answer.

As she snacked her way around the kitchens she acquired knowledge of many new foods, and of a surprising array of familiar ones. Food being a subject dear to her heart, she couldn't stop herself from asking questions.

"We brought many seeds and plants with us when we came; others are natives to this planet. Some of the plants didn't thrive, but others loved their new home." He gestured to a monstrous parsnip on a cutting board.

"Tell me brussel sprouts didn't make it," she begged.

"Never heard of it," he said with a smile.

"Sweet." Even drowned in cheese sauce, she'd never been able to stand brussel sprouts. Martian heads, they used to call them.

He led her out another door and into formal herb garden, smiling at her exclamation of pleasure. "The pride of our kitchens," he said, gesturing to the knot garden. "We have fifteen varieties of thyme alone."

"Cool." She bent to sniff a hedge. "Mint! I love this stuff in cocoa."

The herb garden led into the orchards. It was long past noon by the time they'd toured the vegetable gardens, greenhouses, seen the berry plot and done a quick walk through the livestock area. Tired, but in a pleasant mood, she let him lead her back toward the Citadel.

They'd nearly reached the entrance when they met up with a group of three young ladies and a matronly sort. One look at Jayems and the young ones were all shy smiles and giggles.

Wiley rolled her eyes. Those girls were all around her age--old enough to have more sense. Granted, Fallon was good looking in a brutal sort of way, but anyone could see he would be a totally dominating husband, completely unsuited to any woman with a brain.

It didn't stop the giggling trio, who looked like they spent half their day preparing to wow men. Their hair trailed in elaborate braids down their backs, as if a maid had spent at least an hour on each of them. They wore subtle makeup, expertly applied, and their perfect nails had surely never seen hard labor. Grecian-style gowns of flowing silk adorned perfect bodies, and all of the girls were pretty.

Wiley disliked them on the spot.

Smiling in a sweet, demure way that had never come naturally to Wiley, the girl with the light brown hair greeted them. "My lord. It's good to see you again." A light shown in her blue eyes as she looked at him. "Who is your guest?"

Jayems looked at the girl gravely. "Good afternoon, Lady Nilla. May I present Lady Rihlia, daughter of Lady Rhapsody and Lord Crewel Sotra."

The light drained out of Lady Nilla's eyes as the title sunk in. She stared at Wiley for a long moment and said hollowly, "The pleasure is mine, my lady."

"Wiley," Wiley interjected. "My name is Wiley."

Jayems ignored her. "This is Lady Carr, Lady Nilla's mother. Her companions are Lady Stair and Bella, daughter of the chief cook."

"Pleasure," Wiley said politely.

Lady Carr, a slightly plump woman with too much jewelry, looked Rihlia over quickly and then stared reprovingly at Jayems. "I'm sorry for any discomfort, my lord. We had no warning."

"It happened quickly. Lady Rihlia was only discovered yesterday," Jayems answered; his tone even.

Lady Nilla looked down and seemed to be blinking rapidly. Wiley was no slouch. Nodding to them all, she said, "If you'll excuse me, I have to use the ladies room." She got two strides before Jayems' hand closed around her elbow. She glanced at him. "Don't you have things to talk about here?"

He looked back at the women, who were no longer smiling. Lady Nilla looked ready to break down. He spook gently to her. "If you'll return to your apartments, I'll meet you there in a few minutes. I must escort my lady to her room."

Wiley shook his grip off as soon as they'd stepped into the Citadel. He wouldn't turn loose one second sooner. "Hey, if you need protection from a woman, don't be looking my way. I'm not now, nor will I ever be your lady."

"It was a figure of speech." He looked distracted.

"Sure it was. Let me guess--Lady Nilla there was in the picture before I turned up. No problem. Just tell her that I have no intention of marrying you. She's welcome to you, with my compliments." She ignored his silence. She was feeling flippant. It was her best defense against feeling guiltily. She hadn't done anything wrong. Jayems had messed up his own life by dragging her here. If he'd just left her alone, they'd all be happy now.

They reached his rooms and he stopped inside, looking at her for a moment. Then he stared out the window, not seeming to focus.

With a shrug, she tuned him out, went to her room and shut the door, curiosity nipping at her.

To her surprise, some of her gear from the campsite had been left in her room. Thrilled to see her backpack, she rifled through it and came up with her MP3 player and spare batteries pack. Clutching it like Monty with the Holy Grail, she sent up a prayer of thanks and plugged in.

Chapter Five

Jayems returned to his room feeling pensive, both about the heart he'd just bruised and the explanations he still faced. Expecting to be greeted with either sulks or a tantrum, he was unprepared for the amount of noise he heard as he approached his room. The guards at his door, with their more sensitive hearing, looked pained.

"What's going on?" Jayems demanded of the guard, shouting to be heard over the music. His steward must have been waiting for him, for he hurried up to the door as Jayems came up, clutching an armful of musical instruments.

"Sir," he said respectfully, slightly out of breath. "It seems your lady likes music." The strains of a man's voice singing, "Bang your head," came through the door.

As Jayems prepared to enter, the steward warned him, "You won't be able to talk in there, milord. May I report out here?"

"Make it quick," Jayems said, burning with curiosity. What a racket! It sounded like an entire raiding party, not one lone woman.

"It started out with her banging on pots and pans," the steward said. "She looked spooked when we burst in, so I offered to get her a drum set." He winced, as if regretting that idea. "It got out of hand from there. Next, she asked what other instruments we had. I offered to bring her some samples. Somehow the technicians figured out how to make her music play over your sound system ... well, she's been very busy."

He'd only been gone two hours. How had she gotten so much done? Jayems nodded at them to open the door, wondering what kind of mayhem he'd turned loose in his life. A song was starting up, and he walked in to find his betrothed dressed in black pants, stripped down to her black halter top and gleaming with sweat as she banged away on the drums, singing, "You've got to be cruel to be kind," at volume.

The first surprise was that she was very, very good. He wouldn't have known just by listening through the door. The second was that she had a black tribal tattoo of a wolf on her left arm. A rebellious acknowledgement of who she was? He wouldn't have expected it of her.

To spare his men's sensitive ears, he shut the doors. She saw him, but ignored his presence while she finished her song. Then she turned it down and looked at him. "I was in a band in my spare time," she said by way of explanation.

He looked around at the furniture shoved up against the wall, piled with instruments. "We'll set up a music room for you."

Her teeth flashed white. "I could dig this princess gig."

"So glad to please you," he said dryly. "If you're finished for the night?" He gave orders to move the instruments to a room down the hall. As soon as his furniture was returned to normal, he claimed a seat and ordered a stiff drink. A cocoa was brought for Rihlia, who flopped down on the sofa opposite. Her musical interlude seemed to have relaxed her, and he had a little more insight as to how she'd survived the build up of pressure without resorting to the *change*.

She took a sip of her cocoa. "Mmm! Chocolate mint. You remembered," she said, looking at him in surprise. Perhaps she was unused to such gestures.

He inclined his head. Your friend will be arriving tonight. Perhaps you would like to change your clothes to greet her?"

She laughed and brushed her loose hair off her face. "She's seen me in worse."

"Yes, but perhaps she would see you in a position of power if you dressed the part? It may reassure her. I wouldn't want her to think you were mistreated." He didn't care what the human thought, as they'd never see her after tonight, but he wanted to emphasize Rihlia's position to her. The sooner he started creating a gap in their relationship, the better. Rihlia belonged here and the human did not.

Rihlia stared at him for a long moment. "Okay. I'll dress up ... if you tell me why you'd rather marry me than that little Nilla wafer you just saw."

He thought about putting her off and decided to be blunt instead. A small part of him was angry for her lack of interest, both in him and in Nilla's pain. How could he bind himself to such a brutally self-centered woman? "There are many reasons. Political--you're the daughter of the former lord here, a powerful man. Legally, as your betrothed, I'm bound to see to your welfare, and your welfare in this situation includes the protection of marriage to me. There are those who will not welcome you back. Religious--we were bound together by the priests, who spent a great deal of time in prayer before sanctioning the match. I believe that we were preordained to be together, and disobedience to that divine decree is sin."

She stared at him over her cocoa. "Or maybe my escaping to Earth was divine deliverance for us both? Maybe you messed it up by bringing me here. Newsflash: priests aren't perfect."

"I didn't blindly follow their edicts. I spent a great deal of time in prayer over this myself before signing the betrothal. I knew I would have to wait years before I would have a wife if I accepted you."

"And you have a direct line to the Almighty? Wait a minute, what do you mean 'you'd have to wait years'? How old were you? Are you?"

A trace of humor lightened his face. "Twenty years ago I was twenty-seven."

Her mouth opened slightly. "You're forty-seven? No way! *No way* are you more than thirty."

His mouth twisted. "Our race lives long. Three hundred is considered old age."

After a moment she shook her head like a dog shakes off water. "That would be a mess at the DMV."

Unsure what she was referencing, but satisfied that they'd miraculously broached a great many subjects without major fallout, he suggested, "I have to check with Keilor, who is your cousin, by the way. He'll be bringing your friend here. Why don't you freshen up and I'll tell you the news when you're finished?"

As it happened, Keilor had already left. Refusing to let the upcoming interview shred his already abraded nerves, Jayems sat down at his desk and opened a ledger. The work would help calm his mind while he waited.

Half an hour had ticked peacefully by when Rihlia's door opened. He glanced at it absently, and then did a double take. He'd thought he'd known she was beautiful, but he truly hadn't seen.

Beads of pearl and topaz graced her long braids, weaving in and out of the dark strands like winking stars. White and gold silken robes outlined a body like that of a young goddess, inviting his eyes to linger. Even her eyes looked younger, darting to the door in anticipation of her friend's arrival.

"Beautiful," he said softly, and her eyes shot to his in surprise. Surprise? How could she not know she was lovely?

"Ah, thanks," she said. Sending him an uneasy glance, she took a seat on the couch.

Jayems tried to think of something to relax her. Before he could speak, Keilor strode into the room unannounced. "She is here."

Chapter Six

Relieved to have the subject changed, even by this, Jayems shut the heavy ledger he'd been perusing. He boots remained crossed on the desktop as he waited for more details.

Rihlia wasn't nearly as calm. She leapt up off the couch and demanded breathlessly, "Where?"

Keilor lost the smile he'd had on seeing her. "There's a problem," he informed Jayems darkly. "She's a Sylph."

Ah, no. Not this! Wasn't his life difficult enough already? Jayems' feet uncrossed, dropping with deliberation to the floor. He slammed his palms down on the desk and leaned forward. "A what?"

Keilor shook his head slowly. "She could be nothing else. I'm certain of it."

Jayems swore and got to his feet, pacing with barely controlled frustration. Sylphs possessed a special pheromone, a mutation on the human norm. It had little effect on human men but caused the Haunt males, with their more sensitive noses, to become their mindless slaves.

For thousands of years, her kind had been used by humans to lure and trap the men of the Haunt. The best of their warriors had been enticed by the unique, bewitching scent of the Sylph and killed by their masters until there were few of them left. That, combined with the unrelenting fear and hatred of humans, had driven his kind to seek their own world, free of the hunters.

The best defense was to simply kill one whenever you had the chance, and now his betrothed's best friend, the woman he'd sworn not to hurt, was one of them. His night just couldn't get any more complicated.

Rihlia looked between them in angry confusion. "What's the matter? You told me she could—"

Jayems whirled to face her, and his temper made his words harsh. "I gave permission for you to say goodbye, and I will still allow it, but the minute you are finished, she goes." If word of this got out, he'd have a pack of outraged council members on his hands. In the old days, Sylphs weren't allowed the freedom to come and go. Entire communities died if they did.

Maybe this one didn't know what she was. Maybe there were no hunters with her, but he hadn't been made Lord of the Haunt to take those chances.

Her eyes flared. "Well, of course, *darling,*" she agreed acidly. "After all, we wouldn't want any unsavory humans loitering about, now, would we?"

Scenting trouble, he stalked her, stopping inches from her and bending his head to stare her down. They were not going to fight about this issue. It was going to happen his way. "I'm gratified we understand each other, wife." Before she could snarl out a denial, he snapped, "Bring her, Keilor. Let's finish this."

Keilor opened the door and a petite young woman, surprisingly young, hurried in. Dressed much like Rihlia had been in pants, boots and a short-sleeved shirt, her brown hair was slightly flattened and rumpled, as if she'd recently removed a hat. Reeking of fear, she relaxed only when the door was safely shut behind her. The black and white dog at her side gave a glad bark and charged forward to greet Rihlia.

She laughed and knelt down to hug her dog, fondling her ears affectionately. "Good girl, Lemming! You found me, didn't you?" Then she looked up at her friend, and her eyes glittered with tears as she stood up. "Aren't you a sight for sore eyes," she murmured, and embraced her in a crushing hug. "I thought you'd never get here."

The girl pulled back and gave her a wobbly grin. "Blame it on your map. You forgot to mention that last curve in the road." Her smile faded as she glanced at Jayems and Keilor. "What's going on, Wiley?"

"It's ..." Rihlia broke off and looked at them. Jayems stood with his arms crossed, making no attempt to appear friendly. Already he could smell the insidious pheromone, and it was trying to scramble his thinking. He'd expected to feel the surge of arousal, but hadn't expected the pheromone to make him feel favorably inclined toward the girl. Protective, even. It made him scowl harder and think dark thoughts.

Keilor perched on his desk, feet crossed at the ankles, his expression cool. He must have been similarly affected, but was hiding it well.

"I don't suppose we could have some privacy?" Rihlia asked coldly. Jayems inclined his head, indicating that he had heard her, but he didn't move. He wasn't about to let them make plans in secret.

She muttered something under her breath and led their guest to the far end of the room, sitting down with her on a couch. Lemming came up and nudged Rihlia's hand, and she absently stroked her while she explained.

"We're on another world," she began slowly.

Her friend glanced at the triple moons visible through the huge window and looked back at the door. She nodded slowly in agreement. Oddly enough, she looked more thoughtful than rattled.

Rihlia watched her carefully. "I was born here."

"It explains a few things. Go on."

The men exchanged glances. Her calm acceptance was light years beyond Rihlia's wild panic.

Rihlia took a breath. "The guy who brought you here is my cousin, Keilor."

Jasmine's eyes darted in surprise to Keilor, who watched her with wary distaste. He raised a dark brow at her in mocking acknowledgment of the introduction.

"You have my sympathy," she snapped.

Jayems hid a reluctant smile. It was refreshing to see a woman repulsed by his handsome cousin. In other circumstances he'd love to tease Keilor about it.

Rihlia smiled wryly. She didn't even look at Jayems, just jerked her head slightly in his direction. "The other guy is called Jayems." They were both quiet for a moment. At last Wiley said stiffly, "They won't let me go home, and they want you to go back right away and forget you ever saw me."

Jasmine sat back. Her expression was cold, but a dangerous smile turned up one side of her mouth. "Two words, my friend." She said something in a foreign tongue.

Wiley laughed and looked relieved.

Jasmine smiled slyly back at her, squeezed her hand and then stood up. "It's been real, Wiley, and I'm glad to see that you're all right." She turned to Keilor. "I'm ready to go home now."

Keilor was looking back at her with a knowing expression. He turned to Jayems and made a few signs with his hands. *"The girl is planning to bring back help."*

Jayems glanced at her darkly and signed back. *"I see it."* This was not how they'd planned this. The girl was supposed to be scared out of her mind, begging to go back home. Just look how Rihlia had behaved, and she was one of them. Keilor was supposed to have terrified her. Hadn't he tried?

"I could take care of her," Keilor offered. His face was carefully blank. He'd never harmed a woman before, but both of them knew the stakes.

"I swore not to harm her." He didn't want to admit it, but his options had just narrowed to one. *"Take her to the room down the hall and place guards at her door. Legend has it that the* change *protects us from the pheromone. We'll screen who comes in contact with her until we figure out what to do with her."*

"Right." Keilor signed back. He moved towards the girl. "Why so hasty? You just got here. Perhaps it would be best if you waited to return until morning after all." He watched her closely, ready for her to run.

Panic flashed across her face, and then disappeared. In a carefully modulated tone, she said, "I thought you were in a hurry to get rid of me. Not that I mind staying to talk to a friend or anything, but this place gives me the creeps."

She was an awful liar, and it was the final straw. Jayems straightened from the desk and prowled toward her until both he and Keilor towered over her. She wouldn't look at him.

"Friends," he mussed. "That's not what Rihlia called you. Sister of her heart, she said. Closer than blood. Odd that such a one would desert her so quickly." He grasped her chin and forced her to look at him. "Would you be planning trouble, little sister?"

She met his eyes with difficulty. "Who would believe my story?"

He studied her for a moment and then softly snorted. They would never have trouble reading this one. They'd better pray that she was all that Rihlia thought, though. It was difficult to make sane decisions with her scent in his nose.

Releasing her, he said aloud, "Find her a room down the hall and see that she's comfortable, would you, cousin? And post guards at her door." His smile was less than pleasant. "We wouldn't want anything to happen to Rihlia's loyal little sister."

She stiffened as Keilor's hand closed around her arm and he started to drag her off.

Rihlia got in his way. He canted his head to the side slightly and paused to acknowledge her effort. "Cousin."

Alarmed, Rihlia looked around him to rail at Jayems. "What are you doing?"

His eyes narrowed. "Sending her away before I break her neck for lying to me." He glanced at the wide eyed Jasmine grudgingly. "Though I suppose she can be forgiven, as she does it out of loyalty to you. There is a limit to what I will forgive those who try to deceive me, though."

Rihlia stiffened and said plaintively, "You said that she could go home."

His face hardened. "Keilor."

Without another word, Keilor gently moved the resisting Rihlia aside and continued toward the door.

"You be nice to her!" Rihlia shouted as the door shut behind them. She turned on Jayems. "I can't believe you did that! Why can't you just let her leave?"

"Are you willing to swear that she won't be back with reinforcements? Keep in mind that your word is your only coin here."

Her hands curled into fists. "Why shouldn't she be? You're breaking the law! You should be arrested for this."

"You're welcome to complain to the council. I'll walk you down there myself."

"Hah! You wouldn't offer unless you had them in your pocket." She kicked her hem out of the way and began to pace.

"To hear you tell it, I'm actually doing her a favor. After all, without you she's all alone in her world."

She shot him a killing look.

He raised his brows. "You'd feel better if you *changed*. I spoke with the medics today. They said for someone with your history of self-denial, it would be best if you spent *at least* five minutes a day in Haunt. I told them I would see to it."

That stopped her. "Oh you would, would you? How do you plan to do that?" The sneer on her face was pure provocation.

He stalked her. "Given your dislike of me, I thought I'd start with a promise. If you don't shift, I promise to kiss you until you see stars."

"What!" She backed up, giving him a look of horror.

His pride was pricked, so he deflated hers as well. "Not that it sounds especially appealing, given your waspish attitude and the lengths you go to be unpleasant. I will do it, however." His smile was pure evil. "I'm responsible for your health."

"You don't--stay back!" They rounded the couch once, and this time she jumped it, tangling her legs in her skirts in panic. Cursing, she bounced off the cushions and tumbled to the floor, ripping her skirts in her haste to get to her feet.

He didn't even have to hurry to catch her. Taking her wrists, he leaned toward her. "*Change* or be kissed," he warned her.

She did, faster than he expected. One minute he was the captor, the next he was grappling with a she Haunt every bit as strong as he was. Fortunately, he was experienced in warfare and she was not. In one fast move he spun her from him and released her, the momentum carrying her a few steps away.

She looked at her arms and stiffened with fright. In seconds she was back to human form, her face paper white.

"Scared yourself, did you? You'll get used to it. It's been under a minute, however." He moved toward her.

She cursed him and dashed for her door.

He got there first and slammed it shut, backing her against the panel. "*Change* or be kissed," he warned her again.

"No!" she tried to kick him. Blocked, she squirmed and tried to rip loose, but she was firmly caught. "Please …"

He ignored her anguish and kissed her ruthlessly, thoroughly. She ripped her mouth free and gasped for air, but he captured it again, showing her he meant business. This wasn't about seduction, and they both knew it.

But a funny thing happened. She began to shake in his arms, and her mouth softened. His automatically became gentler to match, and his hand loosened on her hair, cupping the back of her head. A heat started to rise--then she tore away with a roar and shoved him back, shifting once again to Haunt.

They stood there panting for long moments. She was trembling, but she didn't move or try to shift back. When he'd judged five minutes had passed, she turned back to human form.

Shooting him a look of pure venom, she hissed, "Don't do that again!" She ripped open her door and darted inside, slamming it with brutal force.

Chapter Seven

She still hadn't forgiven him the next day.

Jayems stood up from the dining table when Rihlia left her room, her dog at her heels. "Ready for breakfast?" he asked politely. He had no intention of fighting about what he intended to make a nightly ritual. Not that he expected to kiss her again--after last night he doubted it would be necessary.

"I want to eat with Jasmine," she said coldly.

"As you wish. What about your pet? What does she eat?" Any neutral subject had to be better than frozen silence.

She looked at her dog with a small frown. "Dog food, but I doubt you have a grocery store that sells kibble. I guess now's a good time to put her on that raw food diet I heard about."

"What is in that?"

"Raw meat, bones and a little cooked veggies. I'm not sure about the portions, though."

He nodded. "I'll speak with the cook. You might also consult our animal doctor--she'll likely have an idea how to look after her."

Gratitude flashed in her face; then it was tempered by wariness. "Thank you," she said grudgingly. She headed for the door, hesitating as she put her hand on the knob. He'd never allowed her out by herself before, and he could see her wondering if he would let her go.

He would, though not unaccompanied. He had an escort waiting, having anticipated her desire to see her friend. Between his man Knighten and the maids who'd be conveniently cleaning, the room would be full of ears. Later, he'd hear the reports.

He had other business to see to.

Keilor arrived for their breakfast appointment. "I'm hungry," he said as he took his chair and filled his plate. "Training those stripling recruits is hard work."

"Maybe you'd like to try wife-taming instead?"

Keilor shuddered. "How goes that?"

"She's dining with her friend. I'm not a favorite right now." With a ready excuse just down the hall, Jaymes expected Rihlia would stay away from him as much as possible, but even she couldn't spend every waking moment with the Sylph. "How old is that girl, anyway? She doesn't look of an age to be such fast friends with Rihlia."

"Older than she looks," Keilor guessed. "She's very small. It might protect her some, her youth."

Jayems dissected a steak. "Don't count on it. The older council members will not be forgiving of this, and the younger men can be volatile. I expect trouble."

"We're ready for it," Keilor said calmly. "Will you explain the danger to Rihlia or leave her in happy ignorance?" It was a jest, for as Master of the Hunt, the head of the military, Keilor made sure he was aware of everything that went on around him. He had to be. He wouldn't advocate leaving Rihlia in ignorance, not when knowledge would make her more cautious.

"Not directly, not yet. First I'm going to hire tutors--she has twenty years of history and politics to catch up on. I've already sent a message to her mother, who I expect in a matter of days." He grimaced. "Don't tell her. She has such explosive reactions to these things, and I'm not ready for that storm yet. I'm hoping to use the days in between to build her trust. I'd like to become a source of support to her instead of just an enemy."

Keilor smirked. "Has Lord Romantic lost his touch? Last I saw, you had no trouble getting women to adore you."

Jayems adopted a mild expression. "I would have said the same of you, until I saw how the Slyph loathed you."

Keilor lost the humor. "I don't want her to like me. I'm not a man who is led around by the nose or anything else. I haven't forgotten that she's dangerous. You'd do well to avoid her yourself, or to find your way into Rihlia's bed very soon. You know the pheromone has no effect on a mated man."

An image jumped to mind at Keilor's words, but Jayems swiftly thrust it aside. A spike of possessiveness stabbed him instead. He didn't want any man speculating about his woman. "Be careful how you speak of her."

"Noted. You do need to marry, however. You *will* marry. I'd just like to see you hurry it up."

Jayems snorted. Keilor was a practical man, as long as they weren't discussing his marriage. Keilor was happy as a bachelor and had his share of ambitious huntresses trying to catch him. Any mention of them usually sent him running to the practice fields to grind out his frustrations.

He was right, though. The political situation would calm down once the marriage was consummated. Rihlia's father had some fierce supporters in his day, and they would rally around his daughter. As a man in power, Jayems had to be careful who he wed. He'd been devoted to Rihlia's father, a factor that had moved him to agree to the betrothal; inherited supporters could make such a difference.

The other side would do anything to destroy that support.

They might try to kill Rihlia.

He sighed. He wanted her here. Duty was part of it, but he wanted the little girl they'd lost to find her way home. He knew a part of her was gone forever, but something remained. His Rihlia was lost in a maze of thorns, and it was up to him to cut her a way out. She might not like his methods, but he was looking for results. He would find a way to bring her back.

* * * *

Wiley would do almost anything to get home, so she let Jasmine convince her to try her scheme, even though she doubted it would work. She knew the capabilities of their guards far better than Jas. Without explaining how she knew, it was impossible to convince Jas to give up. Who knew? Maybe her crazy plan would actually work.

It wasn't hard to get outside, near the woods. Either her guards had been ordered to be especially lenient, or they had confidence they could keep her under control. She suspected both, knowing Jayems. She had an uneasy feeling that he'd also been informed what they were up to. She opened her mouth to caution Jasmine, but it was too late.

"All right, start counting," Jas said, and took off into the brush outside the Citadel. Their guards watched, but didn't interfere with the game. That made Wiley even more uneasy. She just couldn't see this plan working, but Jas never gave up.

The idea was to play hide and seek, with Lemming doing the tracking. Gradually, Jasmine was going to work her way back toward the gate to Earth. Having been conscious when she was brought in, she actually knew where that was. She'd assured Wiley that it wasn't far.

As agreed, they played the game five times. On the fifth try, Jas made her run for it.

She didn't come back.

Wiley bit her lip as she watched the woods. She couldn't shake the feeling that something was wrong.

Jayems' steward, Knighten, appeared at her elbow. "Come along, milady. Your lord wishes to speak to you."

Her eyes narrowed with worry, and she glanced at the trees. "My friend's still out there."

"Lord Keilor is seeing to her." He herded her along by the simple expedient of stepping into her space.

Resenting his presumption, she let herself be ushered into Jayems' rooms, prepared to act angry. It was hard when she was worrying what Keilor's "seeing to her" entailed. If he hurt her, it would be Wiley's fault for agreeing to the scheme. Jasmine was too impulsive sometimes, but Jayems had promised not to hurt her. She just hoped he was as good as his word.

Jayems looked up from the papers on his desk when she came in. "Please be seated, Rihlia." He flicked a glance at Knighten, who left the room.

"I was in the middle of a game," she said curtly.

"I heard." He looked at her for a long moment. "I think it's time I explained my position more fully. My duty is to protect my family and the people under my authority. I suspect an invasion of humans from the gate would violate that agreement, don't you?"

His words confirmed that the guards had overheard them. She looked aside. "We just want to go home."

"Secrecy has protected us for three hundred years. How do you think your rescuers would react to discovering the Dark Lands and the Haunt? The television reporters would become involved, the military, your late government. Use your imagination."

She shivered. He was painting an ugly picture. "Just let us go, then." Her voice had gotten smaller.

"No." He didn't qualify it or try to soothe her sensibilities. He looked back at his work. "You may go."

"What about Jasmine? You promised not to hurt her."

He met her gaze with eyes the color of polished bronze. "I haven't touched her."

She heard the subtle emphasis. Seriously spooked, she shut herself in her room and paced. When she'd worked up enough nerve, she went back to demand to see Jasmine.

Keilor was there, leaning against Jayems' desk. His eyes were dilated, and he held a drink in his hand.

She froze like a doe scenting fresh blood.

"She's in her room," he said. He took another drink.

Wiley raced to Jasmine's room and burst in, expecting to find Jasmine half dead. Instead she was curled up on her tan and chocolate velvet couch, brooding.

"Where's your keeper?" Jas asked.

Wilting with relief, Wiley waved her hand. "Gone. But how are you?" She knelt in front of the couch, concern clenching her stomach. "Did he hurt you?"

"No." Before Wiley could question her, she added, "How did he know? There shouldn't have been enough time for them to figure anything out."

Guilt pricked her. Pretending she knew less than she did, Wiley moved to an armchair, tucking one long leg under her. "Lights," she ordered and then, "Shutters."

Hoping to avoid more in depth questions, she said, "They figured it out right away. The Haunt brought me back here and Jayems told me that they knew." She shivered, remembering what else he'd said. Her eyes swept down. "I was afraid of what Keilor would do when he found you." She peeked through her lashes to see Jasmine busily avoiding her eyes. Her voice ached when she asked, "What did he do, Jas?" She was afraid of the answer, but she needed to know. If it was the worst, then she wanted to help make it better.

Jasmine looked at her and up at the ceiling, then took a deep breath. "He tied me up to a tree and kissed me," she confessed quickly, and blushed.

"*What?*" Wiley hadn't expected that. The way Keilor had looked ... she knew Jasmine's taste in men. Hadn't they traded opinions for years? Keilor was just her type, and if all he'd done was kiss her friend ...

"How was it?"

Jasmine bounded off the couch, putting an armchair between them as if to stop the flow of curiosity. "Wiley! How could you ask me that?"

Wiley regarded her with the knowledge of years of friendship. "I know you're attracted to him. I saw you eyeing his backside earlier." When Jasmine flushed and mumbled, she went on knowingly, "And if he'd hurt you, or you'd hated it, you'd be upset in a different way. So come on," she coaxed. "Spill the beans."

Jasmine kneaded the back of the chair and grumbled, "It was ... okay."

Wiley's eyes brightened and she sat up, drawing her other leg under her. "Just okay?"

"Bah." Jasmine hunched her shoulders. "All right! Better than okay. More like … all the stars fell and lit up my sky," she finished softly.

"Wow," Wiley breathed. Oh, Jasmine had it bad, and for her cousin, of all things. Gleeful anticipation distracted her for a moment, until she remembered that she didn't want Jasmine falling for that particular cousin. They were supposed to be trying to escape.

But if they didn't, Keilor was in trouble.

"But it's not going to happen again," Jasmine said forcefully. She walked around the chair and sat down. Drawing her knees to her chest, she hugged them protectively. "I'm not going to let that snake get within ten feet of me next time."

That was unlikely, though Wiley kept it to herself. She had a feeling that Keilor was going to be underfoot a lot, keeping an eye on them. After their aborted escape attempt, she'd lay money on it.

She sighed with regret. "I guess we won't be going home any time soon."

Jasmine grunted. "A gun," she muttered, scrubbing her face. "That's what I need the next time. A gun to shoot the son of a bitch before he gets his hands on me."

Wiley turned troubled eyes on her. It was happening, the thing she'd feared. Already her loyalties were being divided. She could kill Jayems! "I don't want anyone to get hurt, Jas. Besides, he doesn't seem like the kind of man to take it well if you turned a gun on him. He might ... take it personally."

That silenced her. Jasmine sat there for a while, and then asked, "So, Jayems wants to marry you. Has he kissed you yet?"

Wiley stiffened. "Nosey, aren't you?"

"He has." Jasmine studied her. "Was it repulsive?"

"I don't want to talk about it."

"Wi, this is me. Talk. I've been going crazy, praying he hasn't hurt you."

"He hasn't hurt me."

"But he kissed you."

"It wasn't that bad," Wiley insisted, glossing over the truth. She'd had enough kisses to know when one held potential, but it didn't matter. "I'm not marrying him for his kisses."

"Then you're going to marry him?"

"No! Don't put words in my mouth. I don't even know him. I don't even like him!" But she was starting to. Know him, that is. She couldn't like him, not after he'd scared her to death that afternoon. Grudgingly, she admitted that he'd kept his promise not to hurt Jasmine, but that wasn't a reason to like him. It was a tiny point in his favor that he'd keep his promises, though.

Too bad she couldn't make him promise to send her home.

Chapter Eight

Jayems was half dressed.

Wiley stopped in the doorway, surprised to see him sliding away a sword. He was barefoot, wearing only a pair of loose maroon pants. A light tracing of hair trailed down his hard chest to his waistband and disappeared.

Knighten, who was similarly dressed, bowed to her and stepped around her.

Uneasy with how much she'd noticed of Jayems, Wiley remembered the Haunt guards at her back and stepped inside. They shut the door behind her, leaving her alone with him.

"Did you have a good visit?" Jayems asked cordially, pouring himself a glass of water. She tried not to notice how the sweat trickled down his throat as he tipped his head back.

"Yes." She took a seat on the couch, adjusting a throw pillow. "You guys still use swords here? They have guns these days, you know."

"We have guns. He sat down opposite her. "We practice all kinds of armed and unarmed combat. Guns do nothing to exercise the body." Judging by his, he exercised regularly.

She averted her eyes from his. She'd been sneaking a peek again. Focusing firmly on his face, she asked, "Do women do that, too?"

"If they like. Would you like instruction?"

Was he planning to teach her himself? She chewed her lip, pondering how unwise that would be.

"Tomorrow I'm bringing in a tutor for you. You've missed a great deal of history. I thought you might want to catch up on some of it. I also brought you this." He reached over to the side table and picked up a folder. He handed it to her.

Inside was a picture of a man. She stared at it, but it didn't ring any bells.

"It's your father, Crewel Sotra," he said softly.

Wiley looked at it, feeling numb. She didn't remember his face, had forgotten long ago what he looked like, except for the dark hair. Dressed in the black uniform of the Haunt, he had an indigo shirt under the leather vest, and a red Celtic knot, a symbol of rank, on his shoulder.

"He loved your spirit. He would have been proud of you for surviving the way you did. He was a good man," Jayems said quietly.

An ache started in behind her eyes and spread to her throat. She looked down to hide her expression, but her eyes kept returning to her father's face. Afraid to cry in front of Jaymes, she laid the picture on the coffee table and got up to look out the huge window. The three moons were rising as the world faded to dusk. The child moon was closest to the father moon that night, while mother moon looked coldly on from a distance.

Jayems came and stood beside her, silently offering her support. In the pain of the moment, she took it. "I was such a brat when I first came to the orphanage. I remember having screaming fits, especially at night. I'd yell until I was hoarse, "I want my Daddy! I want my Jayems!" They kept asking me who my daddy was. I don't think they understood when I told them he was Crewel. They asked if Jayems was my brother. I remember thinking they were stupid. I just kept telling them that he was 'my Jayems'." She'd rarely revisited the memory. Only now did she realize that she'd been calling for the man beside her.

Chagrined, she turned her back to him. "You wanted me to *change*, didn't you? Fine." It was easier to hide in Haunt form, where he could not expect her to talk. While she would never admit it, there was a soothing power in becoming half animal. As if someone had poured cool oil over her burning nerves, her muscles would relax.

Too bad the pain in her heart wasn't as easy to tame.

His hand came to rest on her shoulder. She started, surprised that he would touch her in Haunt form. Then again, the *change* was nothing to him.

"I'm here, little one. If you need a friend, I will be right here. I never left." His thumb made soothing little circles on her shoulder, a silent comfort, an unspoken invitation.

Unable to bear it anymore, she shifted back to human form and threw herself at him, crying in his arms while her heart broke. Taking fistfuls of his waistband, she anchored herself to him, needing a support that wouldn't move.

He didn't. He let her cry until the sobs nearly doubled her over, then carried her over to his armchair and held her on his lap. All along, she cried like a child who'd just lost her father, the pain as fresh as if it had happened again.

In her heart, she knew things would never be the same again.

* * * *

She was asleep.

Jayems peered at her face, then settled them more comfortably in the chair. The last hour had been draining for both of them. Good, though. She'd brought him hope.

"I want my Jayems!" His heart had jerked when she'd said she'd called for him. They'd had a special friendship when she'd been a child, and he'd loved her. It was an innocent love, and an unexpected joy, watching the child who would become his wife, grow up. Of course, there'd been nothing of lovers between them, and he'd respected the boundaries that he would with any child. But he had been her Jayems, and when she'd disappeared ...

He flinched, unwilling to revisit those memories. The important thing was that she was opening to him now. It had been such a relief when she let him in, and he planned to keep the lines of communication open.

It was different, though. He smoothed the hair from her face and felt again that tender wash of desire. She was no longer a child, and he was already bound by their betrothal. Although political marriages tended to also be celebrated in public, the only wedding their law recognized was a very private one.

They needed to talk about that, but the morning would be soon enough. She was exhausted. So he carried her to bed, removing only her boots and socks before covering her. He wanted her to know that she could trust him in her most vulnerable moments, waking or sleeping.

"Goodnight, sweet one," he whispered, kissing her temple. He turned and walked away before he could be tempted further.

* * * *

Wiley woke to a sense of comfort that went deeper than her down pillow. She'd been loved last night.

Jerked out of sleep by that thought, she looked frantically around, then felt her body. She was fully clothed. Then what ... memories flooded back, and she groaned, burying her face in the pillow. She'd bawled like a baby and then fallen asleep in his arms. It was a wonder he hadn't taken it as an engraved invitation--most men would have.

Feeling battered, she got out of bed and washed her face, grimacing at her puffy eyes. Maybe he wouldn't notice. Stupid thought; she'd bawled like an orphaned calf last night. Of course he would notice she was red-eyed this morning.

Straightening her spine, she joined him at the breakfast table, keeping her eyes averted. A slave to her appetite, she filled her plate with baked fish, crusty rolls and sweet potato wedges. It was different than the Frosted Favorites she'd grown up on, but tasty. Best of all, she wasn't the one who had to cook it.

Jayems let her eat in peace. He didn't say a word until she'd taken her last bite. "Your tutor will be here in an hour, and the riding lesson you requested will happen after that. Until then … you hinted that you had experienced intimacy, but that you had never finished the act?"

Stunned, she blurted, "Holy cow! You just dive right in there, don't you?"

Before she could lambaste him, he added calmly, "There are things about your body you're probably unaware of. It sounds as if your instincts saved you, but I wanted to make certain that you hadn't come to harm."

"Nobody harmed me," she said coolly. It was tricky deciding what to add. Did he want a history? He wasn't getting one.

"Then you were aware that, once mated, there is no going back for us? You knew that once the male and female sexual fluids mix, you cannot mate with anyone else without going insane?"

"Huh?" She blinked at him, feeling stupid. First off, his choice of mealtime conversation was stunningly blunt, but what was he talking about? A blush crept up her neck. Where was he going with this?

He searched her eyes, and then nodded gravely. "It's a chemical reaction, one that takes about a year to subside, sometimes a little longer. Most of us wouldn't dare to resume intimacies with someone else for at least fourteen months."

"Fourteen?" Her mind boggled. It wouldn't be worth the bother if that's how long someone had to wait. What if you met the love of your life right after having sex with the wrong person? What a disaster!

Feeling a little green, she asked tentatively, "Can this insanity be treated?"

"No. Usually the afflicted one has to be committed or executed, depending on the severity of the case. Extreme aggression and a tendency to repeat the act, with or without a willing partner, are usually the results."

Now she was seriously worried. There were times when she felt out of control herself. Before she'd sworn off men, she'd certainly felt the need to spoon often. It was the unsatisfying conclusion to those encounters that made her give them up. Men just didn't understand when a woman brought them to the edge, then told them no.

Compelled to make certain she wasn't losing her mind, she said hesitantly, "I've had my share of boyfriends, and I've made out, uh, up the point of no return, but I haven't, um, completed the act. Am I in any danger?"

"We can touch and kiss as much as we wish, as long as the man does not

penetrate the woman with--"

"I get it!" She threw up her hands to ward him off.

He smiled and looked down, then slanted her a boyish look through his lashes. "But you didn't do it. I'm glad to hear it."

Heat pooled in her cheeks like liquid flame. Unable to meet his gaze, she looked around. "So, is that all you wanted to say?"

"That was all." There was laughter in his voice, but he didn't tease her.

"Fine. I'm going to talk to Jasmine before this tutor of yours shows up. I want to see how she's doing." She wanted to get away from his laughing eyes, too.

He was getting to her.

Chapter Nine

Jayems dismounted from his stag and helped Rihlia down. It had been an uncomfortable hour physically--he ached in places not normally tensed by a riding beast.

They were intelligent animals, but few would call them beautiful. With heads like rhinoceros, scales like dragons and the spiked tails of stegosaurus, the muscular beasts would happily trample anyone who didn't watch their back.

No, he ached from the sweet smelling body that was Rihlia. It had been both bliss and torture to ride with his arms around her, directing her use of the reins. They'd both been tense, and his stag hadn't liked it one bit.

Keilor pulled up beside them and handed Jasmine down. If he looked a little pained as he swung down, Jayems wouldn't tease him over it. There weren't many men he'd trust to ride in such proximity to the Sylph for over an hour and not get out of control.

Eyes slightly unfocused, Keilor told him stiffly, "I'm going to … go take care of a few things. I'll meet you back at the Citadel later."

Assuming Keilor was either going to lose his mind in a bottle or go bash a few soldiers on the practice field, Jayems smiled and waved him off. Part of him couldn't help thinking that Keilor had met his match in the feisty little human. It would certainly solve his problems if his cousin would take the girl for his own. Until then, he tried to hold his breath and walk upwind. The medics were working on some kind of nose filter to combat her pheromone, and he was watching their progress with great interest. He had dibs on the first one.

Lemming had been walked on a leash while her mistress was riding, and she sniffed Rihlia all over when she took the lead.

"Stags must smell as funny as they look," Jasmine said as Lemming nosed her as well. "It's too bad horses couldn't survive here--they're much nicer."

"But an inferior steed," Jayems said dismissively. True, he'd never ridden one, but he knew his history.

"What's that?" Rihlia gestured to a grove of log posts to their right. Each log was covered with plate sized and smaller, frilly yellow mushrooms.

"Honey fungus. You had some in your dinner last night. We cultivate the mushrooms on the logs, and then use the spent wood for fuel or mulch. We raise other kinds of mushrooms, but those are the most popular." They passed the mushrooms and came to a grassy park bounded by flowering shrubs and hedges. Children were running full tilt, or playing on the equipment, watched by their mothers or fathers.

Rihlia stopped and looked over the low hedge. He couldn't tell from her expression what she was thinking.

"Still want to have a dozen?" Jasmine said with grin, poking her lightly in the ribs. She dropped down on the bench to watch the children in comfort. "Yikes! If I only had half that energy."

"You need to exercise more," Rihlia said absently, then frowned. "I said five, not a dozen. Just because you don't like children doesn't mean you need to tease me."

"I didn't say I didn't like them. I just can't see myself pregnant, you know? And giving birth! I'd rather adopt. There are lots of kids out there who need homes … better yet, someone else already went through the labor for them."

Jayems hoped she truly did want to adopt. The odds of her producing offspring with his race was practically nil. The bloodlines did not cross gracefully, and most babies miscarried in the first three months. Of course, they still had to find someone who'd accept her as a wife--he had no question she'd be wanted for a lover. The pheromone made sure of that.

Rihlia wanted children. He hid a small, pleased smile. He'd love to start on that project, if only she would let him. He'd wanted a family for years now, and the idea of a small son warmed his heart. Not that he'd shun a daughter, but all men dreamed of a son.

"Let me introduce you," he offered. He knew several of the parents there, and it was a good way for Rihlia to start making connections.

She looked at him uncertainly, and then glanced at Jasmine.

Jasmine shooed them off. "I'm resting. Have fun."

Jayems hesitated and led Rihlia off. When they were out of earshot, he looked at Rihlia questioningly.

"Don't take it personally," she advised him. "You wouldn't think it, but Jas can be shy around strangers."

"No, I wouldn't think it," he said dryly, remembering how much cheek Jasmine had shown that first night. They came abreast of one of the fathers, a captain under Keilor's command. "Jiaral. May I introduce my companion, Lady Rihlia?"

Jiaral made his bow, a slight lowering of the head for several seconds. His chin length hair swung free with the movement, temporarily hiding the fresh laser burn along his left cheek. "My pleasure," he said in his heavy county accent.

"Oh, what happened to your cheek?" Rihlia said with concern. "Have you seen a doctor?"

Jiaral frowned. "A doctor? Oh, you mean a medic? No need. It will be mostly gone by tomorrow."

She blinked, but held her tongue. Jayems knew she was unused to people healing as quickly as she did. Even broken bones healed in a matter of two weeks. Jiaral would think nothing of such a piddling training accident.

A small boy crashed into Jiaral's legs, throwing him off balance and causing him to laugh. He couldn't have been more than four. "Easy, Mot. What's the rush?"

"Dai, Dai! Mai said we could have tarts when we were done. Are we done, Dai?"

Jiaral chuckled. "Rascal. We haven't been here five minutes, and I have company. Be polite and greet Lord Jayems and his lady."

Mot peeked up at them. "Hello," he said uncertainly.

Rihlia grinned and squatted down to his level. "Hello. My name's Wiley. I betcha I can run to the slide faster than you can."

Mot's eyes got big in excitement at the discovery of new playmate. "Last one there has to eat dirt!" He took off like a shot for the slide.

Jiaral laughed in surprise as the pair shot off, Rihlia carefully staying a stride behind. "She must enjoy children. Thank you. My wife is tired from staying up with the baby and wanted a nap. I promised not to come back for a least an hour."

"You're welcome, though Rihlia deserves the credit."

"I thought she said her name was Wiley?" Jiaral looked his question. Surely he'd heard about the lady's history by now. It was all over the Citadel.

"It takes time to adjust to new things," Jayems said, leaving it at that. "How is your little daughter?"

Pleased to discuss his family, Jiaral related the baby's latest achievements.

Jayems used the time to study his betrothed. She needed to play more. From all he'd gathered, it seemed as if she'd been robbed of her childhood. Watching her now, he saw the remnants of the wild little girl he'd once known playing with a little boy who could have easily been her son.

Jayems lowered his eyes and his smile was bittersweet. He was ready to grant some wishes.

* * * *

They walked past the gardens on their way back to the Citadel, and Wiley noticed a woman using a hand pump to fill a bucket. Since they were in the area of the family garden plots, she asked, "Why don't you have hoses or something? I know you guys have electricity--some of your technology is ahead of Earth's."

Jayems smiled at her. "Would you like to spend your life in a factory, assembling electronic pumps? We only use technology for certain things, like pumping the water into our rooms and running our lights, or communication. Some of us still use candles and oil lamps, as well as pack our own water. The exercise is good for us, conserves resources and promotes a simpler, more relaxed way of life. You'll notice that woman is using a wheeled cart to haul her bucket around? It has a spigot on the end, and a hose. If she were pregnant or infirm, she could still manage the chore with ease."

"Hmm." They'd stopped by a rich plot of freshly turned earth, perhaps as long and wide as a school bus. She'd always enjoyed tending her houseplants, and it might be fun to start a garden. "I think I'd like to have a garden, too. What do you think, Jas? Want to help?"

Jasmine shrugged. "Yeah, why not? It'd give us something to do around here. Besides, it might be fun to grow one of those." She pointed to a monster squash sitting in a neighboring plot. "We could see which of us could grow the biggest."

Jaymes smiled. "We'll see which plots are vacant and arrange it. I have a number of books on horticulture you may look at, or you can check some out of the Citadel library. The master gardener would be happy to introduce you to a tutor; he loves to meet others with a love for the soil."

Wiley thought about the rarely used kitchen in Jayems' rooms. It had a large pantry, mostly empty. "Is that what you're supposed to be doing with that huge pantry in the kitchen? Storing vegetables? Where would we keep all the potatoes and stuff, though?"

He looked faintly embarrassed. "I don't have the time to grow and preserve my own produce, though we are educated on the importance of agriculture all our lives. If you don't know how to prepare food for storage, I can make the time to show you. Each garden also has cellar space available."

"You know how to can jelly?" Jasmine asked dubiously.

Jaymes' cheeks turned bronze. "We're taught in school," he muttered. "It's not hard."

Wiley smiled. She liked this side of him, an embarrassed school boy. "Cool. Assuming we can actually grow something besides weeds."

"Speak for yourself. I am a gardener extraordinaire." Jasmine put her hand on her chest and struck a pose.

"Hah! The only thing you manage to grow is mold on the leftovers in the fridge," Wiley retorted.

"And beauties they are," Jasmine agreed, walking on. She was oblivious to the women in a far corner who looked at her, then turned to each other and whispered.

Wiley wasn't. She frowned and glanced at Jayems.

He let Jasmine get ahead of them, out of earshot, before he said quietly, "She is a human and a Sylph. Don't you see the way the men look at her? Many women won't like that."

Wiley had noticed the unusual attention men showed Jasmine, but had put it down to curiosity. Word had gotten around that she was an alien, after all. Heads turned everywhere she went. No matter how keen the interest was, no one dared to approach her, not with four Haunt guards shadowing her every move.

A daydreamer, Jasmine never quite focused on the world around her, never noticed the attention or the danger.

For once, Wiley was glad. Jasmine would hate it if she realized what was going on. "Send her home."

"To what? You said she'd be alone there."

She hated it when he was reasonable.

"She can do as she likes here ... she can be with you. I see the way you look after her--she's a bit of a dreamer. She doesn't even notice the way men look at her, and I think Keilor would miss her."

Her eyes narrowed. "You're making that up. He'd get over her leaving in about two minutes."

He smiled. "Less, right now. I've known him all his life. He's looking at her the way I've never seen him do with another woman, though he doesn't realize it yet. He's going to fall in love."

She shivered at the way he said it, with fondness and pleasure. He truly wanted his friend to be happy. Unable to bear this tender side of him any longer, she lengthened her stride and caught up to Jasmine. "Come on, Jas. I'm ready for a snack."

Chapter Ten

"Come on, Wi. This will work. It has to." Jasmine was pleading now.

Wiley closed her eyes and groaned silently. Jasmine wanted to go home, and she couldn't blame her. This latest scheme was so far fetched, it was laughable. Oh, she believed they could get Jayems and maybe Keilor into a poker game. Jayems had been very agreeable all afternoon. She had a feeling he'd welcome any kind of overture from her.

Bribing the Haunt guards with their ill gotten gains was idiotic, however. The product of a desperate mind.

The sad thing was, she was going to go along with it. Oh, she fully intended to talk some sense into Jasmine later. She had a feeling that it wouldn't be hard. Not only was Jasmine afraid of the Haunt, she hated looking stupid. Once she calmed down, she'd realize that was exactly what she'd look like if she tried to bribe one of Jayems' hand picked soldiers to take them to the gate. It was never going to happen.

Crazy or not, she found herself in Jayems' rooms late that afternoon, setting up a poker game. Jasmine had found a way to persuade the men to bet money against their worthless markers.

"We wager with real money while you use snails?" Jayems asked with a scowl, pulling out a chair.

"What are we supposed to wager, our virtue?" Jasmine retorted, getting up to grab a glass of juice.

She didn't see Keilor's expression as entered the room, but Wiley did. Jasmine might have hesitated if she'd seen the rawness of his gaze. He looked like a man who'd been pushed too far, and was ready to snap at the bait.

Worse, Wiley had *not* known Jasmine was going to say that. She had a feeling that Jasmine was making it up as she went along, and screwing it up, too.

Jayems looked at Wiley out of the corner of his eye.

Her eyes narrowed. "Forget it." She was not participating in this lunacy.

"I don't know, I think the idea has merit," he answered smoothly.

"You would." His naughty smile made her uneasy. He'd never openly flirted with her before. Was he stepping up his campaign?

Keilor acted unconcerned as he took a seat. "If I'm going to be playing with real coin against shells, I'd have to agree with Jayems. We should at least get a kiss if we win the game."

"No!" Rihlia said it forcefully, but nobody was listening. She wasn't willing to kiss Jayems for a plan that wasn't going to work, anyway.

Jasmine hesitated, and then said, "No tongues."

"Jasmine!" Wiley cried. She couldn't believe Jas was going through with this.

Eyes narrowed like a tiger contemplating a stray doe, Keilor bargained, "If you sit on our laps while delivering it."

Wiley slapped a hand on the table, embarrassed. "Stop it, you two!" She was ignored.

Cupping her chin in thought, Jasmine ran a thumb over her lips. "Gold coin for every shell."

Keilor smiled wickedly. "I'll give you two for every shell if you sit astride."

That gave her pause. Her eyes flickered as she looked down. Maybe she hadn't thought about the actual consequences until that moment.

Wiley had pictured nothing but. She was in a sweat just thinking about it. "Don't you dare," she warned Jasmine, breaking the tense silence.

"*Oda ouya aveha anothera away ota etga oneyma orfa ibingbra ehta aurdsga, Wi?*" *Do you have another way to get money for bribing the guards?* Jasmine asked casually and then added in English, "Don't be a baby, Wiley. It's just a little kiss." Even as she said it, she blushed.

Wiley had about five seconds in which to object.

Jasmine shot her a pleading look.

Growling in disgust, Wiley slouched in her chair. She'd beat Jasmine for this later.

"The winner gets the pot, the losers take a shot," Jasmine told them and then explained the rules.

Wiley shuffled the cards in nervous silence. They had better slaughter the guys in this game, because she couldn't handle kissing Jayems more than once or twice. Her face heated at the thought, but she kept her eyes on the cards and refused to look at Jayems.

Predictably, the women won the first few hands, pulling in money by the fistful. Wiley had just begun to relax when Jayems laid down his first winning hand. She blinked, but the cards didn't change.

Slow color flooded her cheeks. Jayems pushed his chair back and laced his hands together over his stomach, a warm flame of anticipation in his eyes.

Okay, she could do this. Taking a quick breath, Wiley gulped her liquor, squared her shoulders and then straddled him. Closing her eyes, she aimed for his cheek. Any second she was going to go up in flames from the heat of her blush. Jasmine was dead!

But her lips didn't land on his cheek. A mouth gave softly under her lips, and he truly had to have great reflexes to have gotten it there in time. His hand came up and cupped her cheek; a butterflies' caress.

She forgot why she was in a hurry, forgot they had an audience. For one aching moment, it was just the two of them, alone.

When Wiley finally slid off of Jayems' lap, she was clumsy with more than alcohol. She knocked her chair sideways as she sat down.

Jasmine laughed as she helped set it to rights.

Then she lost.

"Huh," she said. She reached for her drink, in no hurry to pay up.

Before her fingers could close around it, Keilor grabbed it. With a glint in his eye, he toasted her. "I'd hate for your senses to be dulled for this, Dragonfly."

Wiley was too embarrassed to look. They took their time about it.

Maybe Jayems felt the same thing, or maybe he took pity on her, for he finally said, "Do you think we should leave him to her mercy or have pity and toss water on them?"

She heard Keilor groan, then the sound of Jasmine fumbling for her chair.

The men stole several more kisses before the game was over, and Wiley couldn't even hide behind a liquor haze. Jayems and Keilor kept stealing her and Jasmine's drinks, claiming chivalry. Unfortunately, they didn't fall into a stupor, either. In fact, the liquor had little noticeable effect on them.

"You must be cheating," Jasmine muttered, eyeing the pile of shells in front of their opponents. Keilor raised the bet and Jayems folded. Wiley was already out, and Jasmine couldn't cover the bet.

Wiley had never been so glad to finish a game in her life. The moment Jasmine left, she slunk off and hid in her room. Unfortunately, she knew that Jayems wouldn't leave her alone for long. He was determined to see her change every night--doctor's orders!--and he wouldn't believe she'd do it if left in the privacy of her room. Determined to save face, she acted like she was in need of some reading material and went to check out Jayems' extensive book shelves.

She'd been strictly a cable girl herself and had rarely picked up a book back home. She'd seen Jayems reading in his library from time to time, settled in one of the two leather chairs. Ottomans were positioned in front of each chair, and end tables on each side held lamps for when the daylight faded. The shelves were behind the chair and lined three walls. A handsome rug warmed that corner of the wooden floor.

She hadn't had an interest in exploring that section of the room before. Now she looked at the polished red bookshelves in some surprise. Every book was handsomely bound, and many of them had gilt lettering. Normally that was a turnoff for her, because she always figured those kind of books were boring old classics. Deprived of her TV, however, she was willing to investigate closer.

A book on the side table caught her eye, and she picked it up. It was titled, "Her First Time." Her jaw went slack. Glancing to make certain Jayems wasn't in the room, she hastily set it down and moved to the shelves, blankly studied the spines.

It was a few moments before she actually read the titles. He'd been thinking about her first time? Their first time? Flames licked her cheeks. Her first experience with the opposite sex had happened years ago, and she'd had her fair share since. Was he thinking of her first time graduating to full-blown sex?

With a shiver, she tried to put it out of her mind, but she kept flashing back to it. Curiosity was eating at her. What was in that book?

With an effort, she made herself focus on the other titles in front of her. He had books on negotiating, battle tactics, history, agriculture ... boring. Didn't the man read any fiction? There was a book on stained glass working that looked mildly interesting, but she kept scanning the shelves, hoping for something more enticing. Her search was rewarded. There, right in the middle of his shelves at eye level, was an entire shelf of books devoted to lovemaking.

Wiley's eyes boggled as she read the titles. *An Illustrated Guide to the Sensual Arts. A Woman's Climax. Emotional Need and the Sensual Virgin.* There were dozens of titles.

Holy Hannah! What was the man, some kind of gigolo? She started to wonder if the book on the table was a new book or an old favorite. Certainly he'd started his collection long before she'd entered the picture.

Disturbed to see him as a sensual being, considering the restraint he'd shown around her most of the time, she backed off. Maybe she'd be better off going straight to bed after all.

He was there, behind her. His gaze took in her expression and shifted to the shelves behind her. He raised a curious brow. "Something disturbs you?"

Oh, he was bold. A surge of annoyance made her cross her arms. "Well, yeah. It's a little disturbing to find I've been locked in with a skirt chaser."

"A skirt chaser?"

She tipped her head at the books behind her. "Your bookshelf reads like *National Pornographic.*"

He smiled. "You sound jealous."

"I'm not! I'm just wondering how many women are going to be running around here." She was defensive and knew it, but she wasn't jealous. Of course, that meant she was righteous instead, and that didn't sound good, either.

"One. You." He drifted a step closer. "Are you curious what I learned from my books?"

"No." She tried to sound firm, but she was interested. Those kisses of his had been unusual, unlike any she'd had before. Her boyfriends had always been in a hurry; Jayems liked to linger. That kind of thing could get addictive. "You come off as some kind of cool dignitary, and here you are reading smut in the evenings!"

He moved closer. "Is knowing how to please a woman a crime? Is wanting to? Should I take my pleasure and leave her none?"

These were tricky questions, and it was getting hard to think. She was sure he was doing it on purpose. "That's not the point! You're some kind of playboy. Admit it!"

"I'm not playing with you," he said, closing the space between them. He put his arms around her, loose enough not to make her fight, but firm enough to make his point. One hand began to stroke her hip, distracting, enticing.

She raised her arms to hold him off, but there was no strength in them. "Stop."

"Am I hurting you?"

"No, but that shouldn't matter when a woman says stop," she said with an edge to her voice.

"You're right," he whispered against her lips. He released her.

Now that she was free, she didn't know where to go. To her room? Her legs wouldn't move.

Smoke gathered in his eyes. "I have an idea ... something I can teach you from my books. With this, I won't even touch you."

Curiosity would be her undoing. Or was it him? "What?" she said warily.

"The power of scent," he said softly, drawing in a breath by her ear.

She shivered.

"Our senses are so much more than sight and sound and touch," he murmured next to her neck, raising chill bumps with his breath. "Seduction is also the perfume of flowers in a woman's hair, the warm scent of her skin, the soap she uses to cleanse her body." He sank slowly to his knee while he talked, his eyes half closed as if in bliss. "I can smell the change in fabric from your shirt to your pants, the musk of the leather belt riding your waist, and more ..." He knelt in front of her now and drew in a deep breath.

Slowly, his eyes opened, and he looked up at her through his lashes. "I can even smell your desire."

Riveted, she stared at him. Sweat broke out on her skin, and he closed his eyes as if savoring the scent. Desire pulsed in her blood, made her fingertips itch to touch him. Oh, he was good ... and that was his undoing.

She stepped back, bumping her hip on the chair as she went. Scrambling around it, she eased toward her room, away from him. He didn't move, just watched her back away from him.

"I ... I'm not one of your women," she said, unable to look away.

He just looked at her.

"I'm not going to let you do this," she whispered. She got another two paces.

"My bed is that way," he said simply, and rose. Moving as if he were the master of time itself, he walked toward his room, pulling his shirt over his head as he walked. He tossed it in the open door and unbuckled his belt. With the door still open, he stripped out of the rest of his clothes as casually as if she weren't looking.

There was a lot to see.

He pulled back the covers and got into bed, then picked up a book. Opening the cover, he began to read.

Wiley blinked, but it didn't clear her head. The light gleamed off his chest, reflecting shadows as he turned the page, illuminating every line of muscle. He'd wound her so tight, his every move was pure temptation.

As if her body weighed a thousand pounds, she turned and slowly walked to her room. It was like a nightmare where she wanted to run, but was unable. If she went in that door, she was going to become a wife.

She couldn't be a wife. She couldn't.

* * * *

Jayems watched her slow retreat. Not tonight then, but soon.

Chapter Eleven

Her mother had come.

Wiley watched the huge double doors open to the family banquet hall and tried to control her breathing. She wasn't ready for this.

Jayems had sprung it on her that morning, told her that her mother was arriving that evening like he was handing her a gift. She'd gone ballistic, cursing him for not giving her more notice, cursing her mother for--she still didn't want to think about it.

It was Jasmine who'd talked sense into her. Jas had faced her own mother, an abusive addict, when she was still in her teens. The interview had not gone well, but it was behind her now, and at least she'd had the courage to face it. "Just get it over with," she'd advised Wiley.

Jasmine stood at her side now, silently supportive, and led the way into the room. She might be a dreamer, but sometimes she had ten times the courage Wiley would ever have.

The room was decorated in simple elegance, as were the people inside. She searched the faces of the two older women there and had a bad moment. Neither of them were familiar. The fading brunette was soft and chubby, her flesh plumped around her many rings, and her purple and burnt orange gown draped around her like a high-priced dust cover. A platinum blonde stood at her side, slim and elegant in a pale yellow, grecian inspired gown. Gold clips held her gown together at the shoulders, elbows and wrists, and blue, red and yellow ribbon trimmed her hem and the wine red sash around her waist. Sprays of yellow and white flowers, fashioned of diamonds, flashed in her upswept braids. A matching necklace circled her neck. Her sky-blue eyes were alive with emotion and wet with tears.

The queenly lady glided forward, her gaze devouring Wiley's face. Her voice was hoarse when she whispered, "Daughter?" Without warning she threw herself in Wiley's arms, shaking her head as if she couldn't believe her eyes. "Rihlia. You've come home."

Wiley stiffened and shot a panicked glance at Jasmine, who shrugged her ignorance. Her mother had certainly never wept all over her. Besides, she seemed distracted by the blond man breathing down her neck. Wiley recognized him as the one called Fallon, the man who'd stumbled on her camp with Jayems and Keilor. Whatever his business had been, he seemed to be back, and he really, *really* seemed to dig Jasmine.

Her dress was getting all wet. Trying not to seem rude, Wiley eased her mother back and tried out a smile. It was a sickly effort, but the best she could manage with her churning stomach. She'd exploded at Jayems that morning, but her anger had turned into anxiety. She was a little afraid of the woman sobbing in front of her, and very wary.

Because her memories were twenty years old, she held them in check, but she had forgotten nothing. "Mother ... how good to see you."

Lady Rhapsody dried her eyes with a little laugh. "Oh, I'm sorry. It's just been so long ..." The tears threatened to start up again.

Jayems moved forward. He'd been hanging back, watching the reunion, but was quick to step up and smooth the awkward moment. He smiled as if Wiley's behavior at seeing her long lost mother wasn't a little odd and congratulated them both. Then he introduced Rhapsody's sister Lady Portae, the chubby older lady.

Wiley suffered through another hug and tried to look happy.

"And this is your cousin Urseya," Jayems introduced a young woman near Wiley's own age. A sloe eyed beauty of perfect dimensions and practiced poise, Urseya contented herself with kissing Wiley's cheek and murmuring hello.

Wiley was grateful. She couldn't take anymore damp hugs without jumping and running.

Fallon managed to tear himself from Jasmine's side long enough for a proper greeting. "I look forward to renewing our acquaintance under these happier circumstances, dear cousin," he said formally, then winked. "I'll try not to tell too many embarrassing baby stories about you."

She welcomed the laugh, and liked him better for it. His loose trousers and gold- trimmed tunic, cut in the Chinese style, made the blond of his queued hair all the more striking. There was little resemblance to Jayems or Keilor in him, unless one counted the strength in his face, or the intelligence in his green eyes. While he looked to be in his late twenties, she knew appearances were deceiving among their kind.

Many things were deceiving.

She was relieved when they sat down at the table. She and Jayems were seated at opposite sides, leaving her mother and her aunt to flank her. Poor Jasmine was looking strained, unsure what to do with Fallon's attentions. He'd taken the seat to her left and spent most of the meal flirting with her.

Or maybe Jasmine was distressed with Keilor's behavior. Wiley's eyes narrowed as she saw the way he was flirting with Urseya. Nobody treated her friends like that.

"Is something wrong, dear?" her mother asked.

Wiley jerked herself back from contemplating Keilor's death. She had her own backside to cover. "No. I was just … trying to remember things. I was very young when I … got lost." She watched her mother closely, but all she Wiley saw was sympathy.

"Oh, let's not speak of it again," Rhapsody implored. "I don't want to cry anymore. So many of our family were lost that day." She held her napkin to her mouth while Urseya patted her gently on the back.

"Happy memories! We must replace our dreary past with happy memories," Lady Portae announced. "Let's start tomorrow. What do you say, Rihlia? Would you like to go shopping? We can have lunch together, just us ladies."

What could she say? 'No' would have required an explanation. "That sounds like fun." She looked at her ivory cup for a long moment, toyed with the gold rim. Memories were robbing her of any desire to play nice. She said slowly, "But I do want to know one thing. I was too young to remember anything at all, but how did I get lost?"

Conversation slowed, then ceased. All eyes moved to Rhapsody.

She took a deep breath. "We were attacked, as you know. The two of us were riding a stag together. When they came, our stag shied and threw me. You stayed on for a moment longer and fell off the other side. I assumed you'd run into the brush when I couldn't find you, but I couldn't get to you. Our own guards pulled me into their circle to protect me …" She let out a shaky sigh. "Most of them died in the battle, too."

Wiley watched her mother, and then turned her eyes back to the cup. That was not what happened.

Something made her look at Jayems. Whatever he saw, he gave her the faintest of nods. Knowing Jayems, he wanted to talk. Maybe the nod meant he would listen, too.

Time for a subject change. "Well, all's well, and all that. Where was it you wanted to shop?" Wiley said, looking at her aunt. She couldn't look at her mother, not then.

Jasmine excused herself early, claiming too much wine. Wiley waited a few minutes after she'd left, then caught Jayems' eye. Maybe she looked as stressed as she felt, for he managed to excuse them without seeming rude.

Wiley endured more hugs, and then gratefully allowed Jayems to escort her to his rooms.

He waited until they were inside and she had plopped down on the couch before saying casually, "Now that your mother is here, if you would like to share rooms with her--"

"No!"

His head came up and he nodded, as if in self confirmation. "All right. Would you like some water, anything to drink?"

She was tempted to order a double, but shook her head. "Nothing. Thanks."

He took the seat opposite her and rubbed his lower lip. "What did you want to tell me about your mother?"

She let the silence stretch as she considered what she knew of him, what her gut said about him. "She lied."

"About?" he asked calmly.

"We were riding the same ... stag." Over the years she'd gotten confused, thought it was a horse, but now she knew better. "She jumped off and ran into the bushes. I got off the stag, but it was a long way down, and I hurt my foot doing it." She took a deep breath. "I ran after her, but I wasn't quick enough. I caught her scent, saw a glimpse of her, but that was all. She never slowed down, never came back. I got lost, running from the battle. I was so afraid they were going to catch me and kill me." She could see the tree, remember parting the ferns ... they'd seemed so huge to a child. She'd known they would smell her trail, so she'd kept running, falling, crawling. "It was some time before I noticed the trees had changed. I didn't think much of it, was too scared to care. I remember finding the road ..." The road that had ultimately led to an orphanage and years of hell.

She met Jayems' eyes. "She lied."

He was silent some time. "There is no way you could have misremembered? You were very young."

"We got off on the same side of the horse ... stag," she corrected, angry at the slip. "I followed her into the bushes, calling her name. She looked back, saw me, and ran faster. She wanted me left behind."

"She was found by the rescuing party with her remaining bodyguards. Keilor and I were there. If she left, we didn't notice it, nor did we see her return alone."

"How big was this battle, how old were you, and how scared?" she asked cynically.

He lowered his eyes as bronze colored his cheeks. "Point granted. We also lost our fathers and mothers that day. We were ... distracted."

She looked down and swallowed, feeling his grief. "Okay."

He mastered himself and met her eyes. "Could she have panicked and made a wrong decision? Maybe she lied about how you were lost, but bitterly regretted her cowardice later? Could she not have truly grieved over you?"

"She left me, and she lied. I don't need a mother like that," she said flatly. She looked to the side. "I've seen some ugly things over the years, and I'm sure you have, too. You're giving her a very mild reason to have run away. Maybe there was something worse."

He drew in a slow breath. "You're talking about conspiracy to kill her own family, Rihlia."

"Wiley," she said fiercely. "You're the guy with all the connections, J. Why don't you check it out?" She left for her room, slamming the door for good measure.

She hated it when he butchered her name.

Chapter Twelve

Jasmine was hung over the next day and refused to come out of her room. Gritting her teeth, Wiley banged on the door one last time for good measure and stalked back to her room. She was going to hate her day.

She'd had a hard time falling asleep last night, then tossed and turned with foul dreams. Jayems hadn't had time for breakfast. Whatever he was doing, his mind had been on it, not her. Not that she cared about that, but she had the morning to look forward to and it would have helped to talk to someone, even him.

Her mother, Portae and Urseya were waiting for her outside Jayems' door. Dressed to kill, they looked wide-eyed at her choice of black pants and her tank top.

Rhapsody smiled uncertainly, eyeing Wiley's tattoo. "Are you ready, dear, or would you like time to change?"

"Nope. Let's go." Wiley refreshed her ponytail, feeling a wicked thrill of humor at their thinly hidden dismay. They reminded her of the rich chicks she'd seen slipping into Nordstrom's, all glamour and glitz. No doubt they would be eager to make her over in their image.

She was right. Their very first stop was in a manicurist's. Since she was just along for the ride, she let the girl there tackle her ragged fingernails. They were just going to get dirty when she dug up her new garden, but it was a novelty she'd had a mild curiosity about.

The hairstylist wanted to do an extreme number on her hair, but after arguing with him for five minutes, she fixed him with a look of promise and said, "Touch up the dead ends and leave it all one length, or I will teach you what a full nelson is."

Her mother, who'd been on his side, paused in horror, then nodded quickly to the man. Maybe she was afraid of a scene.

Smart woman.

Wiley exited the salon with her hair in a French braid, a mild concession to her mother's quest for a new look. Of all the good luck, a merchant was selling guitars across the street. Brightly enameled and oddly shaped, they drew her like cotton candy to a child. Picking up a hot pink and red model, she tuned it by ear.

"Oh, you play?" Portae said curiously, seeming a little relieved. Maybe she thought she was about to hear some ladylike ditties she could show off to her friends at teatime.

Wiley grinned wickedly, then played a few warm up chords, surged into a couple of hard rock riffs, then opened with a little Van Halen.

Rhapsody's eyes got big. She looked left, then right, paling as she realized they were drawing an audience. Undecided, she stiffened and waited for the song to end.

Wiley rocked on, loving the surge in her blood as the music flowed through her. It was a wicked delight to tease her mother, and her smile grew in proportion. She finished the last notes with a flourish and saluted her audience, who clapped and cheered.

She handed the guitar to the bemused peddler with a grin. "Deliver it to Lord Jayems' room. He gives good tips." Adopting an innocent expression, she walked on with her mother.

Rhapsody seemed to be searching for words. "That was … very surprising. I had no idea you had any musical interests as a child, or we would have gotten you harp lessons." 'Something more suitable' remained unsaid.

Wiley laughed. "Good thing you didn't. I like the guitar and the drums. If I'd started out on the harp, you would have ruined it for me." Her eye was caught by a display of ready made clothes. "Oh, nice. I need one of those." She picked up a pair of black pants made of a thick, silky material.

"Oh, you don't want those," Portae said quickly, making shooing motions with her fingers. "Those are male attire, for doing labor and such."

"Exactly." Wiley took two pair, one black and one brown, into the curtained alcove in the back of the merchant's stall. They fit perfectly and felt even better than jeans.

"Sold." She said when she came out. She picked out a few more pairs, some long sleeved shirts and a few shirts with tulip sleeves and Chinese collars and arranged for delivery. She even tossed in a couple for Jasmine, knowing she'd appreciate it. Dresses had their place, but she didn't want to be stuck in them for the rest of her life.

Satisfied she'd covered the basics of her wardrobe, she turned to the rest of her party and took pity on their distress. Well, the older two were distressed--Urseya looked amused. "So, where else did you want to go?"

She was ushered into a dressmaker's shop so fast her feet barely touched the ground. If the outside of the store had looked feminine with its pink and white striped awning and fancy mullioned windows, the inside was even more plush. Muted fawn walls washed with lime glaze surrounded a grouping of plush velvet couches and chairs. The ceramic tile floors were softened with delicate floral rugs. Several ladies were waiting already, sipping tea. They looked at Wiley with curiosity.

The proprietor, a pretty redhead dressed in cream and strawberry robes, met them at the door and bowed her head respectfully. "My ladies. What may I do for you?"

Rhapsody took over. "My daughter needs an entire new wardrobe. We're going to need simply everything."

"It will be my pleasure to help, my lady. Please, follow me." They were led to a private parlor and served tea and dainties. An assistant brought pattern books and swatches of material while the ladies looked through books.

Wiley was unsurprised to find that her tastes differed wildly from her mother's. "I don't do pink," she said firmly when her mother pointed out a picture. "No pastels, no ruffles. I like this," she said, pointing to a calf-length tunic. She liked both the sleeveless version and the one with sleeves. They looked especially good with a sash around the waist.

Her mother frowned. "Perhaps as daily wear, but you are a lady of rank. You should wear something that says as much. How about this?" A soft, delicate dress of sea green was favored this time.

Wiley shivered. "Yeah, I can just see wearing that into a bar. Why not just say, 'rape me'?"

"Rihlia!"

"Sorry, but I am not wearing that." She did find a few dresses she liked; not as many as her mother would have wanted, but Rhapsody did agree they were in good taste. She ended up ordering the tunic set and four dresses. They took her measurements, made an appointment for a fitting and escaped.

Well, she escaped. The others left reluctantly, already discussing a side trip to the shoe store.

Desperate for a distraction, she looked around and spied a man selling weapons. Knowing it would aggravate

Rhapsody, she drifted closer and inspected his wares. A throwing knife on the black velvet caught her eye.

"May I help you?" the man asked politely. Seeing her interest, he handed her the knife. "Finest blades in the Citadel."

She looked it over, wondering if that were true. Glancing around, she looked to see if there was anyone she could ask when her eyes fell on her Haunt bodyguards standing a discreet distance away. At first her courage failed her, but she stiffened her backbone and met the eyes of the captain. She'd heard Jayems call him Piper. "Could you, er, *change* so I can talk to you?"

In moments, he had obliged, shifting into a large, rather homely looking fellow. "How can I help, my lady?"

Figuring Jayems wouldn't hire anyone but the best, she handed him the throwing knife. "Is it the best in the Citadel?"

He turned the blade over in his hands and smiled. "It's off balance and of inferior make." He handed the blade back to the flustered merchant without expression, then looked back at her. "If you'd like to accompany me to the armory later, I'd be happy to help you choose suitable weapons and arrange for your instruction in their use."

She laughed. "I'd like that." She liked him, but she looked away as he *changed* just the same. Some things were still too hard to watch.

The pace was wearing her down. To escape, she said, "I'm starving. Is it lunch time yet?"

They had lunch in a classy, energetic café that catered to an upscale crowd. The walls were white and decorated with flowering plants, mirrors and stained glass lamps. Green wrought iron chairs graced each table, and the seats were upholstered in red and white striped canvas. Wiley had to admit the food was good, though her mother was doing her best to give her a belly ache. It wasn't anything she said, it was the way she watched Wiley's posture, scrutinized the way she ate. Wiley had never been accused of being Miss Manners, but she'd never seen the point of having no elbows on the table or chewing her food one hundred times. Content to live and let live, she ate in silence, in her accustomed way.

Until her mother dropped a bomb into the conversation, that is.

Rhapsody smiled fondly and said, "We must start making plans for the wedding ceremony. I can't wait to see you finally settled."

A muscle jumped in Wiley's jaw. "You'll be waiting a while. I'm not planning to get married for a long time."

"Oh, but Jayems--"

"Isn't my concern. I'm not marrying him."

There was silence for all of five seconds. "But you're betrothed!"

Wiley took a deliberate bite of her pot pie, savoring the rich wine gravy. "Not my doing, not my problem. He'll have to find someone else to marry."

Rhapsody opened her mouth and sucked in air, but Portae laid a hand on her arm, cutting her off. "Not here, sister."

Rhapsody snapped her mouth shut and applied herself to her wine instead.

Enjoying the fact that her mother wouldn't make a scene in public, Wiley took her time finishing her meal and made sure to order dessert. If the only enjoyment she was going to get out of the day was Drunken Nut Cake, then she was going to savor every rich bite.

She collected Jasmine as soon as she got back to the Citadel and persuaded her to come to the armory with her. Opposed as she usually was to exercise, Jas had a fatal attraction to martial arts. With her escort and Wiley's trailing behind--all except for Piper, who lead the way--they made quite a parade. Between the two of them, they attracted a lot of attention.

Even Jasmine noticed. "Check it out. You're the center of attention. 'Lost Princess Returns.' If I'd had any idea, I'd have pre-sold the movie rights."

"Very funny."

"Hey, there are worse things than being rich and famous."

"I'm not rich."

"You sure? I thought it kind of came with the princess gig."

"Technically, I'm not a princess."

"No problem. We can still make our fortune. We'll just set up a table in the marketplace and fleece passing shoppers at poker."

Wiley laughed. "You didn't do so good when you played Keilor. Seems to me you spent more time losing and paying with kisses."

Jasmine flushed and looked around guiltily, as if their guards hadn't already heard every word. "Shh! Besides, that whole kissing thing was his idea."

"You liked it."

"Did not!"

Wiley just looked at her.

Jasmine's color deepened. "Besides, I'm sure he's some kind of womanizer. Just look at the guy. He's got trouble written all over him."

"Sometimes that's the best kind of man," Wiley purred, enjoying herself.

Jasmine changed tactics. "Yeah? Is that why you like Jayems so much?"

That instantly sobered her. "You don't know what you're talking about."

It was Jas' turn to look superior, and she looked relieved to do it. "That's good to know. It means I can stop carrying around that heavy fire extinguisher whenever you two get together. Though what you see in …" She put her hand on Wiley's arm when she saw her expression. "Hey, I'm sorry. I didn't know … I'll shut up."

"Thanks." Wiley's throat ached. She didn't want to talk about Jayems anymore.

Jasmine looked around for a moment, as if searching for something. Her gaze landed on a low stone wall. "Oh, look! Betcha I can walk on it longer than you." She boosted herself up on it, ignoring the odd looks sent her way. She gave Wiley a wicked grin. "Don't be shy, now."

Wiley laughed at the idea. If Jas wasn't in her typical dreamy mode, she'd be the one nervous about the attention she was getting. Still, she was trying to make her feel better, so Wiley swung up. "Don't blame me when you break a leg."

"Contrary to popular opinion, I do have some athletic ability. Balance is one of my highlights."

"Oh, yeah? Look, there's Keilor!" Wiley pointed, then instantly regretted her teasing as Jasmine's head whipped up. She tipped and would have fallen if Piper hadn't quickly reached out and steadied her.

"Th - thanks," Jasmine stammered, unnerved by her close encounter, either with the sidewalk or the Haunt. She gave Wiley an evil look. "Brat."

Wiley shrugged, thumbs tipped out, in apology.

With a snort of disgust, Jasmine stomped on along the wall's edge. As it happened, the wall went right across from the armory. Ignoring Piper's offered hand, Jasmine jumped down, landing rather heavily. As Wiley alighted next to her, she offered a small smile. "You're going to have to get over this man-shy thing you have." It wasn't that. She knew what Jas was really afraid of, but if Jas wanted to bluff it out, she would let her. Wiley herself wasn't all that comfortable around the Haunt yet.

Jas looked at her dead on. "I'm no coward, Wi."

Affection and pride made Wiley smile. "No, you're not. Come on. Let's see if we can find something pointy to annoy the guys with." She followed Piper into the armory, still smiling.

Chapter Thirteen

Jasmine was poisoned that night.

Jasmine had taken one drink of Wiley's wine and stiffened. The glass had shattered in her hand, and moments later she'd been screaming, doubled up on the floor. Keilor and Fallon had worked frantically to help her, and somebody had called the medics. Jayems had dragged Wiley back from the scene, calming her frantic struggles with gentle force. Even now, after they knew that it had been Jasmine's dessert that was poisoned and not the wine, Wiley couldn't shake the feeling that she was responsible. Jasmine wouldn't even be here if it weren't for her.

Wiley sat in the hospital waiting room, scared to death that she was about to lose her best friend. They'd been having a family dinner. Things had been a little strained, what with Keilor and Jasmine trying to ignore each other and her mother trying to monopolize Wiley's attention, but they'd almost finished up with no major problems. That was, until Jasmine snatched a taste of Wiley's wine.

Whimpering silently, Wiley put her face in her hands, then ran them through her hair. Jayems was there, lending silent support as Keilor and Fallon quietly argued who could have been responsible.

The medic finally came out and gave his report. It was grim. He mentioned possible brain damage and internal injuries to her organs. They wouldn't know more until she woke up, and the recovery was bound to be slow.

The tears came afresh at the medic's report. Fallon swore softly and Jayems put a supporting arm around her. She leaned into him and he kissed her hair. Poor Jasmine.

There was nothing more they could do there that night, so Jayems led her home, promising to let her spend all day with Jasmine tomorrow. Tonight, the medics were still working on her.

Wiley made it to their room and then collapsed on the couch. "I'm going to go back tonight, even if all I do is watch Jasmine sleeping. She needs to have someone with her."

Jayems smiled and looked down, kissed her hand. "Keilor will be with her all night."

She frowned at him. "It's hardly going to cheer her up if she wakes up and sees him."

"She might surprise you. You'd have to take a sword to Keilor to make him leave her tonight. He feels responsible."

"Why? She wouldn't even be here tonight if it weren't for me," she said in self-reproach.

He shook his head and brushed the hair away from her face. "You would have followed her, if things had been reversed. Keilor is head of security here. Among other things, he feels he should have kept her safe. How can he feel he's doing his job if someone is poisoned at the very table he's sitting at?"

"It's not his fault!"

"I'm just telling you how he thinks. I've known him long enough to know."

She gave a little shuddering sigh. "Why couldn't it have been me? I probably could have recovered from something like this."

He shook his head. "Don't be so eager to court death, sweetheart. You both have enemies. It's nothing you did to earn them. We just have to do a better job of protecting you. That's our responsibility."

She looked at him with wounded, vulnerable eyes. "It's not."

He couldn't help it. He kissed her, swearing with his kiss what he couldn't express with his voice. She needed him, and there was an age old comfort he could offer that neither of them would argue against.

She folded against him, needing the touch, craving the contact with his body. She was hesitant at first, afraid. He could hurt her right now.

As if he knew it, he slid her gently to the couch, his touch still comforting even as it explored her body, gently passed over her breast. The contact made her gasp, made her clutch at him as fire spiked through her. Oh, yes. She needed this. She knew where lovemaking could take her. It was making love with *him* that worried her.

He'd already stepped up the aid and comfort, though, and she was fast forgetting her worries. The man had his hand under her skirt, on the inside of her thigh. He didn't touch the obvious place, though. Instead he caressed her hips slowly, traced her lower belly, massaged her thighs. Only when she made a desperate sound and parted her legs did he place a hand over her patch. The hand remained still.

Wiley whimpered and tugged at his wrist. He started to pull away.

"No! Please, right there." She shuddered and tried to shift his fingers. His hand moved and his thumb caressed the inside of her thigh.

"Are you sure?" he asked in a husky voice. "I won't ask again, sweetheart. I won't let you change your mind."

She pulled him down for a kiss.

Satisfied with her answer, he shed his restraint. His fingers slid home, and she lost track of time. The man was magic, and he was everywhere. She'd never known it was possible to be undressed without her awareness, but suddenly she realized that she was naked. Jayems had lost his shirt, one leg was between hers, riding against her as he slid down and tasted her breasts like a prisoner on his last meal. Or maybe his first real meal since being released. His hot, open mouth moved down her body, shocking her into sudden realization. She grabbed his head. "Wait! I ... I've never done that."

"Good." He actually growled as he shook his head free and deliberately lowered his mouth.

She could not lie still. Sucking in air, she gasped in pleasure, the sounds coming from her mouth getting louder and louder until she was shouting, a prisoner pinned between his hot, slick mouth and the couch.

Finally he slid up and ripped open his fly. He fell over her and looked her in the eye. "I told you I wouldn't ask again." He slid inside.

She arched up and dug her nails into his back. It was so tight, and he was huge. It hurt, and a hell of a lot at that, but he worked his way in, kissing her neck, running his tongue over her ears, massaging her thighs and breasts. The look on his face was mindless, but it was obvious he knew what he was doing. Desire built and built inside her, though he was barely moving. Just the thought of him there, of what he was about to do ... she threw back her head and screamed in climax.

Jayems shook and then pumped into her, driving her deep into the couch. With a roar, he climaxed inside her, joining his seed to hers.

* * * *

She slept hard that night, so deeply that it was well into the morning when she woke. Then she remembered and sat bolt upright. "Jasmine!"

Sore muscles between her thighs made her wince. It was then, as the sheets slid against her naked skin, that she remembered what else had happened that night.

Jayems was already up and dressed. He walked into his bedroom moments after her exclamation. "She's still resting, but we've transferred her to her room. If you'd be willing to eat some breakfast, I'll take you right over." He leaned over and kissed her good morning. It was a gentle hello, nothing like the flaming kisses of the night before.

She looked down, tugging the sheets around her. There'd never been a morning after for her. She didn't know what to do.

He made a low sound, much like a growl. "Don't tempt me, sweetheart. I'm a newly mated man--I can't see you in my bed and not want you."

Fire licked her cheeks as she scooted around him. Walking was uncomfortable, but she assumed it would heal quickly, maybe in time for that night ...

She shivered and got dressed in record time.

* * * *

Jasmine was so pale, but when she finally opened her eyes, they were lucid.

Wiley put a hand to Jas' brow and found it cool. "How are you doing, Jas?" she asked softly.

While better, Jasmine was still tired. After a short conversation and a visit to the bathroom, she drifted back to sleep. Still worried, but relieved, Wiley let the nurse take over and went back to her room. Seeing Jayems, she said with a smile, "She just went back to sleep, but she's feeling better."

He smiled and slid his hands around her from behind, pulling her close. "I'm relieved. I know how worried you were." His hands wandered.

She couldn't help a low moan. "What are you doing?"

"Expressing my relief. Appreciating your amazing breasts," he said as his fingers closed over the right one.

She choked on a laugh. "Amazing, huh?"

"Mmm." He eased up the back of her skirt and bent her gently over the back of the couch. He made a noise of impatience at the sight of her satin panties. "Why do women wear these things?" He slid them down to her thighs and left them there, nudging her legs apart. Kissing the back of her neck, he slid the dress over her shoulders, kissing skin as he bared it. With her breasts hanging loose over the couch, he took his time teasing them, lifting and pushing them together, gently pinching and rolling the ruby tips.

He bent over and whispered in her ear, "Open yourself for me." He breathed in her ear and licked the rim.

Matching heat spiraled down between her thighs. Shocked, she whispered, "What?"

With a wicked laugh, he took her hands and guided them back, placing them on either side of her slick opening. Naughtily, he pushed the tips of two of them just inside her.

She gasped and tried to pull away. "Jayems!"

He chuckled and firmed her fingers on either side, making her spread herself. Giving her clit a wicked little tweak that made her squeal--he had to retrieve her hands again--he slowly slid home.

Wiley quaked. The man had spent too much time reading those books. He was killing her.

"Ah, sweet," he purred, rocking her softly. "I want to lick you so badly, sweetheart, but I can't stop moving inside you."

Unable to focus, she groaned and gripped the couch. A whimpering sound trembled on her lips as he gripped her behind and rotated. She started to pant.

"That's it. Feel me. You know what I'm going to do to you. I'm going to climax inside you, Rih. I'm going to give you my baby."

The climax hit her like a sledgehammer. She went crazy, bucking against the couch, screaming until she thought she would black out. He joined her, driving into her like he'd been shot up with molten lightning.

As she trembled with aftershocks, he slipped a hand under them and pressed. She splintered into another climax, jerking uncontrollably.

She didn't know where he found the energy, but he carried her into the bedroom and shed the rest of their clothes.

The first time must have been a warm up, because he slid into her again, pinning her arms above her head, lacing his fingers with hers. His kiss was wild and tender, restrained yet ardent. He drove her crazy with his kisses, yet made her take it slow even when she begged. His self control drove her wild, and in the end, he joined her.

Even as they lay there, his fingers continued their play between her legs.

It was somewhere after the third time and a nap that she woke up, feeling his body lying against hers. His arm was draped possessively over her waist, and she could tell he was awake.

"What did you mean when you said you wanted to give me a baby?" she asked tentatively. Though he'd kept her too busy to pursue it, his words had consumed her.

He yawned and let his hand trail down her thigh, gently stroking. "You want one, don't you?"

"I – I'm not sure right now. I mean, in theory, yes, but now? With you?"

"It's what husbands and wives do." He rolled her over on her stomach and began to massage her back. "I like the idea. I especially enjoy the practicing part." He nipped her shoulder playfully.

Happiness made her throat tight. The man was offering her a child. He couldn't have offered her anything more precious. "You ought to be tired."

He just laughed and showed her otherwise.

Chapter Fourteen

Jasmine was weak for some days, and spent most of that time asleep. While Wiley would have preferred spending most of her time with her, she wasn't left in peace. Her mother wanted to spend time with her and she was a stubborn woman.

Wiley came back to her room the day after Jasmine had woken up, in search of her guitar. She was going to play something soothing to help Jas relax. Granted, Jas had just slid into sleep, but she was fretful when she woke up, with little appetite. Wiley had to admit she wouldn't want to eat much, either, if she were forced to live on liquids.

Her mother was waiting for her when she entered the room. She'd ordered tea. It was only when she saw the food that Wiley realized she was hungry.

"Come, join me, daughter. Do you care for honey in your tea?" Rhapsody was already pouring a cup, a look of pleasant determination on her face. "We've barely had a chance to visit in the last few days."

Casting a wistful look at her guitar, the one instrument she'd managed to keep in the suite--Jayems had banned the drums to the music room--Wiley reluctantly joined her. "I've been busy looking after Jasmine."

"So devoted of you. I understand she sleeps most of the time?" Rhapsody took a sip of tea.

"Good thing, too. She feels terrible when she's awake." Wiley devoured a dainty sandwich in three bites. She restrained herself from burping. The anger she felt for her mother hadn't resided.

"How sad. Keilor visits her often, I hear."

Wiley pursed her lips. "Twice is not often."

Calmly buttering her toast point, Rhapsody observed, "For a man such as he? Depend on it, the gesture has been marked. He's always been an unconventional man, but I do hope he realizes what he's doing. Tongues are busy."

Wiley stared at her, hard. "Whose tongues? Why would anyone care?"

Rhapsody set her toast aside, untouched. "Your friend is a Sylph, my dear. The older generation still remembers the destruction they brought. Why, your own father was nearly captured by one, before we crossed over." Her face contorted for a moment, then resumed its careful mien. "Human is bad enough. Sylph ... well, you have seen the lengths some people are willing to go to eliminate her."

Wiley's hand tightened on her cup. "She's no threat to anyone."

Rhapsody canted her head in acknowledgement of the comment. "As you see it, my dear, but even those of our people who would see you kindly still consider her a danger. The fact that our Lord of the Hunt visits her ... there are whispers she has him in her thrall."

"They're fools, then."

"Very well. How do you propose to influence them?"

Caught off guard, Wiley blinked at her. "What?"

Rhapsody patiently considered her. "You're the daughter of a very old, respected house. If you would learn to use that power and influence, you'd gather support--or at least, tolerance--for your friend. Learn to trade on your social influence, my dear. Gain allies. Only by changing the political climate will you ensure her safety."

Wiley considered. She was making a lot of sense, but ... "I don't know how to do that."

Rhapsody just smiled. "Leave it to me, my dear."

* * * *

Wiley would later remember that smile with misgiving. Sadly, it was not before she'd made another visit to the dressmakers. Somehow, her mother also saddled her with a hairdresser who insisted on grooming Wiley every chance she got. Between her history tutor, her mother's unending discussions of politics, the round of visits, luncheons and shopping excursions her mother convinced her would help both Jasmine's and Jayems' popularity, Wiley barely had time to breathe, let alone visit Jasmine. To her mother's eternal annoyance, she took the time to check on her friend every day.

Jasmine was first surprised, then amused that Wiley had accepted Jayems as her lover. "Didn't think you'd go there, Wi." She was sitting in an armchair when she made the comment, propped up more by force of will than anything else.

Wiley could see she was getting tired. "Well, I'm glad you're amused. Shouldn't you go back to bed?"

Jasmine glowered tiredly at her and moved her chess piece. "All I do is lay in bed. I can rest after I finish this game, and stop trying to lose on purpose so I'll go there quicker. At least Keilor doesn't do that."

Wiley smiled and deliberately moved her queen into jeopardy.

Jasmine ignored the queen to take a pawn instead. "Stop grinning. He feels guilty. That's all it is."

"Hmm. Okay, I'll humor you. Is this better?" She put Jasmine's king into checkmate.

Jas grunted. "I hope your mother makes you shop for hours. Here, give me a hand up, will you?"

Wiley settled Jasmine in bed and then went home to find Jayems. It was after dinner, and he was reading in his library. Not one of his racier books, she was relieved to see. Taking the opposite chair, she frowned at him. "Who do you think tried to poison Jasmine?"

He marked his page and set the book aside. "I don't know. I'm sorry, but we could not trace the poison. Is she very weak tonight?"

She shook her head. "No, she's getting better every day, but slowly. It's just that my mother is constantly telling me she's in so much danger ..."

He sighed and motioned for her to come to him. Hesitantly, she let him pull her down on his lap and leaned into his arm.

"Your mother is manipulative, my love. She's going to beat that drum as long as it makes you jump."

"So you don't think it's true?"

"I think that your being forced to attend your mother's social carnival is unlikely to result in my removing the bodyguards from her door."

She digested that. "My mother also claims it makes you look better in 'the people's' eyes."

He shrugged. "I think my making responsible choices will make a bigger impact. You're welcome to try, though."

She twisted around to frown at him. "You're not making me feel very important, here."

He smiled. "I didn't make you mine in order to please the political harpies, sweetheart. I made you mine to please me. Fortunately for both of us, you seem to enjoy it." He twisted a lock of her hair around his finger, a glint in his eye.

She moved her head away, but was firmly caught. "You sound sure of yourself."

"You've done nothing but boost my confidence. In honor of that, I'd like to boost yours." He released the hair and began stoking her neck, the long muscle under her left ear.

"How?" She was drowning in sensation, her body humming. The night had grown quiet, intimate.

He smiled. "Stand up. Strip for me."

She blinked at him, thinking about that.

He winked. "Something new, sweetheart. Be bold."

Trembling a little, she drew a breath for courage and stood up. His direct stare made her blush as she worked the fastenings on her gown, clumsy with anticipation.

"Slowly, love," he purred.

Daring herself to meet his eyes, she slowly peeled the bodice of her gown apart, let it slide to her elbows and wiggled free. The gown clung to her hips.

She desperately wanted to cover her breasts.

His eyes darkened. "Lick the tips of your fingers."

Her eyes widened.

His narrowed. "Do it."

She obeyed, shivering at the feel of her tongue on her fingers.

"Pinch your nipples." His look compelled obedience.

Unable to meet his eyes, she pinched her nipples, hissing at the shock that zipped through her. They were stiff, standing at attention. She'd never realized how pebbled they were.

"Cup them, raise them, squeeze them together."

With each order, she blushed harder, but he wouldn't release her. Her breasts were heavy, silky, and she squeezed them really hard to try and soothe the ache. He was watching her!

"Raise your hands over your head and slide them through your hair."

Biting back a moan, she let the silky strands tumble through her fingers.

"Slide your hands down over your breasts and grip your butt. Wiggle out of your gown."

Her hands were more eager this time, her body more desperate. The feel of her hands gripping her butt made her moan aloud. Naked, she fell to her knees between his spread legs. "Please."

He smiled and stood, leisurely stripping out of his clothes. He sat back down and canted his head at her. "I'm all yours."

She made a hungry sound and crawled astride, kissing him to forget her embarrassment, aching for him to fill the damp hollow his watching had primed. She fumbled with him.

He laughed and set her back, slid her down until her knees settled on the rug and her breasts cradled him. His finger rubbed her lips, slid inside. He withdrew the finger, touched it to the tip of himself and hissed at the contact. When she looked at him questioningly, he repeated the gesture, and then caressed her breasts with a growl.

She'd never liked the idea of taking a man inside her mouth, had never done it. It had always seemed dirty, gross. There was nothing bad about the way he was making her feel, though. There was no force, only seduction.

Tentatively, she licked the tip.

His entire body hardened. He said a muffled curse. When she hesitated, he caressed her hair, her face, her breasts, encouraging her.

She kissed him with little, careful kisses. When she finally grew bold enough to close her mouth on him, his head fell back with a moan.

It was a new power, the ability to make him weak, but that first time was about exploration, of discovering him with hands and mouth and tongue. Oddly enough, the experience only intensified the ache between her legs, causing her to cry out with sudden climax.

Jayems' head came up with a snap. In seconds he had surged to his feet and tossed her over his shoulder.

He took off for the bedroom at a dead run.

* * * *

The next few weeks passed in a happy blur. Jasmine and Keilor's romance progressed, Wiley became better at fending off her mother and Jayems found endless ways to make love to her. Wiley was even starting to make some friends among her peers, though she gravitated to the ladies her mother found less than suitable. Oh, they were ladies all right, but they were very into sports and highly physical, or else had a wicked sense of humor. Worse, they had little rank. Two of her favorites were Shanra, daughter of a preeminent musician, and Kayless, whose mother designed many of the dresses for women of status. In their middle twenties, the women still lived with their parents as was the custom. When they weren't hanging out at Wiley's suite, they visited at each other's houses or went shopping. Three days before the public celebration of Wiley's wedding, the girls were lounging around Shanra's house.

"I'm in love," Kayless said, admiring her newest sketch. "Such a pity Fallon will never notice me." She was seated on a floor cushion, her red hair French braided into pig tails. There was amused resignation in her blue eyes.

Shanra laughed as she tried another combination on her lap harp. "Last week you were in love with Lord Keilor." Of medium height and a brunette, she seemed to think she was nothing special. Wiley often thought she'd be surprised to know men noticed her laughing green eyes and long lashes.

Kayless shrugged and played in the smoke from the tripod incense burner. "I'm afraid I'll have to leave him to Jasmine's tender mercies. It's obvious they're in love, even if they don't know it."

Wiley chuckled. She lay belly down on a earth toned, brocade cushion, just listening to Shanra's magic fingers tease music from the harp. Her new friends had met and liked Jasmine, who returned the affection. "Oh, Jasmine's figured it out. I think Keilor's just working up the nerve to do something about it."

"Regardless, that leaves Fallon. It's so hard to find a man like him still unattached," Kayless complained.

Wiley shifted onto her side, the better to smirk. "Oh, yes, tall redheads with blue eyes should complain. That waiter yesterday couldn't pull his tongue off the floor."

Kayless colored. "He's a waiter! I notice you didn't marry one."

It was Wiley's turn to flush. "I didn't exactly pick him."

"Granted, but given a choice between the two? There's just no comparison to a man like that. I mean, he's handsome, commanding, he loves you ... doesn't hurt that he's rich, though I wouldn't need that if I were in love."

Her friends exchanged looks. Kayless was a woman in love with love, and desperate to have it happen to her. Unfortunately, the right man hadn't happened along yet. It didn't help that her mother squelched most men who tried. All she had to do was give them one of her infamous icy looks and they fell back.

Kayless was right--she needed someone with more backbone than a waiter.

Wiley studied her nails. "You know, what we need to do is get out. One of my favorite things to do is go watch

Keilor and his men train. Talk about entertainment! Sweaty men, flexing muscles …"

Kayless wrinkled her nose. "There's nothing sexy about sweat, my dear. Besides, half the time they're in Haunt. There's nothing sexy about that."

Wiley shrugged and stood up. "Just come along. Too bad Jas still needs her afternoon naps, or we could have her come."

"How is that coming?" Shanra asked as she put aside the harp. "I thought she was mostly recovered."

"Oh, she is, but it was near fatal, you know. She's lucky all she has to do is take naps."

Shanra grimaced in sympathy. "Poor thing."

The ladies headed for the practice field via the gardens, taking their time, Wiley's bodyguards trailing behind. They were joking, laughing, when all of a sudden a huge gray body jumped over the stone wall and flattened Kayless.

Wiley's bodyguards jumped forward, but it was too late. The runaway stag had knocked Kayless flat, and she was lying on the ground, gasping for breath.

Just then a man vaulted over the wall, looked frantically around. "Oh, no! How bad is she hurt?" He dropped to his knees beside the girl, elbowing aside the concerned guards.

Kayless drew in a shuddering gasp, then groaned.

"I'm sorry! Lie still." The stranger started looking for broken bones.

"Who are you?" Shanra demanded. "What do you think you're doing, letting that animal run loose? You could have killed somebody!"

His jaw tightened. "My cousin lost control of the beast and it jumped the fence. I was trying to stop it before something like this happened. The other riders should catch it shortly." Satisfied that nothing was broken, he offered Kayless a hand up. "I can take you to a medic, if you like. My name's Hytal, by the way."

Wiley looked at him with interest. She'd heard of the red sash Hytal. A loner famed for his skill with a blade, he was every maiden's dream.

Kayless staggered back and pulled her hand away. "Don't touch me!" She hunched over and wrapped her arms around her ribs.

His expression hardened as he looked at the guards. "I'm going to take her to the medics. Radio for a chair." He looked at Shanra, who had an arm around her. "Let's find her a seat. They'll be here in a minute."

Unable to help without getting in the way, Wiley had the luxury of watching the warrior fuss over her friend. It was obvious he felt badly, though technically the accident wasn't his fault. More interesting was watching her normally flirtatious friend hissing and spitting at one of the most eligible bachelors in the Citadel.

By time they'd whisked Kayless off to the medics and sent word to her mother, Wiley was feeling tired herself. She joined the others in the waiting room until word came that Kayless was resting, her worst injury a couple of broken ribs. In a few weeks she'd be fine, they said. As only her mother was allowed to stay with her, the rest of them went home.

Chapter Fifteen

"I'm tired of my friends getting hurt," Wiley grumped to Jayems that night.

"With luck, you've met your quota," Jayems soothed her. "That sort of thing doesn't happen every day."

"Thank God." She sighed. "So, are you ready for this wedding thing?"

He laughed and snuggled her close. "I've already had my "wedding thing." The celebration is just in honor of it."

He smelled so good. She snuggled her nose into his chest. "I'll be glad when it's over. I don't like being the center of attention."

"Oh, you won't be. Didn't I tell you? Keilor and Jasmine are celebrating their vows at the same ceremony."

"What!" she sat up in bed. "What are you talking about?"

Even in the moonlight, Jayems looked smug. "I got word earlier. They're celebrating their wedding night right now."

Her mouth dropped open. "She didn't tell me!"

He chuckled. "It sounded as if they just couldn't help themselves any longer. I doubt she meditated on it before she gave herself to him."

Wiley just stared at him. Jasmine, married! "Well, she should have found a way to tell me. I'm her best friend, after all."

He pulled her down for a kiss. "Some things are better celebrated in private," he murmured suggestively, then rolled her on her back.

* * * *

She found her wedding celebration anticlimactic.

Yes, there was food, music and a few people she knew there, but she would have been much happier if the crowd had been smaller. As she thought about it, she began to plan a more intimate gathering of friends for a later time. It helped to get her through her mother's posturing and the endless line of people waiting to greet her.

She, Jasmine and their new husbands had stood on a pavilion and been married by a priest in a slick brown robe. Flowers were twined around the pavilion posts and strewn about the floor, raising a heavenly fragrance when stepped on. Masses of flowers were dotted around the garden wedding, providing the primary decoration.

She lost track of Jasmine in the crowd. She'd given Jas a good scolding for not letting her best friend in on the good news first, then laughed when Jasmine admitted she hadn't known herself until Keilor let her come up for air. By then, of course, it had been too late.

She hadn't seemed unhappy about it.

Kayless had been able to attend, but she spent a great deal of time in a chair, poor girl. The last time Wiley had seen her, Hytal had been speaking to her. Kayless had been frowning, but her mother, oddly enough, had not been.

Shanra was lost amid the dancers.

"It's getting late. Do you think anyone would mind if we slipped away?" Wiley asked Jayems.

He looked at her and smiled her favorite smile. "We can do anything you like."

So they slipped away and held a very special, very private celebration of their own.

* * * *

"Jasmine's been kidnapped."

Wiley froze with her eyes locked on Jayems'. Reflected in the mirror, they were grave and worried. Slowly she turned around and looked at him.

"She was taken last night. Keilor is in the hospital in critical condition. They caught him by surprise."

Wiley quickly shed her robe and ran to the closet for her clothes, throwing on a shirt and pants. "This is why they got you out of bed last night? Why didn't you tell me?" She vaguely remembered rolling over and going back to sleep at Jayems' soothing whisper.

"I was busy coordinating a search. It was better that you rest. Someone should be with Keilor when he wakes up-- he's going to be beside himself. I can't be two places at once, and he'd only yell at me to get out and do something if I were. He needs family now."

She nodded, choking on emotion. "Jasmine?"

"We're doing all we can. Go and do what you can for him," Jayems said. The strain was evident in his face. This was family.

She kissed him quickly. "I'll go."

Rabid with worry, she nearly ran to the medics, her Haunt guard tense beside her. Keilor was heavily sedated to keep him in bed. Not that it should have been a problem--his attackers had disemboweled him. He should have been dead.

He recognized her. "Rihlia. My wife … I'm sorry." His voice was a whisper, thick with grief and rage.

She shook her head. "Stop. Rest and heal. Jayems is doing everything he can. He's sent out Jasmine's bodyguards and your friend Mathin. They'll bring her home." She prayed that was true. She couldn't lose Jasmine.

"Mathin." He tossed his head restlessly. "I should be there." The words were faint. He was already going back down. He was so pale.

She kissed his brow. "Rest, Keilor. Jasmine is one tough nut. She'll come out of this okay." Words of hope, but she wished someone would say them to her.

Her mother came to sit with him after a while, with a promise that his aunt and cousin would also take their turns. Meanwhile, those of the family not on watch stayed in Jayems' suite and tried to comfort Wiley, with marginal success. She couldn't help pacing.

Jayems finally had word to share. "We know who took her--a woman named Yesande. She's an old enemy of Keilor's. We think we know where she's headed. The only trouble is, there's no way to get ahead of them, not with the lead they have, at the pace they're going. The good news is that Mathin is right on their tail. He'll find a way to get to Jasmine."

"Why? Why did they take her?" Wiley asked. "It doesn't make sense."

Jayems put his arm around her. "I don't know yet. The important thing is that we get her back. Don't worry--we'll bring her home."

But she did worry. The days became weeks, and there was still no word. Thanks to his Haunt blood, Keilor was rapidly recovering, but he was still in no shape to go after Jas.

Her worry was bad enough, but Wiley's mother made it worse with her 'comforting.'

"You know," she suggested one afternoon at tea, "all things happen for a reason. Perhaps this will work out for the best, after all."

Wiley's eyes narrowed. It was just the two of them, and she felt less and less inclined to be civil. Her mother had been wearing ever thinner, but this was the first time she'd openly suggested that Jasmine's disappearance was a good thing. "I fail to see how."

Rhapsody delicately sipped her tea as she considered. "As loyal as you were to her, you must consider how out of place she must have felt. Sometimes, nature has a way of correcting the balance. Both you and Keilor can now proceed with the natural course of your life. Surely Jasmine--if she'd loved you--would have wanted that for you."

Rage like she'd never known poured through Wiley, consumed her. She stood up slowly, and it was all she could do not to launch herself over the table. Summoning her voice through the white anger was hard enough. "Get out. Start walking, and don't stop, or so help me, I'll bitch slap you to the ground right now."

Eyes wide, her mother stood. "How could you--"

"Get out!" Finger shaking with adrenaline, she wanted nothing better than to choke the life out of the woman. "Don't you ever walk through that door again, or so help me, I'll throw you out it myself."

Amazingly, the woman stood her ground. "I can see that you're upset--"

Wiley started for her.

Finally, Rhapsody realized she'd gone too far. She ran for the door, narrowly escaping.

Wiley slammed against the carved wood, snarling her rage. Outraged, she slammed it again and then gave it a good kick.

How dare she? *How dare she?*

Jayems must have been summoned from wherever he was, because he showed up not five minutes later. One look at the couch cushions scattered in every direction told him the depth of her anger. "What did she say?"

She told him, and she didn't watch her mouth as she did so.

His eyes widened and then he advanced on her with tenderness, folding her into his arms.

It was the tenderness that broke her. "She's no mother to me, Jayems! How could she say something like that about Jasmine? She's been more a sister to me than that woman has ever been a mother. She's jealous, and mean, too."

"I know. It's all right; she won't come back in here unless you decide to make your peace with it." He rubbed her back.

She pulled back. "Make my peace! Are you crazy? How am I supposed to forgive her for that?"

He offered a lopsided smile. "That's why they call it 'make your peace.' Nobody's implied it's easy."

She grunted and allowed him to hold her again, but there was no softening in her heart for her mother.

* * * *

They got word the next day that Jasmine had been rescued. Mathin and his two friends were running with her deep into the swamps to avoid pursuit. Jayems sent out men to clear the path for them for the run home.

While relieved, Wiley found it hard to sit home and wait. It was on one of those dark days, when her friends Shanra and Kayless were trying to cheer her up, that Wiley realized something important. She hadn't had her period since before Jasmine was taken.

Shanra saw the arrested expression on Wiley's face and immediately went to her. "What is it?"

Wiley blinked at her, dazed. "I think I might be pregnant."

Jayems lit up when he heard. Knowing that the glad news would bring hope to Keilor, he quickly passed it on. Her family was ecstatic; there hadn't been a baby in the family in years. Even Rhapsody bragged to all her friends about the new heir. The fact that her own daughter still refused to talk to her was not discussed.

All told, Jasmine was gone almost two months. If anything, the experience changed her in positive ways, for she returned a stronger, more confident woman. She and Keilor had a fiery reunion. When she came up for air, she and Wiley exchanged hugs and tears. But this is not the end of the story…

Teasing Danger
Available now from New Concepts Publishing

Printed in the United Kingdom
by Lightning Source UK Ltd.
115834UKS00001B/38